The Chri

"Becca Freeman gives a much-needed update to classic holiday tales. Told over the course of eleven Christmases, this witty and heartfelt debut tracks a group of four young New Yorkers as their friendship solidifies into a chosen family, one with its own traditions, tensions, and drama."

—Carley Fortune, #1 *New York Times* bestselling
author of *Meet Me at the Lake*

"If you adore Christmas and loved *Friends*, then this is the perfect book for you. I would happily abandon my husband and kids to spend Christmas in New York with Hannah, Finn, Theo, and Priya. A festive, funny, hug of a novel about love in all its forms."

—Clare Pooley, *New York Times* bestselling author of
Iona Iverson's Rules for Commuting

"I'm completely in love with this book! . . . Becca Freeman's debut is witty, heartwarming, and hilarious, and the most delightful thing you'll read all year."   —Jennifer Close, *New York Times* bestselling
author of *Marrying the Ketchups*

"Freeman's writing is filled with wit and insight, and her dialogue crackles."
—Grant Ginder, bestselling author of *The People We Hate
at the Wedding* and *Let's Not Do That Again*

"*The Christmas Orphans Club* has everything you could want in a holiday book-treat: sweetness, laughs, and delicious rom-com moments that'll make you jump up and yell, 'Kiss him! Kiss him!' Thank you, Becca Freeman, for an ensemble cast so lovable I wish they were real and could be my friends."   —Mary Laura Philpott, author of *Bomb Shelter:
Love, Time, and Other Explosives*

PENGUIN BOOKS

THE CHRISTMAS ORPHANS CLUB

Becca Freeman is the host of the popular books and lifestyle podcast *Bad on Paper* and the co-creator of RomComPods. She is an alumna of Boston College and lives in Brooklyn, where she enthusiastically celebrates Christmas every year.

CONNECT ONLINE

beccafreeman.net

BeccaMFreeman

The Christmas Orphans Club

BECCA FREEMAN

PENGUIN BOOKS

PENGUIN BOOKS

UK | USA | Canada | Ireland | Australia
India | New Zealand | South Africa

Penguin Books is part of the Penguin Random House group of companies
whose addresses can be found at global.penguinrandomhouse.com

First published in the United States of America by Penguin Books,
an imprint of Penguin Random House LLC 2023
First published in Great Britain by Penguin Books 2023
001

Set in 10.81/17pt Baskerville
Designed by Alexis Farabaugh
Printed and bound in Great Britain by Clays Ltd, Elcograf S.p.A.

The authorized representative in the EEA is Penguin Random House Ireland,
Morrison Chambers, 32 Nassau Street, Dublin D02 YH68

A CIP catalogue record for this book is available from the British Library

ISBN: 978–1–405–95749–6

www.greenpenguin.co.uk

*To anyone who has ever been alone
on Christmas: I see you, I love you.*

*And to the Mangy Ravens:
thank you for giving me the kind of
friendship worth writing books about.*

Hannah

This year, December 24

'Twas the night before Christmas, and all through Manhattan, not a creature was stirring, not even a mouse.

Scratch that. Manhattan at six o'clock on Christmas Eve is a complete and utter shitshow.

The mice—fine, rats—are frolicking through mountains of day-old garbage bags heaped on the curb. It's pornographic, really. "Stirring" would be putting it mildly.

As for the people, Grand Central is a pulsing sea of bodies rushing to catch a train to whichever tristate suburb they hail from. At Citarella, the fancy West Village grocery store where a pint of berries starts at $10, the fourth verbal altercation of the day has broken out in front of the prepared-food case as two women spar over the last container of scalloped potatoes. Those who opted

to order in aren't faring any better. Han Dynasty's delivery estimate is creeping toward three hours.

So I shouldn't be surprised to be stuck in bumper-to-bumper
traffic, stop-starting my way up the West Side Highway in the
back seat of a yellow cab. I've given up hopes of doing my makeup
on the drive. Winged eyeliner was too optimistic; anything short
of puking from motion sickness will be a victory.

"You a city kid?" my sixtysomething cab driver asks in a thick
New York accent.

"Nope, Jersey girl," I tell him, trying to strike the right balance between politeness and making it clear I don't want to talk.

"You got family in the city, though, right? Aunts? Cousins?"
he asks. "Bet you're heading to spend Christmas Eve with them."

"Nope. No family, just me."

He looks at me through the rearview mirror and I see pity in
his crinkly gray-blue eyes.

He feels sorry for me, but I feel sorry for everyone else with
their boring, conventional Christmases. Some people think it's
sad to be without family at the holidays, but Christmas is my favorite day of the year. And this is poised to be our best one yet. It
has to be, after the twin disasters of the last two years' celebra-
tions. Tonight is only the appetizer.

I consider correcting the driver's assumptions, but I feel the
burrito I had for lunch roiling in my stomach as he taps the brakes
for the three hundredth time, and I decide to shut my eyes and
fake sleep instead. Let him think whatever he wants.

When I race into Theo's apartment, barefaced and vaguely nauseous, Finn yells, "Hannah, is that you? *Finally!*"

"Come on, then," Theo hollers. "If the food gets cold it's all going to be shite."

"Cute scarf!" Priya remarks as I make my entrance into the dining room, where three of my four favorite people are seated around a long table.

"I know Hannah didn't pick it out because it's not neutral or the color blue," Finn jokes. "So who's it from?"

"Hey!" I retort. "But also . . . fair. It was a gift from David," I say as I finger the bright red cashmere scarf wrapped around my neck.

"For Christmas?" Finn prods.

"No, we're doing gifts tomorrow morning. It was a 'just because' present. He saw it in a store window and thought it would look nice with my hair."

"I think he liiiiikes you," Finn sings, stretching out the word like Sandra Bullock in *Miss Congeniality*. "He wants to kiiiissss you."

My cheeks flame at his teasing, but I'm also grinning. David is always bringing home little gifts. I know he likes me—loves me, actually. I've never doubted how he felt about me, not even in our earliest days of dating. But the warm thoughts about my boyfriend are chased by a trickle of guilt. For a minute, I think about spilling everything: how off we've been, what I found a few weeks ago. But tonight, as an extension of Christmas, is sacred. A time-out from real life. No work, no family, just us. I don't want to mar it with my relationship woes.

After I strip off my winter layers, gently arranging the scarf on the back of my chair so it doesn't drag on the ground, I notice the tablescape I missed in my haste. The table is laden with silver trays piled with burgers in paper wrappers. There are crystal bowls with fries of every variety—thin, curly, crinkle-cut, sweet potato, and steak fries. There's even a bowl of onion rings and another of tots. Each place setting has ramekins of what looks like ketchup, mayo, and special sauce.

"I'm sorry," I say. "Did I miss the part of the evening where you all got stoned out of your goddamn minds?"

"You've heard of the feast of the seven fishes, right?" Theo asks. "This is the feast of the seven fast-food burgers."

"We're going to taste them all and pick a winner. He had scorecards made." Finn points to a piece of cream cardstock beside his plate with *Christmas Eve Burger Brawl* written across the top in swirly red calligraphy.

With these people I could have fun in an empty room; just being with them is special. But this is delightfully ridiculous. I can't help but laugh at the spectacle.

"First of all, this is absurd because Shake Shack is definitely going to win, but also, what are you going to do?" I ask Priya, who is vegetarian.

"I'm judging sides," she chirps. "But you should know, Theo has his money on In-N-Out."

"There's not even an In-N-Out in New York," I begin. But sure enough, one of the platters is stacked with burgers with their signature red-and-white wrappers. "How?"

"He had them flown in from California," Finn says with an eye roll. I don't want to know how he did it or how much it cost, but I'm still positive there's no way they'll win, especially reheated.

"Shall we?" Theo asks.

I take a seat next to Finn and shake out my napkin. Everyone begins serving themselves, except me. Instead, I click the shutter button on my mental camera. I want to remember everything, sear this night into my mind as a core memory. Because in addition to being our best, it may also be our last Christmas together.

Finn reaches over to squeeze my hand, silently asking if I'm alright. The truth is, I'm anything but alright. I'm devastated he's leaving, taking half my heart with him, like one of those plastic best-friend necklaces fourth-grade girls trade as social currency. It feels doubly unfair because I only just got him back. A whole year lost to our fight. I'm not ready for whatever comes next. But I paste on a smile and look back at him, pretending to be happy. And I am, for him, but I'm also sad for me. Sad that everything is ending.

Everyone else has something new on the horizon—Priya is still giddy over her new job, Finn has his move to LA, and Theo's whole life is plane tickets and parties. But all I have to look for-ward to is less. A Finn-sized hole in my day-to-day life.

"What?" Finn asks, giving me the side-eye, not buying the smile I've plastered on.

"Nothing," I say. "I'm just happy being here with all of you."

I swallow the next thought that pops into my mind: *I don't know how I could ever be happier than this.* These people are all the family I need.

ONE

Hannah

Christmas #1, 2008

I, Hannah Gallagher, am kind of an expert on depressing play-lists.

Sure, it's a dumb superpower. I'd much rather be able to fly or read minds or turn into a puddle of metallic goo like Alex Mack, but we don't get to pick the hand we're dealt. Don't I know it.

I add "Brick" by Ben Folds Five to the playlist I'm working on and follow it up with "Skinny Love" by Bon Iver. I throw in "Vindicated" by Dashboard Confessional for good measure. If you ask me, the problem with music today is there are too many songs about being dumped or someone you love not loving you back, and not enough about the disappointing state of the whole damn world.

I've spent the past four years honing my craft, and tonight's playlist is going to be my opus.

I minimize a browser tab to check my LimeWire downloads.

Damnit! The progress bar has barely moved, and my laptop's fan is whirring like it's about to blast off my lap.

If I really want "Hide and Seek," I could buy it. But ninety-nine cents is a lot of money for a song, and I'm still mad Marissa Cooper got her pretty, popular stink all over that one. On the other hand, my playlist is a little dude-heavy, and why should men have a monopoly on angst?

Oh, screw it! It's Christmas. I deserve this, at least.

I hop down from my lofted bed and make the arduous journey— all three steps—to the desk where my backpack is slung over the back of the chair. My wallet is somewhere in the bottom, along with a semester's worth of dried-up pens and half-finished Spanish worksheets.

Aha!

As I close my fingers around the wallet, there's a knock at the door.

That's odd.

It's not one of my friends, because I don't have any friends here. And even if I did, they'd be home for winter break, eating ham with their happy, whole families.

When I open the door, I'm face-to-face with a willowy boy with light brown skin, who's dressed like he escaped a Ren faire. He's wearing a ruffled tuxedo shirt tucked into slim-tailored trousers, so slim they might actually be girls' pants. The look— and that's what this is, *a look*—is finished off with a green paisley ascot and black velvet cape. I'm pretty sure he's wearing eyeliner, which, to be fair, he is definitely pulling off.

"Who are you?" I don't bother being polite because I'm positive he has the wrong room.

"I'm Finn Everett," he announces like it's obvious, even though I know I've never seen him before in my life. I would remember him.

To punctuate his statement, he throws the cape over one shoulder, revealing a flash of crimson silk lining, and plants a hand on his hip. He stares down at me like he's waiting for an answer, even though *he's* the one who knocked on *my* door.

"Okay, Finn Everett, what do you want?"

"What are you doing on campus on Christmas? You know you're not allowed to be here, right?"

I've known him for thirty seconds and I'm already exasperated. But I know how to get rid of him: "I'm an orphan."

I'm gratified to see him flinch at the word. I wouldn't usually describe myself this way, but I'm keen to get back to my night, and over the past few years I've learned nothing kills a conversation faster than the *o*-word. It sure sent me running for the door when a middle-aged social worker in a lumpy brown blazer sat across from me and my sister and opened with, "Now that Hannah's an orphan, we'll have to figure out what to do about her guardianship."

Finn Everett looks me up and down, taking in my plaid pajama pants, oversized Boston College sweatshirt, and greasy hair that's been in the same messy bun for the last three days. "No," he says, shaking his head like I'm a math problem he can't solve. "You're too pretty to be an orphan."

"Excuse me?"

"All those white ladies would have been fighting to bring you home from the orphanage. You're cute. Underdressed, but cute." When I don't respond, he adds, "That was a compliment, by the way!"

Well, shit. He's not one of the people who clam up when they hear about my parents; he has questions. There's nothing worse than the question people. *How? At the same time? How old were you? How do you feel about it?*

"Not that kind of orphan. I'm not some Cabbage Patch doll, or whatever you're thinking. My parents died when I was fifteen."

"Oh, okay. Well, we're going on an adventure." My whole body unclenches when I realize he's on to the next topic.

"We are?" I haven't left my dorm in two days because the entire campus is closed, even the dining halls. I've been subsisting on boxes of Special K with Red Berries and microwaved bean and cheese burritos from the convenience store down the hill. What kind of adventure could we possibly have?

"Did you have something better planned?"

I do not. I'm going to listen to my playlist while I eat an entire pint of Ben & Jerry's Milk & Cookies ice cream, and then maybe I'll watch *Die Hard*, the least sappy Christmas movie, so I can tell myself I'm in the holiday spirit. But I don't want to tell him this, because I get how it sounds.

But Finn Everett doesn't need confirmation. He nudges past me and looks back and forth at both sides of the room, each equipped with a bed, a desk, and a dresser. "Which closet is yours?"

One side has a generic navy blue comforter. Every square inch of cinder block wall is plastered with band posters. Guster, O.A.R., Weezer, Wilco, the Postal Service. The other side is decorated with a Lilly Pulitzer bedspread and a single poster of Jessica Simpson vacuuming in her underwear. I think it's obvious which side is mine, but I point to the closet on the right side of the room anyway. He starts flipping through hangers. I'm not sure what he's looking for, but I'm positive he won't find it. I live in a rotation of concert tees bought off merch tables at Paradise Rock Club and the Orpheum.

"That's it?!" He sighs so dramatically I swallow an apology for my lack of evening gowns.

"What were you looking for?"

"Something better than"—he motions at my pajamas and pulls a face like he smelled spoiled milk—"this."

"And where are we going that has such a strict dress code?"

"Now we're going to have to make a pit stop. Grab your coat. Let's go." He snaps his fingers twice to punctuate his demand.

I must be stunned into compliance, because I find myself grabbing my puffer coat and sliding on a pair of salt-stained Ugg boots. I guess we're going on an adventure.

We spill out of Welch Hall into the brisk night air. Snow flurries dance in the wind. What's most striking isn't the snow, it's the silence. Usually there are ten thousand students rushing to a Perspectives on Western Culture seminar or a spin class at the Plex, or at night—let's be honest, sometimes during the day, too—ambling to off-campus parties in Cleveland Circle to play flip cup. But tonight it's just us.

We cross into the unfortunately named Dustbowl, which isn't dusty at all. Most of the year it's a grassy quad ringed by stately stone buildings, but now it's covered in two inches of hardened snow. When I toured the campus, it was spring, and the lawn was dotted with pairs of girls tanning on beach towels while groups of boys playing Frisbee maneuvered around them. It was exactly how I thought college should look from episodes of *Dawson's Creek*. *This* was the slice of normal I was craving.

"How'd you find me?" I wonder aloud. Maybe I should have asked more questions before agreeing to this outing. Not that I ever technically agreed.

"Your music," Finn answers. "But this was the sixth dorm I tried! Trust me, you were not easy to find. I've been *barely* entertaining myself for a week." He gestures at his ridiculous outfit. "I was beginning to think I was the only person on campus."

Finn and I cross into O'Neill Plaza and make our way toward the sad, unlit Christmas tree at its center. Is this where we're going? Some adventure this is. With students home for break, the facilities staff must have decided it wasn't worth the cost of electricity to keep the tree lit, even on Christmas.

"Wait here," Finn instructs.

He leaves me standing under the tree and heads toward the library on the east side of the plaza. I'm not close enough to see what he's doing, but I hear the jingle of keys he produces from underneath his cape and watch him slip inside the building.

I jump from foot to foot to stay warm as minutes pass and he doesn't reappear. For a second, I wonder if I'm being abandoned— again—and he has a getaway horse-drawn carriage waiting on the other side of the building.

I'll give him five more minutes before I head back to the warmth of my dorm and queue up *Die Hard*. As I look down at my watch to start timing him, the tree in front of me flickers on. I crane my neck to gawk at thousands of rainbow twinkle lights. I can feel myself grinning like an idiot. *Okay, Finn Everett, not a bad start.*

I don't hear him approach over the wind whipping through the plaza, but when I look over, he's standing next to me with a smug grin on his face, watching me take in his handiwork. "How'd you know how to do that?" I ask.

He gives a faux-innocent shrug and ignores my question. "We can't have an adventure without ambience, can we?" He winks at me. "Onward!"

"Where are we going?" I trail him down more stairs.

"You'll see. Patience, darling," he calls over his shoulder.

"Hannah," I correct him, realizing he never asked my name. Apparently, the *who* was not critical criteria in an adventure companion. Now I feel even sillier traipsing through campus, probably about to break my neck on these icy stairs, with this weirdo in a cape who doesn't care to know my name.

He pulls to a stop on the landing, and I almost crash into his back. "Hannah," he parrots back at me, rolling the name over in his mouth. "A pleasure," he says with a small bow.

A nervous giggle escapes my throat. I've never been bowed to before. He's so strange, but also maybe kind of endearing? Plus, he was right, what else do I have to do tonight?

"Well, c'mon, before I freeze my ass off!"

After a stop at Robsham Hall to raid the theater department's wardrobe closet and some heated negotiations about my outfit for the evening (he pressed for a corseted Victorian gown, but I bargained him down to a red, fifties-style dress with an itchy petticoat underneath), we're standing outside Lower Dining Hall, which is closed. Except nothing is closed to us tonight with Finn's magic key ring. I'm beginning to wonder if there's a janitor duct-taped to a chair in a maintenance closet, missing one set of keys.

The tea-length dress Finn talked me into wearing swishes around my knees as we make our way into the cafeteria portion of the dining hall.

"And what will the lady be having this evening?" Finn asks.

The options are limited since the dining hall is closed. Without the hot food stations or the salad bar, our options are chips, granola bars, or cereal. "The lady will have your finest Honey Nut Cheerios, my kind sir."

"We can do better than that," Finn says as he ducks behind the service station.

"If you could have anything to eat in the whole world—well,

maybe not the whole world, but that would normally be available at Lower—what would it be?"

We seem to be gearing up for a make-believe tea party situation, but I'm willing to play along.

"So?" he presses.

"Pancakes!"

"That's so boring. Try again, but do better this time."

"Chocolate chip pancakes?"

"Better, but barely."

He bends to open a stainless-steel fridge below the service station and resurfaces with a carton of milk and a stick of butter.

"Back in a flash." He disappears into the kitchen, which I'm positive is off-limits to students. He returns, hugging a mixing bowl filled with dry ingredients to his chest with one hand and dangling an unopened bag of chocolate chips from the other.

"Hop right up." He points to an empty counter.

"You have the most important job of all. You will hold my cape. Guard her with your life," he says, before adding, "No, seriously, I'm dead if I get this dirty. We're doing *Phantom* next semester."

Finn rolls up his sleeves and gets to work measuring milk and cracking eggs into the bowl of dry ingredients. After mixing, he dumps in the entire bag of chocolate chips and flashes me a wink.

"So, how'd you know where all that stuff was?" I ask. I'm surprised at his confidence in the kitchen, especially *this* kitchen, which he appears to know his way around.

He crosses to a different station and turns on a flat-top grill, hovering his hand over it to see if it's getting hot. Satisfied with what he feels, he nods to himself and pulls a ladle from a bin of utensils beneath the countertop. "I work here. It's my work-study job."

"Oh, so that's why you have all the keys."

"No, that's because of my other job. I also work in the provost's office. I'm the errand boy. I have to make a lot of deliveries, hence the keys."

Two jobs. Wow! I managed a straight-B average last semester and I have zero jobs. The upside to dead parents, if you're a silver linings person—which, let's be clear, I am not—is that I have money from the sale of my childhood home to pay for college and should graduate debt-free. The downside, of course, is no parents.

"Is that why you didn't go home for Christmas? Because it was too expensive?"

Finn gives a heavy sigh as he ladles globs of batter onto the grill. "Not exactly."

I decide to shut up. I've become the question person I hate so much. For a minute, we watch the pancakes bubble in silence.

"My dad's an asshole. He cut me off after I came out last summer. It's like marrying a Black woman was his one progressive deed for his whole, dumb life, and now he's done. He didn't even try to understand." His words spill out in a breathless run-on like he can't stop himself from telling me.

"Oh, Finn." My response is inadequate, but I don't know how to comfort him. Hell, I only met him an hour ago.

"I didn't want to transfer schools, so I loaded up on jobs to pay for tuition. But now I'm failing all my classes because I have to work so much. So I guess it wasn't a flawless plan."

He flips the pancakes. The smell is pure heaven. At least there's that.

"What did your mom say?" I ask.

"Not much. Which is a bummer. She doesn't hate my guts like my dad does, but she also won't stand up to him. So fuck them, I guess."

I nod vigorously. It feels rude to say *fuck them*, since they're adults I don't know. Instead, I find myself saying, "My mom died of cancer the spring of my sophomore year of high school and then my dad died in a car accident three months later. Now my sister's off on some round-the-world vacation and didn't even call to wish me a merry Christmas." I have no idea why I'm telling him this. Maybe confessions are contagious.

"Now you went and made my thing look stupid."

"I don't think it's stupid. I think it sucks."

"Yours, too."

Finn pulls out two plates and serves up the pancakes, five for each of us, in heaping stacks. He ducks into the refrigerator and holds up a can of whipped cream, giving me a questioning look.

"Obviously!" I'm offended he has to ask. He doesn't know me very well. *Yet*, I think.

On the way to the dining room, we swipe silverware and load our pockets with syrup packets. "Where would you like to sit?"

he asks. We stand at the head of the dining room surveying rows and rows of empty tables.

"Over there." I point to a round booth in the far back corner that's occupied at all hours, crowded with groups of friends studying over coffee or hanging out for long stretches. For once, I want to feel like I belong. Even if no one else is here to see it.

TWO

Finn

Christmas #6, 2013

My phone vibrates on the nightstand.

Who is calling this early? I don't actually know if it's early, but it feels like it is, and I don't have the strength to open my eyes and check. I wait for the call to ring out and go to voicemail.

The phone starts ringing again. I groan. I am so fucking hungover. My mouth feels like I slurped down a decent portion of the Sahara Desert last night.

"Should you get that?" someone with a posh British accent asks from behind me.

Oh, crap. I brought someone home from the bar last night.

I never do that.

I rewind my memories to see if I have any recollection of who the man in my bed is, his name, or if anything happened between us. Nope. Nothing.

I lift the sheet and peek down to see if I'm clothed. Also nothing.

"Don't worry, I was a perfect gentleman. We only made out a bit," he offers. "Well, quite a lot, if I'm honest."

I'm only relieved for a few seconds, then I'm offended. Wait, I'm a catch. I don't go home with just anyone. Why wouldn't he want to sleep with me? Also, why am I buck naked if we were only making out?

"You fell asleep," the man continues.

Well, that isn't super attractive. But if I fell asleep, why did he stay? That's creepy, right?

"On my arm," he adds.

Okay . . . not such a catch.

Before I turn over to get a look at Mystery Man, I dash off a prayer to the patron saint of one-night stands: *Please don't be ugly, please don't be ugly.*

He is definitely not ugly. Mystery Man is lying on his side with both hands tucked under his cheek. There's a wry smile on his lips like he's enjoying this. One rogue curl of almost-black hair droops onto his forehead and he reaches up to push it out of his eye. When he does, I clock a well-defined bicep.

Heat zips down through my stomach at the thought of him pushing me down on a bed. Did that happen? Or do I just want it to?

The next problem is that I have no idea what his name is, and both my roommates are gone for Christmas, so I have no one to introduce to him so I can lure him into introducing himself in return. Although maybe that's a good thing. Evan and Bryce are fine living with a gay man in theory, but I'm not sure how cool they'd be about meeting a half-naked overnight guest in our kitchen.

My phone starts buzzing again.

"In my experience, when someone calls three times in a row, it either means they're very angry at you or someone is dead." Mystery Man props himself up on his elbow, interested to find out which it is.

I turn onto my back and stretch to grab the phone off the nightstand. Hannah. I said I'd be at her place by ten. I must already be late.

"Hello," I croak out.

"Are you on your way?"

"What do you think?"

"Get up and get over here. It's Christmas!" Clearly Hannah did not spend last night chugging vodka sodas at the Toolbox. She sounds positively chipper. I'm going to need about a gallon of coffee to match her level of enthusiasm.

"Okay, okay. I'm getting up. Give me an hour." It's a blatant lie. I've made the trip dozens of times, maybe hundreds—walk four blocks to the 6 at 116th, ride fifteen stops to Bleecker, switch trains to the F at Broadway–Lafayette, two stops to Essex, then a four-minute walk to Hannah's—and it takes forty-five minutes on a good day. That's when all the trains are running on schedule, which they won't be on Christmas Day. This only gives me fifteen minutes to shower, get dressed, and deal with the man in my bed.

"An hour in Finn time means three hours," she whines. She knows me well.

"It'll be even longer if you don't let me go shower. I'll text you when I'm on my way," I tell her, and end the call.

"Was that your mum?" Mystery Man asks, looking down at me from his vantage point propped up on his side. I'm afraid to lift my head and discover the full extent of my hangover.

"My best friend."

"Ahh," he muses.

This guy is in no rush to leave. "You must have somewhere to be. It is Christmas, after all."

"Nope. No plans."

Fuck. What are the odds? Well, pretty decent. You wouldn't be getting obliterated at a gay bar on Christmas Eve if you had a loving family expecting you bright and early to open gifts. Or maybe you would, what do I know?

"Not spending the day with your family?" I press.

"They're abroad."

"So your friends, then?"

"With their families." He has a mischievous glint in his eye that I do not like. He's full of himself and doesn't know how to take a hint. God, I just want him to leave so I can drink water directly from the bathroom faucet and crawl into a scalding-hot shower.

You can't leave him alone on Christmas, says a voice in the back of my head. This is a massively inconvenient time to find a conscience. But I know the voice is right. I know how difficult it is to be without family on Christmas. I can't believe I'm about to do this . . .

"You could join me and my friends if you want."

"Splendid, I'd love to!" He beams at me with a smile fit for a toothpaste commercial. Definitely veneers. "You already invited me last night, but it felt rude to assume the invite stood given you don't seem to remember the conversation."

I groan and pull the covers over my head. Is it possible to die of embarrassment? Because now would be the time. I wait a minute for death to come in case the universe decides to do me a solid, but nothing happens. So I push myself up to sit against the wall that serves as my headboard, letting the blankets pool around my waist.

The man mirrors me and sits up, too. From this new vantage point, I notice he has a full-on six-pack. I don't stare long enough to count the individual abs—that would be rude—so it's possible it's an eight-pack.

The man reaches his right hand across his body toward me. Is something going to happen right now? It's not like Hannah believes I'll be there in an hour. Maybe morning sex will distract me from my headache, which has fully set in. As long as he isn't expecting a blowjob. My gag reflex can't handle it.

"I'm Theo, by the way. In case you didn't remember."

Oh, the only contact the man—who is apparently named Theo—is offering is a handshake. I awkwardly offer my right hand from in between us to shake.

After showering, I feel slightly more human. I'd put my risk of vomiting around fifty percent, which is not great, but nothing a breakfast sandwich can't solve.

"¿Que lo que, jefe?" Ramón looks up from his Sudoku puzzle to greet us when we walk into the bodega on my corner. "Feliz Navidad" blasts through the speakers. I wince at the volume and almost turn around and walk out, but my need for carbs and grease wins out.

"Can I get a bacon, egg, and cheese?"

"And for your friend?"

"What do you want?" I ask Theo.

He looks confused. "Is there a menu?"

"No, it's a bodega. They have, like, bacon, egg, and cheese; egg and cheese; and I don't know . . . bodega stuff." What New Yorker doesn't have their bodega order locked and loaded? Maybe he's only visiting from England.

"I'll have the same," Theo announces.

Ramón sings along to the music while he scrambles eggs in a little metal bowl. Theo watches him and I take the opportunity to watch Theo, who is now, disappointingly, fully dressed. I home in on his shoes. They're brown and a little scuffed, but from the horsebit buckle I'm pretty sure they're Gucci, and not the knock-off kind from Canal Street I wear. My eyes scan up his body and take in his jeans. Dark wash with no distressing. And his belt, also brown. I try to discern the belt's brand, but the buckle is plain with no details to give away the designer.

"Are you . . . staring at my dick?" Theo whispers coquettishly, interrupting my mental inventory of his outfit.

"No! I'm just . . . uh . . . ," I babble to the display of cigarettes behind the counter, which I suddenly find very interesting. I'm saved by Ramón returning with our sandwiches. He puts them in a plastic bag with a wad of napkins.

Outside, a black SUV idles on the corner. I suggested the subway, but Theo insisted he'd get us a car. After clocking his shoes, I'm not surprised he sprang for a black car.

"Give me your phone and I can put in Hannah's address."

"We need to stop at my apartment first so I can change," he says. "I can't meet new people in yesterday's clothes."

I don't have the energy to argue. "Fine."

I don't pay attention to where we're going. Instead, I focus on my sandwich, which is improving my hangover with every bite. By the time I crumple the foil wrapper and wipe the crumbs from my sweater, we're pulling up to a mid-rise brick building on Central Park West.

"Want to come up?" he offers.

It's better than sitting here with the driver. Before we reach the building's door, my phone starts vibrating in my pocket. I fish it out and see my sister's name on the caller ID.

"I'll catch up in a minute," I tell Theo.

I lean against the building's facade, ignoring the dirty look the doorman shoots me. "Mandy!" I exclaim with all the enthusiasm I can muster mid-hangover.

"Ew. I'm not Mandy anymore. I go by Amanda now."

The last time I was home, Mandy was eleven. She had braces with purple elastics (always purple, it was her *thing*) and a raging obsession with the Jonas Brothers. Nick Jonas, to be exact. Now she's sixteen and goes by Amanda. I have no idea who she has a crush on these days, but she can always be counted on to call on Christmas and my birthday.

"Well, merry Christmas, Amanda!"

"You too. Tell me what you're doing today!"

She loves hearing about the Christmas adventures Hannah and I have. "No big plans this year. We're watching movies and going out to dinner later."

I don't need to ask what she's doing. I'm certain that, as always, she'll be sitting down to a formal dinner at exactly three o'clock in the afternoon. Turkey (never ham), collard greens, my mom's famous cornbread, and macaroni and cheese.

"That sounds way better than here. Uncle Owen is bringing his new girlfriend, and Mom says she's trashy. It's a whole thing."

"Wait, Uncle Owen and Aunt Carolyn got divorced?"

"Yeah, a while ago. Mom's on Aunt Carolyn's side, so she invited her, too. It's going to be super weird." A lump forms in my throat at the idea that my mother, who wouldn't stand up for me, stood up to my father and invited his brother's ex-wife, not even a blood relative, to Christmas. What's more, I can't believe he let her.

"Is Mom around? Can I talk to her?" My mother never initiates the call, but sometimes Amanda passes her the phone and we trade pleasantries for a few minutes. She asks about auditions and my apartment, but never my love life, and in return she fills me in on neighborhood gossip or, more recently, the engagements and weddings of my high school classmates.

"Mom's downstairs. She's making three different pans of cornbread this year. She's on high alert because Grandma Everett made a comment last year about the cornbread being dry."

"Oh," I say, careful to mask my disappointment. "Tell her I say merry Christmas."

"I will. But I gotta go, she's calling me to set the table. Love you, Finny! Bye!"

She hangs up without waiting for my goodbye.

Before I head inside, I take a deep breath and try to shake off the call. I appreciate Amanda's calls, I really do, but sometimes it's easier to pretend I don't have a family at all. Especially on days like today. Talking to her feels like picking at a scab that never quite heals.

A doorman in a crisp gray uniform opens the door for me and I step into the building's wood-paneled lobby. The lobby's only concession to Christmas are two imposing columns opposite the entrance wrapped in pine garlands and dotted with white twinkle lights. There's not a red glittery ball in sight to junk up the decor. I wince at the squeaking noise my boots make on the marble floors, interrupting the otherwise pristine silence.

Off to the side, behind a desk, is another uniformed doorman, this one in a Santa hat. You'd think he'd be the fun one, but he's the scariest-looking dude I've ever seen and he's scowling at me like he can smell the vodka emanating from my pores, even after a shower.

"I'm with, um, Theo?" I desperately hope he saw us arrive together because I don't know Theo's last name, and I don't want him thinking I'm some vodka-scented riffraff trying to gatecrash.

He gestures toward the elevators without a single word.

For a moment, I'm relieved, until I realize no one told me which apartment I'm going to or even which floor. I'm about to turn back when the elevator doors open, revealing a third door-man (or would this be an elevator man?) waiting to ferry me up to Theo. He presses the button for PH, and we stand in silence as the elevator ascends.

The elevator doors open into the foyer of the nicest apartment I've ever seen. The walls are covered in red wallpaper dotted with zebras leaping through the air, which should be garish or cheesy, but combined with the classic black-and-white checker-board floors, it makes the space look modern and fun. Off to the side, there's a lacquered black buffet topped with a pair of gold lamps buttressing an enormous arrangement of white peonies. *Are peonies even in season?*

I was not ready for a multimillion-dollar real estate situation. First the abs, then the shoes, and now this? My instinct is to cut and run. I may as well call it before I embarrass myself any more. Clearly, Theo is out of my league.

But I can't make myself turn around and press the button to call the elevator.

"Hello?" Theo calls out from somewhere within the apartment.

"Hi! It's me," I say, and then add, "It's Finn," because he barely knows the sound of my voice and I don't want him mistak-ing me for a robber here to steal his art and antiquities. I can only imagine what the security is like in this place. Guess there's no going back now.

"In here!" he calls.

The hallway in front of me leads into a living room. I stop short as I enter. The room has a wall of windows with a jaw-dropping view of Central Park. I make a mental note to check the address on our way out, because I am going to need to Zillow this place. On another wall, floating bookshelves take up the entire wall from floor to ceiling. The shelves are populated with an artful arrangement of knickknacks that look like they might have come with the apartment. There's not a single book or framed photo to give any hints about the man who lives here.

What must Theo have thought of the hovel I call an apartment?

I'm standing in the center of the room, gaping at the view and trying to remember if there were dirty dishes in the sink or what state the bathroom was in, when he walks in, freshly changed into a new pair of dark-wash jeans and a soft-looking forest-green sweater. The color brings out his eyes, which I notice are also green. The sweater must be cashmere. I have the sudden, inadvisable urge to reach out and feel it for myself, but that would be creepy. So I shove my hands in my pockets and try to look casual.

"How'd I do?" Theo asks.

"Good. Fine. Yep!" I say, like I had word soup for breakfast and it didn't sit well.

"Can I use your bathroom?" I need a minute to regain my composure.

"Second door on your right." He points to a hallway at the far end of the living room.

When I'm pretty sure he can't see me, I slow my pace so I can snoop. The first room on the left is an office with an imposing mahogany desk at the center. I'm charmed when I notice a flock of model airplanes floating above the desk, strung from the ceiling with fishing wire so it looks like they're flying.

The desk checks out; he must be important to afford this place. I preemptively dread the moment when he asks what I do and I have to confess that I'm an out-of-work actor with two equally unimpressive side jobs. The first, folding khakis at Banana Republic, and the second, answering phones at Actors' Equity. I thought a job at the theater actors' union might give me an in at auditions, but so far all it's given me is an encyclopedic knowledge of the ins-and-outs of qualifying for the union's health coverage. My only fleeting hope is that we already covered this topic last night and I had the good sense to black it out to save future me the embarrassment.

Opposite the office is a guest room, judging from the nondescript decor. The only other door in the hallway is the bathroom. I slip inside and lock the door behind me before slumping over the marble vanity.

C'mon, Finn, get it together.

I'm far too dehydrated to need to pee. I inspect myself in the mirror; I look tired.

I open the medicine cabinet hoping for some magical eye cream that will make me look dewy and well rested and worthy of the hot young Monopoly Man in the other room. I recently started using Mario Badescu eye cream and wonder what kind Theo uses—probably La Mer, from the looks of this place. The medicine cabinet is bare except for a bottle of Advil. I take two with a handful of sink water and decide enough time has passed. The last thing I need is for it to seem like I'm taking a giant dump. I flush the toilet and run my hands under the faucet to maintain the pretense.

I'm feeling pleased with myself when we pull up to Hannah's building on Orchard Street at 12:25, beating her three-hour estimate by forty-five minutes.

I let us into the building with my spare key, a remnant from when Hannah and I lived here together. We lasted two months before realizing that sometimes best friends make the worst roommates.

Theo pants as we climb the gray linoleum-tiled stairs to apartment twenty-seven, and I'm gratified to have proof that he's not actually perfect. When we reach the fifth floor, I hesitate. Should I knock or use my key? Knocking feels more polite since I'm not alone.

Priya answers the door wearing a pink sweatshirt that says *Sleigh the Patriarchy* in glittery letters. "Oh, it's you! Why didn't you use your key?" She throws a sheet of glossy black hair over one shoulder and leans in to kiss me on the cheek. "Merry Christmas, by the way!"

"Who's at the door?" Hannah calls from the kitchen.

"Just Finn," Priya answers.

"Always nice to get such a warm welcome from my best friends."

"Did you lose your key?" Hannah emerges from the kitchen, wiping her hands on her ratty plaid pajama pants, the same pair she was wearing the night we met. Time hasn't done them any favors, but she wears them every Christmas morning insisting they're part of the tradition.

Hannah looks past me and notices Theo.

She plasters on a weird, manic smile and her posture straightens like she's a marionette and her puppeteer jerked her strings taut. "Oh, you brought someone!"

"Theo, these are my very rude friends Priya and Hannah."

"Lovely to meet you. Thank you for letting me barge in on your plans." He presents Priya with a yellow box of Veuve Clicquot from a canvas tote I didn't notice him carrying. "I brought this for you by way of apology."

"That's so nice of you." Hannah takes the box of champagne from Priya so she can inspect it, too. I'm positive this is the nicest bottle of alcohol that's ever graced this apartment. We make mimosas with André, sometimes Cook's, but only if it's someone's birthday.

"We'll put it in the fridge for later," Hannah says. "Finn, will you join me in the kitchen? I need your help making hot chocolate."

Hannah is a terrible cook, but even she doesn't need help making hot chocolate from a packet. She must be pissed. Priya leads Theo down the hallway lined with Hannah's collection of tour posters stuck to the wall with Blu Tack and into the living room, peppering him with questions about how we met and where he's from in England.

"Who is he?" Hannah whispers once we're alone in her Polly Pocket–sized kitchen. Not in a coy *oooh, who's your new man* way but more in a *who is this stranger and what is he doing in my house* way.

"It's a long story." I grab the kettle from the stove and fill it at the sink.

"Well, let's hear it. You brought someone to Christmas! Are you dating?"

"No."

"You're dressed in matching sweaters. You two look like you stepped out of a freaking J.Crew catalog." I didn't expect this reaction. And we don't match, we coordinate. Me in red, Theo in green. Not that correcting her will make this any better.

Instead, I blurt, "You brought Priya last year!"

"She lives here!"

"Well, I can bring someone, too." I know I should have asked, but she's making a way bigger deal of this than it needs to be. She's also physically blocking my path to the stove, so I'm whisper-yelling while holding a sunny yellow tea kettle with daisies all over it—definitely Priya's—which I fear is undermining how seriously I'm being taken.

"You can't make unilateral decisions about Christmas. Christmas is our thing. We talked about inviting Priya!" Hannah takes a breath and resets. "I didn't say you couldn't bring someone. I asked who he was," she says in a measured tone.

"I brought him home from a bar last night, and he didn't have any plans today, so I invited him. There, are you happy?"

She rears back like she's been slapped. "So you don't even know him. He's some, what? Some stray?"

"You do realize we can hear you, right?" comes Priya's sing-song voice from the living room.

Hannah's hands shoot up to cover her mouth and we exchange a horrified look before she rushes out of the kitchen, taking the corner so fast her socks slide on the hardwood floors.

"I'm so sorry." She addresses this to Theo. "Honestly, I didn't mean anything by it. We're all strays. I'm a stray, Finn's a stray. I guess Priya's not really a stray, but she screens most of her mother's calls."

"Hey, leave me out of this!" Priya protests.

"I'm so, so, so sorry," Hannah continues.

"Please don't apologize. I completely understand why you'd be surprised by a stranger showing up at your apartment uninvited, and on Christmas, no less. Perhaps I should go—"

"No!" Hannah and I shout at the same time.

"Please don't go," Hannah adds.

"I was going to say, go take a walk around the block and allow you a few minutes to chat."

This is his way of making a polite exit. There's no way he'll come back. This will become an anecdote he tells over cocktails and canapés to his rich friends about how the other half lives. "Can you believe how rude they were?" I imagine him saying while someone named Mitzi or Bitsy titters with laughter.

Theo stands up from the beige Ikea couch, and my heart drops into my stomach. I fish my keys from my front pocket and press them into his hand. Maybe some collateral will make him more likely to return. "Here, take my keys," I blurt, "so you can get back into the building. It's the two silver ones."

"Okay." Theo shrugs on his peacoat.

A loaded silence settles over the room while we listen to his footsteps retreat. When the door clicks shut, Priya says, "Do you think he's coming back?" at the same time Hannah says, "Did you sleep with him?"

"No," I answer.

"To which?" Hannah asks.

"To both. He's probably already in a cab uptown. Giving him my keys was dumb. Now I'll have to sleep here until Evan gets back from Maryland and I didn't bring a change of clothes." I sink my head into my hands and sputter out a long "Fuuuuuuck."

I'm in the kitchen doctoring three mugs of hot chocolate with peppermint schnapps. My head is throbbing after the Advil's brief reprieve, and I completely blew it with Theo. Some Christmas this is turning out to be. I'm about to carry the trio of mugs into the living room when I hear a key turn in the lock.

I rush to the hallway to intercept him.

"You came back," I whisper, my voice full of wonder. This must be how my childhood schnauzer Noodle felt when we got home from church on Sunday after he'd been convinced he was being abandoned. Unlike Noodle, I did not pee in anyone's closet to express my distaste for the circumstances.

"Of course I came back. I have your keys," Theo says.

"But we were awful."

"Eh, I know awful. You were garden-variety rude at best."

"Are you leaving again?" I ask.

"Do you want me to leave?"

"No."

"Then it's settled. I'll stay," Theo confirms.

The rest of the group spends the afternoon watching a double feature of *Elf* and *Love Actually* while I spend the afternoon worrying about whether Theo is having a good time. Is he bored? Does he regret coming back? Does he notice the way the paint is peeling on the doorframe? Does he think these movies are childish?

But, remarkably, from my position glued to his side, the miniature sofa providing a convenient excuse, I feel his laughter reverberate through my own rib cage when Buddy's arm goes into hyper-motion throwing snowballs in Central Park. At one point he reaches over and puts a hand on my knee, and I almost pass out. Maybe from relief, but more likely because all the blood in my body has rushed to my dick.

Later, another black car paid for by Theo drops us outside a restaurant sandwiched between a TGI Fridays and a deli. A vinyl sign affixed to the scaffolding reads DIM SUM AUTHENTIC BANQUET with some Chinese characters below it.

Last week I heard a group of boys complaining about their hangovers after a wild night at China Chalet while we waited in a fluorescent-lit hallway for our turn to audition to play an unnamed factory worker in the chorus in *Kinky Boots*. I called for a reservation the minute I left and pitched the plan to Hannah and Priya as a surprise, mostly because I'd been eavesdropping and wasn't sure about the particulars.

"Is it open?" Hannah asks, sounding underwhelmed. The Financial District, which is always quiet outside of market hours, feels abandoned to the point of eeriness, like we've stepped into the opening scene of an *Unsolved Mysteries* reenactment.

I'm surprised when I pull the restaurant's door handle and it opens. We ascend a flight of stairs and emerge into a stodgy banquet room dotted with white-linen-topped tables. Each place setting has a green napkin folded into a fan. The napkins clash with the worn red-and-gold carpet, which clashes with the strip of pink neon lights that ring the room. Only a handful of tables are seated.

"Isn't this great!" I say with forced cheer.

"Jews have been eating Chinese food on Christmas forever," Priya says as the host leads us to our table. "I think they have it right. I mean, nobody even likes turkey, but everyone loves dumplings." I make a mental note to get her a better belated Christmas gift than the rainbow socks I gave her earlier for pretending that this is not a total bust.

Once we're seated, a waitress pulls up to our table with a cart full of bamboo baskets. She holds up items one by one, taking off their lids and presenting them to us like she's the Vanna White of dim sum. By the time she wheels her cart away, every inch of the table is filled with baskets of pork buns and pot stickers and satays.

The addition of food eases the mood. "These are fucking great!" Hannah says through a mouthful of cold sesame noodles.

Having a newcomer gives us an obvious topic of conversation, but Theo is sparse with details, like he's embarrassed by the largesse of his upbringing. Over the course of dinner we eke out a few basic biographical tidbits: He grew up in a townhouse in Belgravia, but left for boarding school in Switzerland at eleven before going on to college in Paris. He has an older brother, so old that he was at university by the time Theo was in primary school. He speaks four languages fluently and a few others less fluently. This we learn when he summons the waitress and requests more shrimp dumplings in rapid Cantonese. She laughs at something he says and ruffles his curls. When she returns, she has an extra basket, even though we only ordered one. His father is skiing in Gstaad for the holiday and his mother is on a beach vacation in Thailand.

"Do you miss home?" Priya asks.

"Not really, no." He rushes to cover: "Does that make me sound awful? I guess I don't think of it as home. I haven't properly lived there since I was eleven. In a lot of ways, it's easier to be away."

A wave of recognition crashes over me, like his words could have been my own. Outside of Hannah, I've never met anyone else who doesn't have a family. I feel blindsided when friends mention going on family vacations or having two birthday parties—one with friends and another with family—even now that we're firmly into our twenties. A reminder that they're part of a set, while I'm a lone Lego piece. Those people I don't get, but this . . . this, I get.

When the check arrives, Theo lunges for it, putting down his credit card despite our objections. "You got me breakfast," he says, "this is only fair."

When the waitress returns with the credit card receipt, she takes inventory of our group. "Are you going in back?"

"In back?" I'm intrigued.

"To dance?" she clarifies.

"We're definitely going in back to dance!" I tell her before anyone can object. "And where do we go to do that, again?"

She points to an unremarkable swinging metal door opposite where we entered, which leads to a mirrored hallway. We follow it deeper into the building before taking two turns and a flight of stairs that deposit us into a cavernous basement, the air thick with cigarette smoke despite the city's nonsmoking ordinances. The floor shakes with the driving beat of "I Love It" by Icona Pop. I'm shocked we didn't hear music in the dining room, there must be some industrial-grade soundproofing. A disparate crowd of revelers—from skater punks to glossy uptown girls—wave their hands in the air dancing with reckless abandon. Here are our people. Here are the other Christmas strays dancing the night away at China Chalet.

Later that night, or more accurately, early the next morning, Hannah and I stagger into her apartment on tired legs. My ears still ring from the music. We left Priya there, her mouth fused onto the face of the DJ, who periodically broke their kiss to switch out the record on his turntable. Theo hopped into yet another black SUV with promises we'd do this again soon.

I could sleep in Priya's room. She won't be using it tonight. But instead, Hannah and I lie face-to-face in her full-sized bed, under the watchful gaze of Florence Welch, whose illustrated form stares down at us from a poster above the dresser.

"Did you have a nice Christmas?" Hannah asks through a yawn. She's already half asleep despite the cacophonous performance the old steam radiator is putting on.

"Definitely top three."

"Because of Theo?"

I'm glad my back is to the window so the slant of streetlight doesn't catch the gooey smile that comes to my face unbidden. I reach up and cover my mouth with my hand just in case.

"Do you like him?" she follows up when I don't answer.

"Maybe."

She kicks my shin. "Okay, yes," I admit.

"I do, too," she says. "For you, I mean. But promise me if you fall in love with him, we can still have Christmas together every year." There's a whiff of desperation in her voice, but I could never leave her.

"Of course I promise." I reach out my pinky finger and she hooks it with her own.

THREE

Hannah

This year, November 14

Sunlight streams through the windows of the Tribeca apartment. Even after five months, it's hard to think of it as mine. Ours, really. Every morning the ample light and space surprise me anew when I walk out of our bedroom, like maybe it was all a lovely dream.

I moved here with David, our first apartment together, after Priya announced her plan to move out of Orchard Street. "You've lived in the same apartment since you were twenty-two, Hannah. Don't you think it's time for a little upgrade?" she nudged. "Wouldn't it be nice not to be on top of each other? To have closets that fit more than five outfits? To have a living room with windows? A dishwasher? And with this new job, I'm finally making enough to get my own place."

Of course those things would be nice, but Orchard Street was my home, mostly for lack of other, better options to claim.

Plus, I loved living with Priya. It was the college roommate experience I never had. Saturday nights doing our hair to a soundtrack of Lana Del Rey and Lorde in the apartment's Pepto-Bismol-pink-tiled bathroom, nursing mugs of cheap white wine. I'd gotten used to her sounds (her marimba alarm tone and her favorite podcast, *Call Your Girlfriend,* which she listened to while getting ready for work) and her smells (the expensive Diptyque candles that were her most-cherished beauty editor perk and the rooibos tea she left half-full mugs of around the apartment). After almost six years living together, Priya was fully ingrained into the fabric of my days.

With her moving out, David suggested we move in together. The idea was as intriguing as it was terrifying. Even though I already spent most weekends and an increasing number of week-nights at David's Flatiron apartment, living together felt like a huge step. What if he was turned off by my apathy toward basic housekeeping, or found me annoying when there were no breaks? After all, Finn and I had only lasted two months as roommates.

"I already know that you have awful dragon breath in the morning and that you prefer the crappy one-ply toilet paper to the good stuff, and I still love you," David joked. "I want all your quirks, Hannah. Bring 'em on." And just like that, his exuberance melted my resistance.

Rather than moving into his apartment, David suggested we find something that was *ours* instead of *his*. I was a goner the second I saw this apartment with its oversized factory windows, exposed brick walls, and a top-of-the-line kitchen straight out of a Food Network set.

But better than the apartment itself was the man I got to live here with. We'd been dating for a little over a year by then, and I felt like I'd gotten away with something by getting his tacit agreement we'd stay together at least the duration of a twelve-month lease.

"What's wrong with this place?" I asked as I poked my head into the walk-in closet in the primary bedroom. If it was in our price range, there had to be a catch. Cockroaches? Professional tap dancers for upstairs neighbors? Ghosts?

It turned out I was right, *I* couldn't afford this place, but *we* could. David had a huge grin on his face when he showed me the Excel formula he made to calculate how much rent we should each pay based on our relative salaries. My heart swelled seeing his nerdy excitement over a spreadsheet. "I really don't mind," he explained. "Please let me do this for us. I want us to be a team." Instead of answering, I backed him against the closed door of our would-be bedroom and pressed a kiss to his lips.

"Is that a yes?" he asked when we came up for air.

"Definitely yes," I confirmed.

I wasn't used to having someone take care of me. Finn once called me violently self-sufficient when I failed to tell him about a two-day stomach flu until after I recovered. He meant it as an insult, but I took it as a compliment.

But here, David had a point: he shouldn't be made to suffer

through the real estate atrocities my salary could afford. It wasn't his fault the radio industry paid peanuts, although technically I made the jump to podcasts two years ago. But my employer is still a chronically underfunded public radio station. I have a cabinet full of canvas pledge-drive totes to prove it.

This morning, I'm camped at the kitchen island getting a head start on my inbox when David emerges from our bedroom in blue-striped pajama pants and a white undershirt with a stretched-out collar. His light brown hair is mussed from sleep and he's wearing an old pair of wire-rimmed glasses he only wears first thing in the morning or last thing at night.

Morning David is the version of David I like best. The private version, just for me, before he pomades his hair, puts in his contacts, and dons his suit for his job at the law firm. Although he doesn't look bad in a suit either.

He wore the glasses on our first date, which I later learned was unusual and only because he ran out of contacts. "I have a really early morning," he said after two glasses of wine at the Immigrant, the dimly lit wine bar in Alphabet City he'd suggested. I thought our date was going well, certainly the best I'd ever been on, but it seemed the feeling was not mutual.

I braced myself for a brush-off. After only a month on the dating apps, I'd learned to read the signs. I chastised myself for daring to get excited about him. But then he surprised me. "Would you mind if I just got a water?" he asked. "Because I'm really enjoying talking to you and I'm not ready for the night to end yet." In that moment I fell a little bit in love with him, and the tally of tiny special moments added to his chart of accounts has only grown since.

"Morning," he mumbles. "Why do you look like someone kicked your puppy? It's barely seven thirty." He shuffles over to me and plants a kiss in my hair. Butterflies flip in my stomach at the sweet, comforting gesture, and for a few seconds I forget about the email at the top of my inbox. I lean into him and can feel the heat of sleep radiating off him. "What's wrong?" he asks.

"Mitch," I groan.

"What did he do now?" David asks.

"He's threatening to shut down the whole project if we don't lock in talent for the pilot episode soon." He marked the email letting me know with an urgent flag, the same way he does every single one of his other emails. Even the completely benign ones.

"How could he do that? I can't believe he doesn't see what a good idea this is."

I'm working on a pitch for a music history podcast called *Aural History*, which I think is a pretty clever name. It would be my first solo project. Each episode would tell the story of a different song. Some chart toppers, other deep cuts with sentimental meaning to the artist, some one-hit wonders. We'd interview everyone involved, from the artist to the songwriters, producers, and session musicians about how the song came to be. I picture it as a hybrid of *Pop-Up Video* and *Behind the Music,* both staples of my teenage TV diet.

My original idea for the pilot was to tell the history of "Konstantine" by Something Corporate, a fan-favorite song that, for years, the band refused to play at concerts. It was the cornerstone of every playlist I made in high school.

"The song is nine minutes and thirty seconds long," Mitch, my boss and the station's newly hired head of podcast development, barely took his eyes off the CNN news ticker long enough to protest. He didn't bother turning off the TV when I came into his glass-walled office, only muted it.

"So? That makes it more interesting. How did a nine-minute song that was only released in Japan become a fan favorite? This was 2003, the early days of the internet. I could make this fascinating."

"To exactly four people, and you're one of them. So your audience is three people. Bring me something with commercial appeal and I'll think about it."

My second pitch was to profile "Candy" by Mandy Moore. What's more commercial than a bubblegum pop hit with a tie-in to the number-one show on television? What nineties kid doesn't remember that lime-green VW Beetle?

"Yes!" Mitch boomed. "My wife loves *This is Us*. Now, how do we get the talent?"

"Leave it to me! I have plenty of music contacts from Z100," I told him as I backed out of his office before he could change his mind.

With Mitch's yellow light, I reached out to Mandy Moore's manager. When I didn't hear back, I tried her agent and her publicist, too. But after a month of silence, despite weekly follow ups, I have to admit they're not going to return my inquiry.

Turns out Z100 has plenty of music contacts, but I have none. Which leaves me back at square one.

"Would coffee help?" David asks.

It's a rhetorical question. He's already filling the carafe with water to pour into the coffee maker and pulling down my favorite BC mug from the cabinet. I could, of course, make my own coffee. But David's a light sleeper and our beloved Capresso grind-and-brew sounds like a jet engine preparing for takeoff. So this has become our morning ritual. After five months here, I cherish the little routines we've built together. Falling asleep in the warm, protective circle of his arms every night and cooking dinner together while we talk about our days—fine, technically he cooks while assigning me the impossible to mess up tasks like chopping onions or peeling carrots, but I always do the dishes—far outweigh the occasional domestic spat. I'm starting to get used to, maybe even enjoy, someone taking care of me.

As the coffee brews, he leans against the counter. "I think I've figured out what I was doing wrong with the pizza crust," David announces. He's been trying to hack the at-home version of our favorite prosciutto and arugula pizza from a little pizzeria in the West Village for months. "How about I give it another whack tonight and we can start that Netflix series my brother was telling us about. Maybe it could be a light at the end of the tunnel after dealing with Mitch all day," he suggests.

"That sounds amazing, but I can't. I'm grabbing drinks with my friends tonight."

I don't need to specify who I mean when I say my friends. I

have work friends—people I brave the Sweetgreen line and trade bits of office gossip with—and I'm happy to double-date with David's college friends from NYU, but I'm always relieved when their wives or girlfriends don't follow up on their promises that we *have to* make plans to hang out without the boys. "My friends" will always refer to Finn, Priya, and Theo.

David gets along with them well enough, but not so much that he's part of the group. Not that there was much of a group to be part of when we started dating. That was the year Finn and I weren't speaking. But even so, we have too much shared history for someone new to catch up. When David joins us, we're constantly having to stop and explain that Elise is Priya's monstrous ex-boss, the one who laid her off at Refinery29, or that one time Finn cajoled us into playing beer pong with gin and tonics and none of us have touched gin since, or that Theo's mother was in a terrible art house movie in the eighties, a contemporary remake of *Madame Butterfly* called *Ms. Butterfly*, and we laugh hysterically whenever anyone says the word "butterfly" in any context.

"Is it someone's birthday?" David asks.

"No?"

"Oh, I just thought . . ." He trails off. "Never mind me. Precoffee brain." He pours a splash of half-and-half into my coffee and sets it down on the counter in front of me.

Even though he didn't mean anything by it, his comment bristles. The implication that we need a reason to get together. But if I'm honest, it's been a while since we've had plans as a foursome.

"No occasion, really. Just catching up."

"Well, can you pencil me in for tomorrow night?" he asks.

"Tomorrow night? I thought you were going to your brother's apartment to watch the game." David's brothers and a few of their childhood friends have a fantasy football league they take way too seriously. They get together on Thursdays to watch whatever game is on and talk strategy. David is their de facto statistician. At the end of the season, whoever loses has to fulfill a silly bet, which is how David ended up sitting for the SATs last spring. He actually enjoyed brushing up for it, going so far as to buy a stack of test prep books. I teased him mercilessly when he brought *SAT Prep for Dummies* to bed with him, but he was the one laughing when his score went up by twenty points since he took the test in high school.

"I can skip this week," he tells me. "I'd much rather spend time with you."

I stand on the footrest of my stool and lean over the kitchen island to catch his lips with my own. "Yes," I tell him. "Don't pencil me in. Use pen."

That night, I'm the first to arrive at Rolf's. In December, there's a line around the block, but in mid-November, it's me and a skeleton crew of regulars.

The regulars at a Christmas-themed bar are a quirky bunch: women in their sixties who look straight out of the *SNL* mom-jeans sketch with feathered hairstyles and sweatshirts with applique flowers. They gossip at length about their husbands while throwing back glasses of merlot and eating from party-sized bags of Lay's potato chips they're inexplicably allowed to bring in, even though Rolf's is also a German restaurant.

I claim a stool in the middle of the bar—close enough to eavesdrop, but far enough away not to seem nosy—and order a warm spiked apple cider. I watch the bartender, a bored-looking kid in his early twenties, fix my drink in a goblet the size of my head.

The women remind me of how my mom was with her friends. What would she be like if she were still alive today? I count the years on my fingers to figure out how old she'd be: fifty-seven. Fifteen years since she died. This Christmas she'll have been gone for as many Christmases in my life as she was alive for, and the thought makes me unbearably sad. Over time, missing her has softened to a dull thrum in the back of my chest, but every once in a while, like now, it floods through me at full volume.

I still picture her as she was before she got sick: smiling out from a sign on a bus bench advertising her as EDISON'S FAVORITE REAL ESTATE AGENT. She wanted the ad to say "top real estate agent," which wasn't technically true. However, she was the undisputed queen of the town's gossip mill, which made her a favorite with certain types. The year of her diagnosis, she got the Rachel haircut, which even then she was a few years late to— Jennifer Aniston was already onto her sleek flat-iron phase—but she was incredibly proud of the haircut nonetheless. I imagine she'd have updated it by now if she were alive, but my mental image of her is frozen in time. An eternal Rachel Greene.

Rolf's is like that, too; never changes. Year-round, every available square inch of ceiling and wall space is covered in faux pine and dripping with Christmas ornaments and fake plastic icicles. Rolf's found its niche and sticks with it. I respect that.

I check my phone to see if anyone has texted, and I find a message from Finn: Running late. I have news!

With Finn, "having news" could be anything from seeing Timothée Chalamet on the subway to meeting the love of his life to discovering a sandwich place with a really good buffalo chicken wrap. Everything is news with him. But spotting Priya and Theo enter the bar, chatting animatedly, puts a pin in my speculation.

An hour later, Finn bursts through the door in a cloud of apologies for his lateness and makes his way to the booth where we relocated to spare Theo the flirtations of the women at the bar.

"Sorry! Sorry!" Finn clucks as he unwinds his scarf and hangs it on a hook at the end of the booth. He leans in and gives Priya a double-cheek kiss and then scootches into my side of the booth. He finds my hand on the bench and gives it a squeeze. I always breathe easier when the four of us are in the same place.

"So, you have news?" Theo prompts him.

"Big news!" Finn looks around the table to make sure everyone is giving him their undivided attention. "I got a new job! At Netflix! Working on shows for actual fucking adults!"

Priya shrieks and leaps out of her seat to wrap her arms around Finn's neck.

"This calls for champagne!" Theo announces.

"This is incredible! You're incredible!" I tell him, my excitement rendering me unable to find words other than "incredible."

"This isn't exactly the side of the entertainment industry I envisioned for myself, I was picturing myself more as the talent, but it's still a step up. So that's something." Despite his dismissive comment, Finn is beaming at our reactions to his news.

Finn has worked as an associate development executive at ToonIn for the past three and a half years, helping to select which shows get picked to air and shepherding them through the production process. For the better part of that time, he's been locked in a heated rivalry with Sparky MD, a cartoon puppy who is, for reasons that are never explained, also a doctor for humans. Finn passed on a pitch for the show six months into his tenure, and *Sparky MD* went on to become the number-one show at their rival network.

These days, Sparky has a ubiquitous presence, popping up on billboards and children's backpacks. Once we were picking up my birth control prescription at Duane Reade when Finn spotted Sparky MD Band-Aids next to the register. He marched outside in a huff. I found him pacing on the sidewalk out front. "It doesn't even make sense!" he raged. "Sparky can't talk! How does he tell people their diagnosis?!"

Unfortunately, none of the shows Finn *had* greenlit held a candle to Sparky's success. This new job is long overdue—he could use a clean slate. I'm proud of Finn. I'm also relieved I'll never have to hear about *Sparky MD* ever again.

"I didn't even know you were looking for new jobs," I tell him.

"I didn't want to say anything in case it didn't work out," Finn says. "I didn't want to worry you for nothing."

"Worried? Why would I be worried? This is great! I'm so happy for you."

He fiddles with a groove in the table, avoiding eye contact. "Because the job is in LA," he says to the wood.

I blink rapidly trying to process this new information. I see Priya's lips moving, asking Finn a follow-up question, but I can't hear it above the roar of static in my brain.

Sometimes I wake up at 4:00 a.m., an old habit from years of working on a morning radio show. I lie in bed trying not to move, so I don't wake up David, and I make mental lists of all my worries. I worry about work deadlines or a snappy comment I made to David when I was hangry, but mostly I worry about my friends. I worry Theo will grow bored with New York and decide not to return from a trip to Paris or Bangkok or Sydney, or wherever he happens to be at the moment. I worry Priya will decide to follow whichever man she's dating; her men are always so transient. Last I heard, she was dating a chef who ran a series of pop-up dinner parties in airstream trailers across the country. But I never even thought to worry about Finn leaving.

And now he is.

Once the initial wave of shock recedes, I realize I'm also angry. Angry Finn didn't tell me separately before he told Theo and Priya. The delivery stings almost as much as the news itself.

Maybe we aren't as okay as I thought.

My attention snaps back to the conversation to find everyone staring at me.

"You look kind of pale. Are you feeling sick?" Priya asks.

"I'm fine, totally fine! Just surprised!" I gulp my drink to buy time and get a noseful of champagne bubbles. I start coughing, which only draws more attention. Now the surrounding tables are staring, too.

A hush falls over the table. I need a distraction. A subject change. I need people to stop staring at me and give me a moment to process. So I overcompensate. "Christmas!" I blurt.

My friends give me puzzled looks like I'm a robot short-circuiting.

"Since Finn is moving, this might be our last Christmas together." I forge ahead. "We have to make it our best one ever!"

"Are we doing that this year?" Priya asks.

Finn gives a noncommittal hum.

"Of course we're doing Christmas this year!" Finn and I have done Christmas together every year for a decade, Priya has been there for six, Theo for five. How can they think we wouldn't do Christmas this year?

"The last couple years, Christmas has been . . ." Priya trails off. She doesn't need to continue; we were there, too.

"But everything's fine now! And we have to do it this year . . . for Finn!" I sling my arm around his shoulder to illustrate how okay everything is. It has to be.

FOUR

Hannah

Christmas #5, 2012

When I wake, Priya is banging around in the kitchen. I hoped she'd be gone, but no such luck.

Priya has lived here since Garrett moved out in June. Garrett, my roommate after Finn, liked to do kickboxing workouts in the living room, which is already too cramped for sitting quietly, never mind jab-cross-uppercutting. I'm also pretty sure he peed in empty soda bottles in his bedroom. Either that, or he was massively dehydrated, because sometimes he wouldn't leave his room for the whole day on Sundays.

The only positive part of Garrett's roommate tenure was that he was gone over Christmas. Back to wherever he came from. I never found out where that was.

In the kitchen, Priya is standing in front of the single square of countertop in a pair of pink-and-red-striped thermal pajamas, her hair gathered in a topknot. The counter is littered with vegetable scraps and broken eggshells. She's humming along to "We Are Young" by fun., which pours out of the tinny speakers of her cell phone. "I'm making us breakfast!" she announces.

I peer over her shoulder into the mixing bowl, where there's a goopy mixture of eggs and what looks like remnants of every vegetable in the fridge. "Thanks," I tell her, despite how dubious the contents of the bowl look.

"My mom always makes this. She calls it kitchen-sink quiche. She takes everything left in the fridge, mixes it with cheese, and puts it in a pie crust. It looks gross now, but I promise it's really good." It wouldn't normally phase me, but today—on Christmas—my own lack of family feels more acute. I'm struck with a twinge of jealousy that Priya has a mother to refer to in the present tense. "Anyway, I was up early and thought I'd make a special breakfast since it's a holiday and all." She glances at me over her shoulder and gives a sheepish shrug. "Plus, what else do I have to do today? For all us non-Christians, Christmas is just a weird day on the calendar when everything's closed."

Her kind gesture makes me feel like an asshole for withholding an invitation to spend Christmas with me and Finn.

"We should invite her," Finn urged last week. "She said she doesn't have plans." I was less sure. She'd been a solid roommate so far. Way better than Garrett, which is a low bar. She's out most nights: PR events on weeknights, dates or bars with friends on the weekend. She brought Finn along to a couple of the press parties and he raved about the signature cocktails, mini crab cakes, and gift bags stuffed with travel-sized beauty products and branded water bottles. He couldn't believe it was all free.

As for Priya and I, we probably wouldn't hit it off if we met at a party—she seems too normal, too well-adjusted—but we have the same taste in takeout and TV shows, which goes a long way where roommates are concerned. But still, I held out hope that I'd wake to an empty apartment this morning. Maybe one of her other friends would invite her to spend Christmas with them. But it looks like she isn't going anywhere.

We eat our kitchen-sink quiche in the living room, whose aesthetic is an odd marriage of our possessions. My Backsälen loveseat next to her lucite coffee table. My Band of Horses tour poster beside Priya's *For Like Ever* one. Even her paperback of *Something Borrowed* looks slightly uneasy on our Billy bookshelf next to my copy of *The Hunger Games*. But at least one of us has taste when it comes to decor. Even I have to admit that the addition of her possessions has made the apartment feel homier.

"I've always wondered," she begins, "what's the deal with you and Finn?"

"We met in college, on Christmas our sophomore year. And we immediately clicked. It's like he's my soulmate, my person." I pause. "Ew, I'm explaining this all wrong. This sounds so cheesy." I laugh.

Her eyebrows rise so high and so quickly, I'm worried they might shoot right off her face. "Wait, are you, like, in love with him?"

"I mean, yes, but not romantically, if that's what you mean. We're just friends. More than friends, really. But not like *that*." I shoot her a pointed glance. "I just mean . . . I don't know how else to describe it. Have you ever had someone like that?"

I cringe at the babble I spewed at her. I'm not good at talking about my feelings. It's as if after so many years of suppressing them in the years following my parents' death and vehemently reassuring everyone I was *fine, totally fine*, I lack the vocabulary to make someone understand, even when I really want them to. This is where the non-biological-twin sense Finn and I share comes in handy. He just gets me, and vice versa.

"Ben," she says, "But we were absolutely *like that*. But I know what you mean."

"Who's Ben?" I ask with a mix of curiosity and certainty that no matter who he is, their connection couldn't possibly be the same as mine and Finn's.

"My college boyfriend." She stares down at her plate of quiche, suddenly guarded even though she volunteered his name.

"What happened? If you want to talk about it, I mean."

"*National Geographic* happened, that's what. He got his dream job as a travel photographer, so he's currently somewhere in the middle of the Amazon jungle. Kind of hard to stay in a relationship with someone that only has cell service like ten percent of the time. We tried long distance, but he might as well have been on Mars. And I guess he loved the job more than he loved me because he's still there and I'm very much single and still not over him."

"I'm sorry." Her admission about Ben makes me feel closer to her. Maybe her loss isn't the same as mine, but it's proof she isn't just the sunshine and rainbows facade she projects either. I reach over to put my hand on her knee, but at the last minute I decide maybe we're not those kind of friends yet and grab my fork to shove another bite of quiche in my mouth. It really is good.

"It's not your fault," she says.

"By the way, um . . . I meant to mention this earlier. Do you want to hang out with me and Finn today?"

"Oh, I don't want to crash your plans," she demurs. "I was going to go to the movies later. Christmas isn't even a holiday for me. Seriously, don't feel like you need to invite me because I told you about my ex-boyfriend drama."

"No, I'd really love it if you came," I tell her, and surprise myself by wanting her to say yes.

At two, we meet Finn in the heart of the Village. Priya's dressed in a sweatshirt I loaned her. Green with a fuzzy lamb on the front that says *Fleece Navidad* in squiggly cursive letters, the arms decorated with crisscrossing strands of Christmas lights. I've acquired quite a collection of holiday-specific attire over my four years of Christmas adventures with Finn. The plan is simple: we're going on a two-person ugly sweater bar crawl through Greenwich Village. Now three, with Priya.

"Whoa, there are way more people here than I expected," Priya says as we sidle up to a high-top table at Wicked Willy's, a pirate-themed bar offering $2 Bud Light Limes on special. They have a steadfast commitment to a tropical theme, even on Christmas.

"College bars are always a good bet," Finn says. "You get a mix of international students, Jewish kids, and the ones that can't afford airfare, but can afford two-dollar beers. There are tons of people alone on Christmas if you know where to look."

Priya looks around, taking in our fellow Christmas orphans.

"What'd you do for Christmas last year?" Finn asks her.

"Took half an edible, went to see the new *Alvin and the Chipmunks* movie, and ate an entire jumbo popcorn and a family-sized bag of Twizzlers. What'd you two do?"

"Oh my god," Finn says, and flashes his gaze toward me, both of us remembering how great last Christmas—our first Christmas living in New York—was. "So it's going to sound super cheesy, but we went to Dyker Heights. You know, in deep Brooklyn where they go all out on Christmas lights—"

"No, seriously," I interrupt, "they go *all out*. I have never seen Christmas lights like this. Like, this is *break the bank on your electric bill* kind of lights."

"So, we did the lights," Finn says, "and then we were walking back to the subway at Eighty-Sixth Street and we passed this Italian restaurant. A real old-school red sauce joint that looks like somewhere the Mafia would eat, and it's packed. So we decided to check it out. Turns out, it was the family that owns the place's Christmas dinner, but they invited us to join them. I've never had ravioli this good before.

"We ended up sitting at a table with Carmela, the great-great-grandmother. Everyone was serving her like a queen. We sat with her taking shots of limoncello while she told us stories about growing up in Sicily."

"Finn was obsessed with her," I add.

"She was like a real-life Sophia from *The Golden Girls*. She sent me a Christmas card this year, you know."

"That sounds really fun," Priya says. "Seriously, thanks for including me this year." She glances around the bar taking in the mix of twentysomethings, shouting and laughing. "I still can't get over how many people are here. Actually, there are some cute guys. See anyone you're interested in?"

"There's nothing here for me," Finn answers without bothering to look. "Everyone here is violently straight."

"Fair enough," she says. "What about you, Hannah?" They both focus their attention on me.

"I don't need anyone else. Especially not today. I just want to spend the day with you guys." I knock the neck of my beer against theirs and take a swig.

Five hours and four bars later, we're huddled around at a sticky wooden table at the Bitter End, a grungy bar–slash–music venue. The game of Never Have I Ever Priya and I are playing is interrupted when a man wearing a T-shirt printed with the bar's logo steps up to the empty stage. He taps the mic twice, sending screeching feedback echoing through the room.

"Sorry about that," he says. "Just wanted to let you know we're going to start the open mic in fifteen minutes and there's a sign-up sheet over at the bar."

"We should sign Finn up," I tell Priya. He stepped out a few minutes ago to answer a call from his sister. He was out of fingers in the game anyway.

"No, that's so mean! I'd be furious if you ever did that to me." Priya looks horrified by my suggestion.

"Trust me, he'll love it."

Finn suggests we leave after the first two lackluster performances—a drunk college kid butchering "Summer Girls" by LFO and a woman scream-singing a particularly angry rendition of "You Oughta Know."

"Let's stay for a couple more," I beg. "Please?"

He gives me a funny look but doesn't protest.

When they announce his name, Finn glares at me. "I should have guessed." But his mouth quirks into a coy smile.

"You don't have to," Priya says with a hand on his shoulder. "I told her it was cruel. Just so you know, it was all Hannah!"

Before she can finish her sentence, he's already strutting up to the stage, performer mode activated.

Priya stands on her chair and wolf whistles when Finn finishes his cover of "Bleeding Love."

"Goose bumps, Finn, I have goose bumps." Priya thrusts her arm in front of his face when he makes it back to our table. "You were amazing. I had no idea you could do that."

"I told you I sing. We had a whole conversation about auditions last week when we went to the launch party for that energy drink."

"Well, yeah," Priya says, "but I didn't think you were actually good." Her hands shoot to her mouth, the lubrication of the four previous stops on our bar crawl having loosened her tongue. She rushes to cover: "I mean . . . why aren't you getting cast if you can sing like that?"

Finn doesn't take offense at her gaffe. "Everyone at these auditions is good. Talent is table stakes. But I don't have any connections or credits. I've had directors tell me I don't have the right look for the part, which is sometimes code for I'm too Black, but other times code for I'm not Black enough. Or sometimes the reason is totally minuscule. Like one time, I almost got cast for a role, but I was too tall for the costumes, and they didn't have the time or resources, or maybe just the desire, to refit them."

"That's bullshit, Finn. That's so unfair," Priya rails.

"Life isn't fair." He shrugs his shoulders. "Does anyone want another?" He holds up his empty vodka soda.

"I'm good," I say. "I have to be up at the ass crack of dawn for work tomorrow." As the most junior full-time employee at Z100, I had no illusions about getting the whole week off. The station is closed for Christmas, playing a preprogrammed loop of music and ads, but tomorrow we're back at it bright and early.

"Hannah Gallagher, rising star of radio, destined to outshine her starving artist best friend as she rockets towards success," he says in a fake newscaster voice.

"I don't know that I'd call my minimum wage job 'success.' I don't think that's what they were talking about at BC when they said to 'set the world aflame,'" I say, quoting the oft-invoked Jesuit motto they lobbed at us during various platitude-heavy speeches throughout college. But secretly, I was overjoyed to be converted to a full-time employee last month after paying my dues for more than a year as an unpaid intern.

No one was more surprised by my post-college career glow-up than me. I figured I'd wait tables or work at the box office of whatever theater's production Finn was starring in. I only applied to the internship on a lark after a particularly frustrating conversation with a counselor at the campus career center. "What do you *love?*" she implored. The only things I could think of were music and my Christmas tradition with Finn, and only one of those was monetizable. Finn, on the other hand, is having a harder time finding his footing.

"Is anyone else starving?" Priya asks.

"Let's get out of here," Finn suggests. "We can still make the Waverly Diner."

"Now *that* I'm on board with," I say. It's one of the few spots that has hash browns instead of home fries, making it our favorite. "Breakfast for dinner is kind of a Christmas thing for us." I tell Priya.

"Okay, highs and lows of your first Christmas," Finn prompts as he leads the way down Bleecker toward the West Village.

"My high was definitely your song, Finn. I'm still not over it. You had the whole bar on their feet." Finn's face lights up at her gushing praise. "Seriously," Priya continues, "I don't have any real basis for comparison, but this Christmas easily takes my top slot."

I beam back at her, glad she gets it. "Want to do it again next year?" I ask.

"I would be honored."

FIVE

Hannah

This year, November 16

Wait for me on the boyfriend couch. Finishing up one thing! 5 mins! Priya texts.

I'm not sure what a boyfriend couch is, but it's self-explanatory when I get to Glossier's Lafayette Street office and spot three men scrolling through their phones on a pink tufted sofa in the reception area while their girlfriends shop for makeup in the attached showroom, sampling the brand's minimalist shades and taking selfies in the perfectly lit mirrors.

Since Priya started her new job in April, it's all she can talk about. She mentions the brand every other sentence like she has a crush. *Glossier is going to be the next unicorn. Glossier gave me stock options. I read on* Into the Gloss *that Priyanka Chopra uses yogurt to exfoliate her skin.* Priya didn't just drink the Kool-Aid, she did a twenty-second keg stand and is wasted on it.

And it's nice to see her excited about work after three years of career misery. Before this, she was cobbling together an income from an increasingly bleak slate of freelance writing assignments. Toward the end, all she was getting were SEO articles designed to bait readers into clicking affiliate links. But now she has her dream job as an editor for the brand's blog.

When she started, I placed a massive online order for products with names like "cloud paint" and "haloscope" despite not knowing how to use them. I was just happy to see Priya so happy and wanted to support her.

After a quick wait, Priya rounds the corner into the reception area shrugging on a furry blue coat that looks like it's made from a Muppet pelt, her eyes rimmed with matching glittery blue eyeliner. "Ready?" she asks.

"Tell me what this class is again?" I ask as we cross Canal Street, making our way toward Tribeca. I've seen a lot less of Priya since she started her new job and we moved out of Orchard Street. The last three times we had plans just the two of us, she bailed with an 8:00 p.m. text that she was stuck at the office. I figured she was less likely to flake if the plan was her idea, but now I'm wary about what I've gotten myself into.

It turns out, I was right to be scared. Ostensibly, it's a dance cardio class, but by the end of the fifty-five-minute session I feel like I showed up to an advanced Navy SEALs training in a pair of water wings and a string bikini. My T-shirt is soaked through with sweat, and I tripped over my own feet no less than five times.

At the end of class, Priya finds me lying prostrate on the mats we rolled out for cooldown. I'm not sure I can get up, never mind wipe down my mat and walk home.

"So fun, right?" she asks once we're on the street outside the studio. "Imagine how ripped you'd be if you did that three times a week." Priya's blue eyeliner is still intact while I have mascara tracks dripping down my cheeks.

"I will never know because I'm never coming back here. I think this fulfilled my workout quota for the next year at least." I hope I haven't accidentally opted into a new tradition. I much prefer the old hits, like Sunday nights eating pad thai and spring rolls from our favorite takeout place while we binge episodes of *30 Rock*. But I guess we've only managed to do that once in the five months since moving out.

"We could have done something else," she offers.

"I wanted to spend time with you, and this is what you wanted to do," I tell her.

"You really are a secret softie." She nudges my shoulder with her own.

"Don't tell anyone," I urge. "It's not good for my street cred. Now, can we please go get a huge plate of fries, and maybe a yellow Gatorade if we pass a bodega on the way?"

She loops her arm through mine, and I lead her to Terroir, a neighborhood spot David and I love. I rationalize that being a regular gives me the right to show up in workout clothes with my sweaty hair plastered to my head.

Once we're installed at a table with a cheese plate between us and an order of fries on the way, I broach the subject that's been nagging at me ever since Finn's announcement earlier this week. "So, about Christmas—"

"I was wondering if this would come up," Priya interrupts. "Hannah, I don't get it. I thought you'd spend Christmas with David's family this year. Are things not going well?"

"Things are going great with David. But this isn't about him, this is about the four of us." I'm frustrated that everyone seems willing to give up on our Christmas tradition so easily.

She arches an eyebrow at me. "You haven't even talked to David about Christmas yet, have you?"

I gulp half my glass of water in an attempt to dodge her question. She knows me too well.

My time apart from Finn brought me and Priya even closer. Before, I would split my confidences between them, never wanting to be too much of a burden to either. But when my relationship with Finn evaporated overnight, Priya was promoted to my sole sounding board. I'm afraid if I give her the chance, she'll talk me out of Christmas the same way she talked me down when I nearly broke up with David twice in our first months of dating.

"Don't you think he sounds a little too good to be real?" I asked Priya after our fourth date. "I mean, first of all, intellectual property lawyer sounds fake, right? That's exactly what a catfish would say. And he asks so many questions—about my job, about all my favorite things, about my childhood. It's like he's trying to figure out my online banking password. Do you think this could be some kind of identity theft scam?"

"Hannah." She gave me a look like I was the densest person in the world, which maybe I was. "I think he's actually trying to get to know you. And I hate to break it to you, but you make seventy-five thousand dollars a year and spend half your post-tax income on rent. I don't think your identity's worth that much. What if he's just a good guy?"

She was right about David, but there are other things she can't understand. Not fully. Not like Finn can. And I'm afraid Christmas might be one of them.

After our first Christmas, I wasn't sure I'd see Finn again. But he showed up to my dorm day after day, always armed with a plan for an adventure. There were plates of French toast at Johnny's Luncheonette, a morning spent wading through the bottom floor at the Garment District where the clothes are in one big pile and priced by the pound, and a movie night where he forced me to watch *Moulin Rouge* and in return I forced him to watch *Garden State*.

Becoming friends with Finn felt like that classic falling-in-love scene in a rom-com, told in a montage over the backdrop of an upbeat pop song. Unknowingly, he broke me out of my haze of grief and self-pity. By the time the rest of the student body was back on campus in January, our friendship was cemented.

And after a decade of Christmases together, I feel like I owe it to Finn to give him one last Christmas to commemorate all he's given me. So I avoid Priya's question about whether I've told David that I can't spend Christmas with him and his family. He'll understand why this is so important.

"We always spend Christmas together, the four of us," I say to Priya. "I mean, were you going to do something else instead?"

"I was thinking about going to Bali," she says, "I looked it up and tickets are really cheap if you fly on Christmas Day. Glossier is closed for the week between Christmas and New Year's, and it sounds better than spending the week freezing in New York."

I've never heard Priya mention Bali in the six years I've known her. It's like she threw a dart at a map, like anything would be better than spending Christmas here with us. The idea that she thinks so little of our tradition stings.

"But why go to Bali alone when you can spend Christmas with your friends?"

"Because last Christmas was . . . awful." Priya grimaces as if the memory physically pains her.

"Well, sure. But that wasn't anyone's fault."

"And the one before?" she asks in a stern voice, like a teacher trying to get me to admit my dog did not actually eat my homework.

"I get it, but trust me, Finn and I are fine now. It was a blip. This year will be different. I promise you, it will be so much better!"

"Hannah, why is this so important to you?"

"Why isn't this more important to you?"

Before she can answer, Priya's phone lights up with a call from Amma. The screen shows a photo of Priya and her mom with their faces pressed close together. Priya's nose is scrunched in laughter.

Priya looks down at the phone and then up at me. The answer

to my question hanging in the air between us. She doesn't *need* Christmas like I do. She has a *real* family. She would never phrase it like that—and neither would I, out loud—but it's the truth.

She flips the phone over, ignoring the call. I'm not sure if it's because she doesn't want to talk to her mother, who calls almost every night to warn her about some mysterious new medical concern based on whichever patients she saw that day at her job as a nurse practitioner, or out of deference to me.

I smear some Brie on a piece of baguette and pop it into my mouth, chewing slowly to try to figure out how to articulate what I need Priya to understand. "This is Finn's last Christmas in New York—"

"So? He can fly back next Christmas if he wants. He's moving to LA, not Antarctica."

"Yeah, but what if he makes new friends? Or has a boyfriend? Or what if we don't do it this year and then the tradition is dead, so he doesn't fly back and is all alone in his sad apartment."

"Why are you assuming his apartment is sad?" she asks.

"I don't know! That's not the point. The point is Finn is my family—you and Theo are, too—and this is our tradition, and if this is our last Christmas we need to do it right: one last time while we're all here together."

Lately it feels like we have so much less time for one another. It used to be a given that the four of us would spend our weekends together. We didn't need restaurant reservations or concert tickets to bind us to a date and time. If we didn't have something to do, we'd find something to do. That's how we wound up spending a rainy Saturday in April at the Dave & Buster's in Times Square trying to win enough tickets for the most expensive prize, which was, disappointingly, a toaster oven that still lives in Finn's kitchen. But now it takes thirty emails and a Google Calendar invite a month in advance to lock in a date, and even then there's a fifty percent chance at least one person bails. I thought Christmas was our one sacred tradition, but now even that's in jeopardy.

She heaves out a sigh. "I know this is important to you, so I'm in. On one condition." She holds up a finger in between us. "No drama this year. You have to pinky swear that this really will be the best Christmas yet. No repeats of the last two years. And you have to convince Theo, too. Or else Ubud here I come." From her smile I know she's kidding, and I breathe a sigh of relief. One down, one to go.

On Saturday, it's time to tackle Theo. I'm waiting for him outside Massey Klein, the art gallery on Forsyth Street where he told me to meet him. I'm convinced the staff will be able to intuit my relative poverty through my clothes or my haircut or maybe my smell, so I'm shivering on the sidewalk listening to Clementine Del's new album while I wait. This new record is much darker than her old music.

My playlist is interrupted by an incoming call from Brooke. I do not have the capacity to deal with her today, although there's never an ideal time to talk to my sister. I let it go to voicemail.

When we were kids, I worshiped Brooke. Of course, our six-year age gap meant I was just her annoying tagalong kid sister. Someone our mom insisted she bring with her to the town pool where she met up with her *actual* friends. But I cherished those days, pretending to read one of my Goosebumps mysteries, while eagerly devouring every morsel of gossip Brooke traded with her trio of girlfriends. I harbored a fantasy that once we were older, we'd be best friends, like the sisters on *Charmed*, Brooke's favorite TV show at the time.

Brooke and I were close for exactly one week in our lives. The week after our dad died.

We weren't surprised when our mom passed. The cancer took over her body in increments. First her lungs, then her brain, then everywhere. When she died, it was like reaching the destination on a long road trip. Everyone was tired, cranky, and sick of the other passengers in the car. We were sad, but there was also relief. After the funeral, Brooke was free to go back to Georgetown and spend the final Saturdays of her senior year partying at Sigma Phi Ep without feeling guilty she should be sitting vigil at our mother's bedside.

But our father's death came out of nowhere. One morning, three months after our mom died, he went to work and didn't come home. He hit a tree driving back from the commuter lot at the NJ Transit station in the center of town. He fell asleep at the wheel, the police officer told me when he knocked on our front door and mistook me for someone old enough to unload this news on. In my worst moments, I wondered if he crashed the car on purpose. If he didn't want to live in a world without my mother.

Brooke and I spent the week after the accident haunting our childhood home in a shared haze of grief. We spritzed ourselves with clouds of Mom's Chanel N°5 perfume and cocooned into the worn flannels and vintage band tees Dad favored on weekends. During the week he wore what he called his "office drag"— a collection of khakis and pastel button-downs—to collect a paycheck as a graphic designer at an ad agency in the city. "Unfortunately, there's not much money in doodling," he'd lament as he sketched caricatures of me and Brooke while we did our homework at the kitchen table. "So you better learn this math stuff." That was the saddest part; he died commuting home from a job he hated.

Brooke and I were alone in the world. We were the only family the other had.

We took turns reading aloud diary entries from a journal we didn't know our mom kept, but found in the top drawer of her nightstand beside a small pink vibrator, which got thrown in the trash amid much shrieking. The entries alternated between funny anecdotes from our childhood and plans for the future she would never have, enumerating the exotic trips she and Dad would go on once I graduated high school. Brazil, Bermuda, Botswana, and that was only the *B*'s.

Our closeness lasted the length of Brooke's allotted bereavement leave from her first post-college job as a junior analyst at Lehman Brothers. Then she got on with her life.

Brooke was appointed to be my legal guardian. There was no one else, really. Dad was an only child; his parents were already gone. Mom barely spoke to her family. "Fundamentalist wackos," she called them. None of them showed up at the end, even for her funeral.

Brooke's role as my guardian existed more on paper than in practice. What did a twenty-two-year-old know about taking care of a sixteen-year-old? Brooke could barely take care of herself.

In our new living situation, we were about as feral as you'd expect. I survived on a diet of pizza delivery and pity dinner invites to friend's houses. Brooke lived at home and commuted into the city, but more often than not she crashed on friends' couches near her office, coming home every couple of weekends to do laundry and make sure I hadn't destroyed the house. It didn't even occur to us to enroll me in a new school in the city.

After a minute, my phone dings with a voicemail notification.

"Hi! It's Brooke. You never answered my text about Thanksgiving, so I'm checking in. Spencer's parents are coming up from Florida and his brother's family is driving down from Maine this year, too. We'd love to have you. Finn is welcome, too. Or David. Or both. Well, call me back and let me know if we should expect you. I need to give a final head count to the caterers by Tuesday."

I can't believe Brooke hired caterers for Thanksgiving. On second thought, I can absolutely believe it. Her commitment to the Stepford Wife persona she invented after marrying Spencer is Oscar-worthy. I shoot off a quick text: Going to David's parents' house this year.

She sends back a thumbs-up emoji, probably equally relieved not to have me as I am not to go. I'd be an ugly stain from her sad past marring the otherwise perfect family she's built for herself.

At ten past one, a black SUV deposits Theo on the sidewalk outside the gallery. He's dressed in a charcoal wool overcoat with a Burberry scarf tied around his neck, impeccable as always. His face breaks into a grin when he spots me leaning against a bike rack.

"Why are you waiting out here?"

"It says 'by appointment only' and I don't have an appointment. Do you?" I point at the tasteful placard in the window.

"They don't mean us. You must be freezing your bollocks off out here."

"Theo, I don't think ladies have bollocks."

He laughs. "Your tits, then. Come on." He leads me into the gallery.

A black-clad gallery girl looks up from her laptop and flashes Theo the barest of smiles. "Let me know if you need anything."

"What are we looking for?" I whisper as he leads me into the first room.

"You don't need to whisper, it's not a library."

"Well?" I ask using my full voice, but it feels wrong in a place like this.

"I'm looking for a piece for the bedroom." He pauses like he's debating whether to say more. "The piece above the bed was Elliot's, but he took it with him when he left."

Elliot is the latest in Theo's string of mysterious paramours.

Over the five years we've known Theo, we've heard rumors of his love interests, but rarely met them. Elliot, the third-chair violinist for the New York Philharmonic, was a notable exception. Theo seemed more serious about him. They lasted seven months, a record as far as I know. He moved into Theo's apartment this summer after two months of dating.

Theo claimed Elliot sublet his apartment because he planned to be out of the city for the summer. The way Finn told it, Elliot was a gold digger using Theo for a lifestyle upgrade. But you could never be sure about Finn's opinions on Theo's romantic partners. He disliked them all on principle. The principle being they were not him.

"Why didn't you bring Finn?" I ask. "Don't you think he'd be better at this?"

"You know that's untrue. He'd like everything because it was expensive."

A snort-laugh sneaks out of me. He's not wrong.

"I was so glad when you called to make plans," Theo continues. "You and I haven't spent any time just the two of us in a while, and I thought we could use an activity." Again, not wrong.

"So, was there a reason you wanted to meet?" he asks. "Not that you need a reason, of course, I'm always happy to spend time with you." He places a hand on my lower back to guide me into the next room, which is full of hyperrealistic paintings that look like photographs if you stand far enough away. There's one of a man wearing small swim trunks with even smaller pineapples on them, only his torso and legs are visible. Another of a young girl facing away from the viewer, wearing baggy jeans and a pink backpack. None of the subjects have faces, but you can tell so much about them from these snippets of body parts and clothing.

"I wanted to talk about Christmas," I say.

"I had a feeling that was the case." He doesn't give any indication of where he stands.

"I think we should do it. Give Finn one last Christmas adventure. One for the record books!" I have a whole speech prepared. I practiced in the bathroom mirror this morning. I wait to see how my opener is received before proceeding. I was fairly certain Priya would cave, but I'm not as sure about Theo. Even though Finn and I mended fences, Theo's kept me at arm's length the last year, and I've let him. But with our possible last Christmas looming, I need things to go back to how they were before the great Hannah-Finn fight, when we were at our best. Just the four of us.

He stops in front of a painting of two sets of bare legs, a woman in sandals and a man in sneakers, and cups a hand to his chin to consider it. I can't tell if he's interested in the piece or stalling. For a minute, I wonder if he has a foot fetish. As far as I'm concerned, the painting is weird, but then I got a D in my required art history elective in college.

"What do you think?" he asks after a minute.

"Of the painting or about Christmas? I told you what I think about Christmas, I think we should do it."

"I'm on the fence about both, frankly. But I think this is too jarring for the bedroom."

He moves to stand in front of the next painting, this one by a different artist. Two bodies float in a blue ocean portrayed with thick layers of paint caked on top of each other to suggest the appearance of waves. I stand next to him and wait for him to say more about which way he's leaning on Christmas. Another thing I've learned from observing Theo's relationships is he usually has one foot out the door, always preferring to leave than be left. I know Finn's departure must be affecting him more than he's let on.

After a minute of silent consideration of the swimmers, Theo speaks, eyes forward, addressing the painting instead of me. "I think you should have Christmas without me. I don't want to get in the way."

After our first Christmas as a foursome, we weren't sure if we'd see Theo again. That spring, we invited him to happy hours at Tacombi and to see Finn's off-off-Broadway play about JonBenét Ramsey's murder where he played her nine-year-old brother, despite being almost three times his age. It was ironic, Finn claimed. But Theo declined every invitation saying he was sorry to miss us, but he was out of town. The more plans he declined the clearer it became his fancy apartment was more storage unit than home.

In his absence, we scoured Google for hints about him, but didn't get very far without a last name.

That year, Finn and I spent endless hours parsing Theo's texts over buckets of dollar beers at Lucky's, our neighborhood bar. Was Theo sending a shirtless selfie—his chest bronzed and a coy smile on his face—because he was coming on to Finn or was it just because he was on a beautiful Caribbean beach? Was the photo of him eating a bao bun in Beijing alongside a text that said, Dim sum always makes me think of you, a nod to our Christmas dinner or was he actually alluding to the night before? And I knew there were other texts, too, ones Finn didn't share with me. Sometimes he'd leave his phone unlocked on the table between us and I'd catch glimpses of long swaths of messages traded between them.

In August, Finn invited Theo to his twenty-fifth birthday party at Wilfie & Nell. "This is the last olive branch," Finn told me. "There's only so much rejection one person can take."

Theo wrote back he would be in Mallorca and was sad to miss it. But at the party, a waiter brought over a bottle of champagne with sparklers sticking out the top, courtesy of Theo. Finn beamed as the waiter set the bottle down in front of him, relishing the spectacle and impressed that Theo had sprung for Dom.

"Does he get another chance?" I asked as I poured Finn a glass.

"Just one," he said, unable to hide the lovesick grin on his face.

The next time we heard from Theo, he was the one who reached out. On November 1, he texted Finn: What's the plan for Christmas this year? Happy to host! And after our second Christmas together, our group of four was cemented. Theo was just as much a part of our Christmas tradition as any of the rest of us.

"Get in the way?" I echo his words back to him. For a moment, I forget about the tomb-like silence of the gallery, and my protest comes out louder than is necessary or appropriate. The gallery girl pokes her head up from her laptop to see if she's missing anything worth eavesdropping on.

I adjust my tone to a whisper and grab Theo's arm, pulling it so he faces me and can see how serious I am. "You could never be in the way. It wouldn't be Christmas without you. You're part of the group."

"Oh? I thought I was a stray?" The left side of his mouth quirks up into a wry smile. He's teasing me. I'm pretty sure I have him.

"It just so happens those are the sort of people I like best." I wind my arm through his and let him lead me to the other side of the room to stand in front of another painting by the same artist, this one of four people swimming. While the other two swimmers looked like they were floating along serenely, these people look like they're having fun, maybe splashing around. I like to think they might be the four of us, even though the "people" are just thick abstract globs of flesh-colored paint.

But after a few minutes of silent consideration, there's no "yes" forthcoming. I try again, "Why wouldn't you come?"

He sighs. "Things are finally good between you and Finn. And I know Christmas is so important to you both, I don't want to upset the peace. I'm worried I don't know the whole story about what happened."

From what I've heard about what Finn told him, he's right. But that's not my place. Instead, I say. "We're great. Truly. Water under the bridge." And even though I've avoided part of the question, it's the truth.

"And you'd tell me if you two were *not* fine, right?"

"There's seriously nothing to tell." I shrug, offering my empty palms as proof.

He mulls this for a minute while he studies the painting in front of us. "Well then, I only have one more question," he says. "Do you want help planning?"

I throw my arms around his neck and squeal into his ear. The noise is too much for the gallery girl, who pops her head around the corner. "Is everything alright in here?" she asks.

"We'll take this one," Theo says, pointing to the four swimmers in front of us.

"I'll start the paperwork," the woman tells him. She returns to her desk and comes back a few seconds later to affix a red dot sticker to the painting's information card. It's a done deal.

SIX

Finn

This year, November 18

I survey my collection of sweaters, which I've taken out of their drawers and stacked in piles on my bed. I'm trying to decide which to bring to LA and which to donate. I can't picture what my life will look like in LA—I've only been twice, once on a family trip as a teenager when we took a bus tour that drove us past what they claimed were celebrity homes, and once for my final round interview at Netflix—but I'm pretty sure LA Finn will wear more T-shirts than turtlenecks, so sweaters feels like as good a place as any to start my pre-move purge.

To avoid making any actual decisions, I've organized them by color and arranged the stacks in rainbow order. I'm saved from my indecision by the door buzzer.

"Hello?" I say into the intercom. I'm not expecting anyone, and I've been trying to curb my online shopping until after the move. I don't need any more stuff to box up and bring to LA.

"It's me," the voice on the other end announces.

I hold down the button to open the lobby door and smile to myself as I crack the apartment door so Theo can let himself in.

Theo comes bearing iced coffees.

"This is a nice surprise!" I tell him and take a long pull of my coffee. Cold brew with oat milk, my usual. I like that Theo knows my usual, and he feels comfortable showing up unannounced.

"I'd sit down, but it looks like the sweaters beat me to all the good seats." Theo gestures to the chaos around us. "Are you going on a ski holiday?"

"I wish. I'm trying to get a head start on packing."

Theo sits down in the spot I clear for him at the foot of the bed.

"I called to get a quote from a moving company yesterday. Did you know it takes two weeks to get your stuff when you move cross-country? So, either I pack everything up by December fifteenth or wait around for two weeks in LA in an empty apartment."

"Easy," Theo says. "Send everything early and stay with me. You can borrow anything you need." He flops down on his back and knocks a pile of red sweaters on the floor. I wait to see if he'll pick them up, but he doesn't notice. He's engrossed in something on his phone. Classic Theo, helpful with the big things, incredibly unhelpful with the little ones.

"Thank you, I'll think about it," I tell him, and pick up the red sweaters.

"What's there to think about? I've solved it. Now, should we nip out for brunch?"

So that's why he's here. This is also classic Theo. Whenever he's single, he packs his weekends full of plans—museum visits, shopping, dinner parties, cocktails, never a solitary moment—and when he doesn't have plans, he instigates them.

"I still have to pack!"

"Can't you pay people to do that? Don't you get some fancy moving stipend?"

"Yeah, and it's paying for the moving truck, which is really freaking expensive." I know he'd offer to pay for a packing service if I'd let him, which I won't. To change the subject, I hold a red sweater against my body. "Should I keep this?"

"You must keep that! You wore it to Christmas the first year I came, didn't you?"

He's right. I'd forgotten. But I like that he remembers. I ate cereal for dinner for weeks to afford the sweater, which now feels tragically out of style with thick cabling down the front. Very Billy Crystal in *When Harry Met Sally*. I fold the sweater and put it in the keep pile.

"What about this one?" I hold up a lemon-yellow sweater.

Theo glances up from his phone. "Not your color."

I bought it a few years ago after I saw a famous singer wearing the same color sweater, but Theo's right, I can't pull it off. Once, I wore it to the office with jeans and spent the whole day worried people thought I was doing some weird Arthur cosplay. I put it in the donate pile.

Next, I hold up a green sweater for Theo's inspection.

"Just so I'm clear, are we doing the *Sex and the City* closet clean-out montage thing?" He flashes me a cheeky grin. "Promise if I do this we can go somewhere for brunch after. I can't watch you waste one of your last Sundays in the city."

I really should keep packing. The yellow sweater is the only thing I've managed to part with, but he has a point. I only have a few weekends left as a New Yorker. The reality crashes into me that soon I won't have Theo's casual drop-ins. He won't be a twenty-five-minute subway ride away, instead it will be a six-hour flight.

I think about the hours and hours Hannah and I have logged watching bad reality TV, hungover on her couch between Seamless orders. All the warm days lounging on a blanket in Washington Square Park, half reading our books, half people watching and gossiping. The endless weekends of exploring every new fad New York has to offer with Priya under the guise of research for a column. I'll be losing those, too. The thought makes my stomach knot.

"Fine," I relent, "but we've gotta get rid of some of this stuff first." I dangle the green sweater into his line of vision to keep things moving.

"I can't tell. Try it on."

I shuck off the navy Henley I'm wearing and toss it on the bed. As I pick up the green sweater, I glance over to see if Theo is looking. He isn't. He's still absorbed in his phone. I take my time putting on the sweater, watching from the corner of my eye to see if he looks up. He doesn't.

It's not like I'm an exhibitionist, but ever since I turned thirty earlier this year, I started exercising for the first time in my adult life. Hannah laughed when I told her. "Wow, I have missed a lot. We're not gym people," she said.

And historically, she was correct. We're more *watch Bravo with a running dialog of snarky banter* people. *The Real Housewives of Beverly Hills* is our sport of choice. Before this year, the only purposeful exercise I got was running my birthday mile. Every year on my birthday, I wake up early and walk to the Hudson River. I blast "My Shot" from the Hamilton soundtrack and run one mile as fast as I can to prove I'm not actually getting old and can still run a sub-six mile, the same mile time I needed to make the varsity track team in high school.

This year, I puked after I finished. But I finished in 5:58, which is the important part.

Another thing that was different about this year's birthday mile was that I laced up my sneakers and ran again the next day. And the next day. And the one after that, too.

It was miserable and I was slow as shit when I stretched my runs to three miles then five then seven—I could hear my high school track coach yelling at me to pick up the pace in my head— but it was also addictive. Running is the only thing that shuts off my brain and lets me be in the moment instead of agonizing over how my life at thirty looks nothing like I thought it would and how I haven't had sex (or even kissed anyone) since I broke up with Jeremy in the spring. I'm beginning to fear I might never kiss anyone again. These days, settling for *like* instead of *love* doesn't sound like such a bad idea.

Now, three and a half months into my running regime, I'm

starting to see physical changes, too. I'm not destined to become some beefcake Instagram model, my frame's too wiry, but the slight paunch I developed around twenty-eight is gone, and if I stand at the perfect angle first thing in the morning, before I eat anything, there might be the faintest outline of abs forming. I wonder if Theo will notice, too.

I cling to the fantasy he'll look up and it will be my Rachael Leigh Cook on the stairs moment in *She's All That*. After the winter of Raj, six weeks of Alex, and the god-awful summer of Elliot, he'll realize it's me. It was always me. That's why it didn't work with the others, because they weren't me. I cringe at my own stupid, misguided hope. Life isn't a rom-com. Instead, I look over Theo's shoulder at his phone and see he's on Grindr. It lands like a gut punch.

"Ta-da!" I announce once I have the green sweater on.

"No." Theo barely glances up.

Okay, then. I take off the green sweater and throw it in the pile with the yellow one. Next, I put on a black and blue patterned sweater. "This one?" I ask.

"You look like a cut-rate David Rose." I paid good money for this sweater. My shoulders slump forward as I study the piles in front of me wondering if any of them will meet Theo's exacting standards.

"Are you alright?" Theo asks.

"I'm fine."

"You don't look fine. You're pouting."

"I'm not pouting!" It comes out as more of a yell.

Theo sits up and places his phone beside him on the bed. It's open to a long message thread with some guy who is not me. "I'm sorry. I thought we were doing the *Sex and the City* try on thing. I was being Samantha. I thought you wanted to get rid of things, wasn't that the point?"

Of course that's the point. But then I went and got it in my head it might be something more. Not for the first time, I feel like an idiot for letting myself believe that. When I don't look at him, he ducks into my field of vision and forces me to meet his eyes. He reaches out a hand and entwines it with mine. "You know I think you look great in everything, don't you? I was only kidding. Please don't be cross with me."

And there's that damn flicker of hope again.

Two hours later, after a stop at Housing Works to drop off a donation of sweaters, we're walking toward SoHo. I tug my coat tighter against the freezing wind. Theo notices and pulls me to his side, maybe for warmth or maybe because he knows I'm still a little mad from earlier.

I relish the sense of rightness I feel tucked into his side, but know it means nothing. Theo has always been an affectionate friend—and not just with me—but after the night we met things have remained purely platonic.

"Aren't the English supposed to be repressed?" I asked him one night between movies during a Lindsay Lohan marathon at his apartment. He'd been lying with his head in Priya's lap all but purring as she played with his hair throughout *Mean Girls*. He'd sporadically turn his head to look up at her and say he was in love with her.

"Good thing no one English raised me," he retorted.

By then, I'd heard all about his childhood governess, Lourdes, a cheerful older Spanish woman who, as far as I could tell, was a cross between a nanny and a surrogate grandmother. I walked into his apartment one afternoon to find him sprawled on the couch gossiping with her in rapid Spanish over FaceTime and he introduced us.

When he was a child Lourdes lived with his family for most of the year, but went home to spend summers in Marbella. Instead of taking the time off, she brought Theo with her, and he bodysurfed in the ocean and ate her homemade tortilla alongside her actual grandchildren. The way he told it, his parents used their best parenting on his older brother, Colin. By the time Theo came along, they were rarely home, mostly because they couldn't stand to be under the same roof together. He still talks to Lourdes far more than anyone in his actual family.

We install ourselves at the bar at the Dutch and order a round of Bloody Marys and a dozen oysters from the ironically mustachioed barman in a denim apron.

"How do you think Hannah took your news?" Theo asks.

"I mean, she was weird about it, but I guess it went as well as it could have, right?"

Last weekend, I broke the news to Theo, and he listened as I puzzled out how to tell Hannah. In public, I decided. Less chance for her to yell or cry, which were equally likely. Underneath her gruff exterior, Hannah is a big softie. But she'd be far less likely to get emotional in public. Theo had taken the news of my move in stride. So much so, I found myself wishing he'd been a bit *more* emotional about it.

"Have you spoken to her since?" he asks.

"No. I thought I'd give her time to process. Why? Do you think I should call her?"

"I can't even pretend to understand the complexity of the relationship between you two. I'm just glad you're speaking again. I'm declaring a subject change. When do you leave for Thanksgiving?"

"Wednesday afternoon," I groan. It took a lot for me to say yes to this trip, to face going back there *again*, but I had to. It's important to me to try. Especially now. "I'm in heated negotiations with Amanda. I'm trying to get her to stay a couple extra nights instead of driving down for the day. I offered to go to the liquor store for her before she heads back to campus, but she has a fake ID now. We never should have gotten her that thing. I'm thinking of offering her straight cash."

"I meant what I said before," Theo says. "If you want someone there with you, I'll go."

"No. One of us should be having fun. And you already have a flight to California."

"Flights can be changed. I don't mind."

"I couldn't ask you to do that."

"You're not asking, I'm offering."

"I'll think about it," I tell him. I appreciate the offer, I really do. But I can't ask him to hold me together at my parents' house. Not again.

We're interrupted by my phone vibrating on the bar between us. Hannah's name flashes on the screen. "Do you think she knows we were talking about her?" Theo laughs.

I swipe to answer and Theo leans close to listen. "Hey," I say.

"Hey! I have good news!"

"Oh yeah?"

At least she's not calling to yell at me. I hadn't ruled it out that after more time to process she'd come back angry I hadn't told her I was applying to jobs outside New York. Before she left her job at Z100, we had months of late-night confabs, curled up on the couch at Orchard Street with glasses of red wine and bowls of popcorn doing our best Olivia Pope–level fixing. The problem: Hannah's dead-end career at the radio station—all her colleagues were lifers and there was no room for promotion. We had a legal pad full of pro and con lists before she finally decided to leave.

I thought about telling her when I applied to this job, but figured it was a long shot. My resume isn't exactly sterling. And I worried if we talked about it, I might lose my nerve to hit the submit button in the first place.

"Christmas is on!" Hannah's voice is full of pride. I was nervous she wouldn't be able to rally everyone after the last two years—both at least partially my fault—but I'm glad she did. This will be the perfect end cap on my time in New York. One last Christmas.

Once he realizes there's no scandal about to go down, Theo pulls out his own phone and starts scrolling through Instagram.

"That's great, Han! It means a lot to me that you got everyone to agree. I'm really excited. One last time for the record books!"

"That's what I told Theo. Speaking of Theo, did you hear that he and Elliot broke up?"

"Mhmm," I tell her, careful about what I say since Theo is six inches away.

The worst part about Elliot was that we look alike. He's tall and half Black and looks like the version of me if I got a movie makeover montage. Shinier, more handsome, better dressed. But the similarity of our features rankles me. Then, of course, there's the major difference: Elliot is successful. He actually achieved his dream of playing with a professional orchestra. Maybe that's why Theo was attracted to him. His type is always accomplished. Meanwhile, I'm coated in a fine dust of failure. I've spent the past three years languishing in educational cartoon purgatory after four years of blundering my way through every audition I ever had. I get it, not a turn-on.

"I was thinking now that he's single, you should tell Theo," Hannah says.

"Tell Theo what?" Theo perks up at the sound of his name.

"You know . . ." I'm positive this isn't a conversation I want to have with Theo in earshot. I hold up a finger to signal I need a minute and point to the window opposite where we're sitting.

"Gimme a sec," I tell Hannah as I wedge the phone between my chin and shoulder so I can shrug on my coat.

"Oh, shit, is he there?"

"Mhmm."

"Oh god, I'm sorry."

I push through the side door onto Spring Street. "It's fine. I'm outside now. What were you saying?" I pace to stay warm, dodging groups of tourists loaded down with shopping bags.

"I saw Theo yesterday and he said Elliot moved out. You're finally both single at the same time and I thought it might be the right time to tell him how you feel."

I've been down this road before. "You'll excuse me if I don't trust your advice on my love life."

"Raj?" she asks. "I didn't know about him. This is different!"

"Yeah, it's different because I'm leaving. So there's no point. It's game over."

"The point is you love him, and you should tell him."

"If I never tell him, he won't have to smash my heart into pieces and stop talking to me because I've made it too unbearably awkward to be friends. I'm not trying to burn it all down on my way out of town."

"Counterpoint: if you never tell him, you might spend your whole life wondering what would have happened if you did."

"I don't have to tell him. I know what he'd say."

I gaze through the fogged window at Theo. The bartender is

leaning in close with one arm bent on the bar between them, laughing at something Theo said. Theo makes friends wherever he goes. He makes people feel special. That's his superpower. I know better than to read into it. I think of this morning and the sweaters. He's not interested. He's had every opportunity to make a move, and he hasn't. He only thinks of me as a friend, and I need to accept that.

"Promise me you'll at least think about it?" Hannah says.

"Fine," I tell her. "But I have to go."

After we hang up, I keep pacing with the phone to my ear to give myself a minute before heading back inside. I stare at Theo through the glass and remind myself of what I know to be true: *He doesn't feel that way about you. You're just friends*, I chant over and over in my head.

SEVEN

Hannah

Christmas #7, 2014

The elevator opens directly into Theo's apartment.

Holy shit.

I thought that only happens in movies. I turn to Priya and see my shocked expression mirrored on her face.

We've heard Finn recount his visit to Theo's ad nauseum over the last year, the apartment getting nicer with every retelling. I assumed he was exaggerating, but realize I owe him an apology.

Priya and I stand glued to our spots outside the elevator gaping at the enormous Christmas tree taking up most of the foyer. It looks like it was plucked from a department store window. The tree is wrapped in rainbow lights and dotted with quirky candy-colored ornaments. A stick of butter, a hot-air balloon, a glittery pink roller skate. Clumps of silver tinsel, the kind my mother objected to on account of the mess, are heaped on its branches.

Finn comes skidding around the tree, eyes wild, and almost

knocks off a hot dog ornament with his elbow. He grabs my arm. "You'll never guess who's here!"

"Okay, then tell us," I say.

"It would have been so much better if you guessed. But get this—Clementine Del is here!" He bounces on his toes waiting for our reaction.

"The singer?" Priya asks, confused.

"Yes, the singer! Here! In the living room! She's even prettier in person. Theo knows her!" he gushes. Only a genuine celebrity could eclipse Finn's excitement over seeing Theo again. Good thing we skipped the guessing, or we would have stood in the foyer all night. Her music is a little too bubblegum for my taste—in her most memorable music video she's unironically dressed in a pink tulle gown in a life-sized replica of a Barbie Dream House—but I'm still impressed she's here.

He leads us down the hallway and into the living room where, true to Finn's word, Theo and Clementine Del are sipping cock-tails on a cobalt velvet couch while Nat King Cole croons from a record player in the corner. Clementine, dressed in black-and-white polka-dot palazzo pants and a cropped yellow sweater, looks at ease here. Her sky-high gold platform heels are cast aside beneath the coffee table, and her white-blond hair is twisted into a messy knot held in place by a pen. When we walk in, a throaty bark of laughter explodes from her like Theo just told a particu-larly bawdy joke. She grabs his arm as she cackles.

Theo pops off the couch when he notices us, somehow every bit as excited to talk to us as he is an actual pop star. "You're here!" He gives us both a double cheek kiss while Finn settles back into an armchair opposite the couch.

Despite the occasional selfie shared by Finn, my memory of Theo faded over the past year, or maybe the camera dulled his chiseled bone structure. His hair is longer, too, the ends curling around his ears like one of the Stark brothers on *Game of Thrones*. It suits him. I'm surprised to realize his good looks go toe-to-toe with the woman sitting on the couch, who if I'm not mistaken is a spokesmodel for any number of makeup and fashion brands.

"First order of business is cocktails," Theo says. "Clem made margaritas!"

"Not very festive, but it's all I know how to make! Unless anyone wants a shot of whiskey, I can make that, too. I've spent too much time on the road with boys. That's all my band drinks." Her voice is familiar from her songs. Her newest single, "Queen of Hearts," is currently inescapable, playing in every yellow cab, Duane Reade, and coffee shop across the city on what feels like a constant loop.

Theo pours two margaritas from a crystal pitcher on the sideboard.

"Okay, introductions," he announces.

Before he has a chance to start, Clementine focuses her attention on me. "Wait, I know you."

"Me?" I point at myself and then glance over my shoulder to see if there's another famous person standing behind me. The way tonight is going I wouldn't be surprised.

"You know . . . her?" Finn asks, his voice dripping with shock.

"Yes, you brought me a tea. Didn't you?" Clementine asks, oblivious to Finn's incredulous tone.

Technically, she's correct. I brought Clementine a mug of chamomile tea when she came into the radio station last year to do an interview with Elvis Duran, the host of our morning show. Over the past three years, I've brought all manner of beverages to every type of celebrity at the radio station: a Diet Coke for Katy Perry, a Red Bull for Snoop Dogg, a venti mocha Frappuccino for Ed Sheeran. Most don't bother to say thank you, and I can count on one hand the ones who ask my name. I certainly didn't expect Clementine Del to remember me a year later. I'm instantly won over by the gesture. "Um, yes. At Z100, right?"

"I knew it! I never forget a face. Names are another story, though. Remind me of yours?" Clementine unfolds herself from the couch and reaches out her hand to shake.

"I'm Hannah."

"Lovely to meet you. Again, as it is." She rolls her eyes at her own forgetfulness. "Everyone calls me Clem."

"Clem," I parrot back as I shake her hand.

"And this is Priya," Theo jumps in. He throws an arm over Priya's shoulder, while her mouth hangs open as she struggles to process this evening's unexpected turn.

"Lovely to meet you," Clementine says. She collapses back on the couch, tucking one leg up underneath her.

"So," Finn prods, "you were about to tell us how you two met before they got here."

"Ah yes," Theo muses. He settles back into the couch next to Clementine and they exchange a look like they're having a silent conversation about whether or not to tell us.

"We dated!" Clementine blurts. She leans into Theo and gives him a playful nudge with her shoulder.

She probably expected a laugh, but her announcement lands like a bomb. The room is engulfed in a shocked silence.

Surely this would have made the tabloids. You can't check out at a grocery store without Clementine staring back at you from the cover of a glossy magazine under a headline about her scandalous trip to Cabo or whether she's fallen out with Princess Beatrice again. So, this must mean it was a while ago, before we met Theo, or surely Finn would have noticed him on the gossip blogs.

"When was this?" I ask, imagining a teenaged Theo in a prep-school blazer, cheeks speckled with acne, dating a pre-Hollywood Clementine Del. I picture her as a drama nerd. Maybe she knew Theo was gay all along and was his beard until he was ready to come out.

"Last summer," Clementine replies. "Well, not this past summer, the summer before, I mean."

So that would mean Theo was dating Clementine Del right before he hooked up with Finn? That was so . . . recent.

"We met at Ascot," Clem continues. "I was there with my old schoolmate, Peach. Her real name's Penelope, Peach is just a nickname. A Clementine and a Peach! We used to try to pass ourselves off as twins, even though we look nothing alike. Although Clementine is my given name."

She notices Finn and I eyeing each other. "Sorry! I'm boring you," she says, "I always do that. Too many details! The short of it is, we met at a ludicrously boring, not to mention inhumane, horse race we were both forced to attend. Meeting Theo was the only redeeming part of the day!"

Theo picks up where she left off. "Clem was on a break from touring and her manager sent her to schmooze some smarmy record exec. Except it turns out the record exec was my friend Ollie's father. His dad got totally rat-arsed the night before and had one hell of a hangover, so he sent Ol in his stead, and I tagged along. We thought it would be a laugh. You know: dress up, get pissed on Pimms, place some bets. So we went. Then imagine our surprise when Clem and Peach show up at our box.

"Not a bad day at all," he continues, "I won five thousand pounds. But Clem was the real prize." Theo and Clementine exchange saccharine smiles on the sofa.

"I told him I wouldn't go on a date with him unless he donated his winnings. I couldn't stand the thought of someone profiting off animal cruelty," Clementine says. "Although if I'd known how loaded he was, I would have made him triple it!"

Theo gives a hearty laugh and I get the sense their lines in this story have been polished over many retellings to captive audiences at swanky cocktail parties. I attempt to school my face into a bland smile and think of a polite follow-up question. But every question that comes to mind is deeply impolite: *I'm sorry, you also date women? You dated her?! What's Theo like in bed? What's Clementine Del like in bed?*

"After Ascot we absconded to Capri for a few weeks. Clem had never been. Can't say she saw much of the island—"

"And it's a small island!" She braces her hand on his arm for emphasis. "We mostly stayed in the room if you get me."

We get it. You banged.

"But after Capri, I was off to Hong Kong to continue my tour and Theo was spending the summer in California."

Theo picks up the story baton. "Suffice it to say, things didn't work out. We were rarely on the same continent, never mind in the same city."

"He's the only person I know who travels more than I do."

"We called it two months later, but she's the only ex I've managed to stay friends with." *How lucky for us!* I remind myself not to roll my eyes.

"We see each other whenever we're in the same place, which is less often than you'd think," says Clementine.

Theo and Clementine share a private smile. Oh my god, are they going to have sex tonight? Or maybe they already did before we got here. I feel weird thinking about this. I had put Theo in a certain box, and if I'm honest, assumed it was only a matter of time before he and Finn got together. That was the whole reason I agreed to Christmas at Theo's, after not seeing him for a year—so Finn could see if there was really something between them, now that Theo is back in New York. But there are some new variables in the mix. I look over at Finn to see how he's taking all of this and watch him drain half his margarita in one long gulp.

"Alas, he's the one who got away!" Clementine teases.

Finn starts choking on his drink and lets out a hacking cough. "Sorry, wrong pipe," he covers.

Undeterred, Clementine smiles beatifically up at Theo and winds their hands together on the couch cushion between them. Theo shows no signs of discomfort.

"Well," he coos at her, "I'm here now!"

"And I leave next week!" she adds with an exaggerated pout, continuing their two-person show.

"Clem's on tour again at the moment," Theo adds for our sake, although I'm well aware. The radio station has been playing ads for Jingle Ball, which Clementine headlined, every fifteen minutes for the past six weeks and it's my job to queue them up. "And I figured Clem would fit in well with you lot. She's a bit of a stray, too."

"Well, that's not how I would phrase it!" she says, taking offense to Theo's word choice. "But my mum's gotten remarried and she's spending the holiday with her new husband's family. It's all a bit new and weird. Didn't think they needed the woman from the telly showing up for pudding."

"But enough about us. I'm sure we're boring you. I want to hear about you all! Theo's spoken so highly of his New York friends."

She must have us confused with other people. We've met once. How could we possibly merit mentioning? My list of rude questions grows longer by the second.

"Should we move into the dining room?" Theo asks, sensing an opening in the conversation.

We stand mutely. I look over at Finn who is glancing around the room in search of an emergency exit.

I clear my throat. "I'm going to head to the bathroom to wash my hands before we eat. You know, subway grime. Finn, do you want to wash your hands, too?"

"Yes, I do! My hands are very dirty, actually," he says.

"Mine are, too," Priya adds, not wanting to be left out.

We are the three least subtle people on the planet. Theo raises his eyebrows, but doesn't try to stop us.

In the hallway on the way to the bathroom, I linger in front of a photo of Theo with Phillip Benson, the eccentric billionaire owner of Infinite Airlines. I wouldn't have taken Theo for one of his legions of fanboys. Maybe he has a kink for celebrities.

Inside the massive marble powder room, Priya is perched on the vanity, while Finn paces the five steps from the toilet to the far wall. I close the door behind me and take a seat on the closed toilet lid. Who has a powder room large enough to pace in? But the real estate gawking has become secondary to the actual pop star in the living room.

"So Theo is bi?" Priya asks Finn.

"He could be pan," I offer.

Finn, who has been conspicuously silent, looks like he might throw up.

"Are you alright?" I ask him. "You didn't know about this, did you?"

"Of course I didn't know," Finn stops pacing and leans against the far wall. "He woke up naked in my bed. Sorry I didn't think to ask in detail about his sexual preferences."

"Well, has he ever mentioned any other women he's dated?" Priya prods.

Finn slides down the wall into a crouch and scrubs his hands over his close-cropped hair. "Guys, I hung out with him one time, the same as you. I had no idea."

"Yeah, but you've been texting," I say. The other week, Finn dropped a weird comment about Gaston into our text thread when I asked if he wanted me to grab him an egg sandwich on my way to his place, before remembering it was an inside joke he had with Theo instead of me. "Did this never come up?"

"No, it didn't come up. It's not like we were exchanging body counts and comprehensive biographies of everyone we've ever slept with. I kind of didn't think to assume he was bedding A-list celebrities."

"You seem kind of upset about it," I say.

"I'm not upset." His body language begs to differ. "Why would I even care?"

"Because you like him?" I ask.

"I don't like him," he scoffs. "I told you on my birthday I'm over him."

And I didn't believe him then either. The past month Finn has been all giddy smiles whenever Theo's name or our plans for tonight come up in conversation. But it's almost as if I can see the mask slide over his face as he shuts down and detaches right here in this bathroom, like this is a role and he's getting into character.

Tonight, the role of Finn will be played by . . . this other robot version of himself. Letting him have this is easier than calling him on his bullshit because we still have to make it through dinner.

"Then what are we even doing in here?" Priya asks.

"I thought we were washing our hands and gossiping," Finn says. "I think Clementine's had work done. Did you notice her nose looks different? I'm not saying we should, but if we wanted to, we could sell a photo of her from tonight for a lot of money."

Our group of five is seated around a dining table that could easily fit twelve. Instead of putting all the place settings at one end of the table, the extra chairs were removed, and we're spaced at odd intervals. It's not just the seating chart that's awkward, the conversation has stalled since we returned from our bathroom confab.

While everyone busies themselves with their salads, I'm staring at the roast in the center of the table—each shank is topped with a little paper hat—and hoping I'm not expected to serve myself, because I wouldn't have the faintest idea of how to cut into that thing.

"It's a crown roast," Theo explains when he catches me staring. "When I was a boy, this is what we'd eat at the holidays. So I asked the caterers to make one for us tonight."

A round of appreciative *hmms* circle the table.

"We always had Christmas crackers on the table, too. But I didn't leave time to order any," Theo tries again to spark a conversation. "One year my father had some custom made with hundred-pound notes inside, except I'd been particularly naughty that year, almost got thrown out of primary for scrapping with one of my classmates, so he made one for me with a lump of coal inside."

Clementine reaches out to put her hand on his arm to console him, but she's too far away and her hand swats at air before coming to rest on the white tablecloth in the vast space between them.

Over her shoulder, I notice another framed photo of Theo, sandwiched between Phillip Benson and an older woman with frosted blond Farrah Fawcett hair and a face frozen into a startled expression with injectables.

"Wow, you must be a major fan of Phillip Benson," I remark for lack of anything better to say. "If you start quoting from his book, I may have to excuse myself."

Tyler, the other assistant on the morning show, is constantly quoting business catchphrases from Benson's book. "Most 'necessary evils' are far more evil than necessary," he likes to remind us whenever he wants to weasel out of grunt work. It would be laughably nerdy, except our boss loves Benson, too.

"Oh, trust me, I'd be the last person you'd catch quoting from his book," Theo assures me. "The ego of that man writing a self-help book with all his issues is appalling. I'm shocked people aren't demanding refunds."

"Exactly!" Then I remember the other photo of him in the hallway. "Wait, I thought you were a fan?"

Theo gives a harsh laugh. "Hardly."

"But the other photo in the hallway?" I look around the table to see if everyone is as confused as I am.

"Phillip's his father, darling," Clementine says. "Didn't you know?"

I certainly did not know, and by the look on Finn's face—his eyebrows basically in his hairline—he didn't know either. I'm peeved we already burned our group bathroom trip, because there's suddenly a lot more to discuss.

"Who would be your dream celebrity threesome?" Priya asks out of nowhere. I'm grateful for the distraction.

Clementine turns her whole body to face Priya and claps her hands together. "Ooh, this is fun! That I've had? Or I want to have?"

"Um, either?" Priya tells her.

"It doesn't matter, it's actually the same. Chris Evans and Rita Ora. You think he'd be the star, but she knows her way around a clitoris."

Finn's jaw drops. Literally drops. I imagine my face must be doing something similar. We're at dinner with the son of a billionaire and someone who's fucked Captain America. Meanwhile, here we are: an assistant, a struggling actor, and an internet columnist. I can only imagine how much they're regretting their choice of dinner guests.

"What about you?" Clementine asks Theo.

"Celebrities are too high-maintenance for me." He looks over at Clementine and adds, "Sorry, darling."

She shrugs, unbothered by his assessment, before turning all her attention to Priya. "Same question back to you."

"Maybe Dominic Broughan—"

"No," Clementine interrupts, "he's an awful kisser. Too much tongue. You know the type." She makes a sour lemon face and darts her tongue in and out like a lizard. The table collapses into giggles, which just eggs her on. She starts groping the air in front of her. "Proper handsy, too," she adds, "and he's pocket-sized. Only came up to my collarbone."

After dinner, Theo switches the record, and a melancholy Irish ballad pours from the speakers. "The Pogues, really?" Clementine asks from where she's sprawled on her back on the living room carpet. The pen holding her topknot in place was lost some time during dinner and her silvery blond hair is fanned around her like a lion's mane.

"'Fairytale of New York' is Britain's favorite Christmas song," he says defensively.

"Let's play a game," she says as the song's tempo picks up. "Theo, do you have any cards? We could play strip poker."

We're all a bit drunk. After the initial tension receded, Clementine managed to win us over. Me with her music taste, Finn with her encyclopedic knowledge of musicals (turns out I wasn't wrong about the former theater nerd assessment), and Priya with tidbits of celebrity gossip. It's not hard to see why she's famous. There's something magnetic about her. Something sparkly and indescribable.

She's also a terrible influence. She appointed herself in charge of refilling our glasses with more of Theo's never-ending supply of red wine and topped us up with liberal pours whenever our glasses dipped below half full. "I'm an optimist, darling," she said as she refilled mine almost to the brim. "I like full glasses."

I have no idea how much I drank, but my wineglass never emptied over the course of our two-hour dinner.

"No cards, I'm afraid," Theo says.

"I have a game we can play," Priya offers. "Do you have a bedsheet?"

"Yes?" Theo answers. He looks confused but leaves in search of the sheet Priya requested.

Clementine hauls herself up to sitting with a giddy expression on her face. "Tell me, tell me. What game are we playing?"

"Sheet game," Priya says.

"Sheet game?" With Clementine's accent it comes out sounding more like "shit game." I giggle. I'm drunker than I realized.

"Tell us how it works," Finn says and moves himself from his chair down to the floor with Clementine.

Theo returns with a white bedsheet and hands it to Priya. "Great, I was about to explain the rules." Everyone listens to Priya with rapt attention. "First, everyone gets ten slips of paper. You can write down anything you want. A person, a movie title, a place, an object. There are four rounds: The first round is like Catchphrase. You can say any word except the words on the paper to get your team to guess. The second round you can only say

one word. The third round is charades. The fourth round is charades under a bedsheet. We use the same words every round, so
people get better at guessing as it gets harder."

"Are there teams?" Finn asks, already excited.

"Yes, we split up into two teams. We go back and forth and
each team gets a one-minute turn to get their team to guess as
many words as possible. The round is over when we get through
all the slips of paper. Each paper your team gets right is a point."

"This feels too complicated for drunk people," I say.

"Trust me, it's fun. The winters are cold at Syracuse, we had a
lot of time to fill."

"I'm game," Finn says.

"Me too," Clementine adds.

"Fine," I say.

"What are the teams?" Theo asks.

"How about boys versus girls. You have one fewer person, but
you can go first," Priya suggests.

Theo moves to stand behind Finn and reaches down to rub
his shoulders like a manager hyping up his prizefighter. "You up
for it?"

"Absolutely." Finn beams like he won the lottery.

After refills and tracking down pens—the only ones in Theo's
office were two Montblanc fountain pens in decorative stands,
plus we found Clementine's hair pen under the dining room
table—we brainstormed our words and threw our folded slips of
paper into a crystal bowl.

"This is way fancier than when we played in college," Priya

says. "We used to use the popcorn slash vomit bowl for this." She heaves the vessel towards Finn, who is going first.

"One minute on the clock. Go!"

Finn picks out his first slip of paper, and grins when he reads the clue. "It's a musical about Oz!" he shouts at Theo who has a blank expression on his face.

"Kristin Chenoweth!" Finn adds.

"Erm . . ." Theo scrunches his forehead in thought.

"Popular!" Finn shouts. When Theo doesn't say anything, Finn tries singing it instead. *"POP-U-LAR."*

It doesn't help. I feel bad for Theo. This reminds me of the time Finn tried to teach me how to play Zip, Zap, Zop, the game they used for warmups in his acting class, and was furious when I didn't catch on fast enough.

"Witch!" Finn screams at Theo.

"Can we pass, then?" Theo asks.

"Oh my god, we're going to need to fix this ASAP if we're going to be friends," Finn scoffs as he picks a new slip of paper.

"Murder podcast everyone's obsessed with."

"Serial?" Theo says.

Before Finn can pick a new slip from the bowl the alarm on Priya's phone rings to signal time. "They got one point."

Theo reaches over and grabs Finn's thigh. "I let you down. I'll do better next time." I watch as Finn stares down at Theo's hand wide-eyed.

"They're cute," Clem leans over to whisper to me. I nod, unsure of how to answer.

Priya takes the first turn for our team.

"C'mon, Priya, you've got this!" Clementine urges, giving her a drumroll by slapping her hands on her thighs.

Theo starts a timer on his phone. "And, go!"

Priya pulls out her first slip. She squints one eye closed while she thinks. "Topless paparazzi photos of Clem," she says.

"Leonardo DiCaprio's yacht!" Clementine shouts, and it's unclear if she is elated by the memory or getting one right.

"People dumping water on their heads on social media," Priya says.

"The Ice Bucket Challenge," I yell.

"The woman from *The Hunger Games*," Priya urges. She picks up a fistful of paper scraps instead of one. Our team is on a roll.

"Katniss Everdeen!" Clementine shouts.

By the time Theo's alarm sounds we have eight slips of paper in our discard pile. Clementine offers Priya a high five when she takes her seat on the couch.

An hour later, we're in the final round, and my stomach hurts from laughing. After a rocky start, Finn and Theo have come from behind to narrow our lead. Coming into this round it's seventy-four for the boys, and seventy-six for the girls. Theo's way too into it, revealing a competitive side that rivals Finn's. The slips left in the bowl are the ones that keep getting thrown back because no one can guess them.

"Guess it's me. Promise you'll still speak to me even if I boff it?" Clementine asks.

"You won't boff it," Priya tells her.

Clementine puts the sheet over her head, bringing along a few slips of paper with her underneath.

"Ready, set, go."

Clementine tips her head back and mimes something with her hands. It looks like she's playing an imaginary trumpet. Then she starts thrusting her hips like she's dry humping something.

Theo is laughing so hard that he has to wipe tears from his eyes. We would be laughing, too, if we weren't so invested in figuring out what the hell Clementine is miming. I never could have predicted tonight ending with an honest-to-god pop star dry humping the air with a sheet on her head. If paparazzi would have paid good money for the photos of her new nose, imagine how much we could get for these. The headline would read: "Clementine Del Suffers Mental Breakdown."

Clementine is back to playing the air trumpet.

"'Drunk in Love'?" Priya guesses. Oh, that was drinking, not the air trumpet.

"You're an ace!" Clementine yells from beneath the sheet in Priya's general direction.

"No talking!" Finn chastises.

"Sod off, I'm not cheating."

Now she starts zooming around the room with her arms spread wide. She dives to one side and knocks over an empty champagne flute. The glass is so heavy, it doesn't break. "Leave it!" Theo orders. This is too important.

Clementine crouches into a squat, her arms held out, and slowly rises while duckwalking across the living room like a plane taking off. "*Thoughts from Thirty-Five Thousand Feet,*" I yell the name of Theo's dad's self-help book.

"Yes!" Clementine cheers. She pulls the sheet back so it sits atop her head like a wedding veil and tackles me into a hug. We go flying backwards in a mess of limbs and high-thread-count linen. Priya throws herself onto the pile.

Across the room Theo grumbles, "Leave it to my father to ruin Christmas without even being here." Finn rubs circles on Theo's back to console him. "I want a rematch."

But the rematch doesn't happen. Shortly after the game ends, Clementine falls asleep, curled like a kitten on the carpet, emitting light snores. But the rest of us are still wired from the game, or the wine, or one another's company, or some intoxicating combination of all three.

As our conversation creeps into the early hours of the morning, there's an electric feeling in the room, it's as if I can feel something clicking into place between the four of us. I gave Finn a hard time about inviting Theo last year, but he was right. He's one of us.

EIGHT

Hannah

This year, November 22

Our rental car, a silver Prius, idles outside David's parents' house in Fairfield. I've been here twice before—once for his mother's birthday and once for David's—but every time the house impresses me anew. Not because it's huge; it couldn't be on two educators' salaries in one of the most expensive zip codes in Connecticut. But because it looks like it was plucked from a TGIF sitcom. White siding, black shutters, a cornucopia filled with gourds on the top step of the brick walkway leading to a bright red front door—it's all so inviting.

"Ready?" David asks from the driver's seat.

"Yep," I answer with more certainty than I feel. My knee bounced the entire hour and a half drive from the city.

"It's going to be great," David tries to reassure me. "My parents are so excited to have you."

As soon as David clicks the lock button on the key fob, the car emitting a beep-boop of confirmation, the front door swings open to reveal his mother like she was standing there in suspended animation waiting for her youngest son to appear so the holiday could begin.

When we're in arm's reach, she pulls me in for a hug. I shove the pie I'm carrying in David's direction to keep it from getting squished. "Hannah! We're so happy you're celebrating Thanksgiving with us this year!" June gives me an extra squeeze.

"And what am I, chopped liver?" David asks over my shoulder.

June grabs David by his upper arms and holds him at arm's length to inspect him, always on high alert for him looking too thin. Like he might have wasted away since the last time she saw him three weeks ago when we met his parents at Grand Central and took them to dinner before they saw *Dear Evan Hansen* on Broadway, the tickets an extravagant birthday gift from David.

June pulls him into a hug and plants a kiss on his cheek, leaving behind a smudge of rosy pink lipstick. "You could never be chopped liver," she coos at him. "You're too handsome. Maybe you could be a corned beef reuben. Everyone likes corned beef."

June loops her arm through her son's and guides us into the house.

"Go say hello to your brothers, they're in the den." He hands me the pie and obediently disappears into the back of the house.

June couldn't be more lovely, but she terrifies me.

This may seem like an odd reaction to a petite woman in a cream-colored sweater set and matching pants who's never said a mean word about anyone. What scares me is how much her approval matters to David.

After I met his parents for the first time, over steak frites at Almond five months into our relationship, David had an extra pep in his step on the walk home.

"They like you," he said.

"Well, good. I liked them, too."

"They didn't like Alexa." His last girlfriend, the only one serious enough to meet his parents. "They thought she was stuck up and 'not very bright.'" Ever since, I've lived in fear of June rescinding her stamp of approval, aware it's not a given.

I follow June into the kitchen where pots are simmering on every burner. The audacity of this woman to cook a full meal in an off-white outfit without an apron or any concern about stains only confirms I'm correct to fear her.

"Where should I put this?" I hold up the pink bakery box. "It's pecan."

June demurred when I offered to bring something. "I've got everything covered, just bring yourselves," she said.

I'm not much of a cook. Not any kind of cook, actually. But food is David's love language, and he inherited that gene from his mother. He courted me over meals at his favorite restaurants, telling me his personal history through the dishes we ate—the *lucky* ramen from a spot on St. Marks he ordered the night before every one of his NYU finals, the seafood tower at Jeffrey's Grocery where his dad took him when he passed the bar exam, the pancakes at Sarabeth's where he brings his mom every Mother's

Day. When I had a cold, he insisted on getting June's recipe for chicken soup, the kind with homemade broth from a chicken carcass. According to him, the soup had mystical medicinal properties. To my astonishment, it really did work.

What I brought to his mother's house on Thanksgiving felt like a test, and I wanted to ace it. I'm not meeting anyone new, but being here for a holiday feels more important, more official than my previous visits.

I spent the past week maniacally researching Yelp reviews of every bakery in the city to secure the best pie money could buy before settling on Pies 'n Thighs in Williamsburg. I took the J train over the bridge at eight this morning to collect the pie I ordered, not wanting to risk it growing stale overnight.

"You can put it over there, sweetie." June points to a square of countertop where two other pies rest on a cooling rack. There's a third in a domed Tupperware from one of David's sisters-in-law. If this was a test, I already feel like a failure as I set my pie with the others, all homemade.

"Can I help with anything?" I ask.

"I've got it. Why don't you go see what the girls are doing?"

"Do you realize how hard it is to get into the right preschool?" Jen, David's sister-in-law, is asking Zoe, his other sister-in-law, when I walk into the living room. "You should be putting yourself on the waitlists now."

Zoe's face crumples. She's on her third IVF cycle in as many years. She confided in me about this over drinks—a glass of wine for me, a sparkling water for her—at a cozy wine bar in Fort Greene, around the corner from the apartment she shares with David's middle brother, Nate. They moved into a two-bedroom a few years ago with hopes of needing the extra room for a baby, but so far, the only new addition is a Peloton bike.

"I didn't realize there was a right and wrong kind of circle time," I say to take the heat off Zoe. We've only hung out alone a few times, but I like her, and Jen is a bully.

"Oh my god, not putting Sophie on the waitlist at Saint Ann's the minute I got pregnant is my biggest regret in life. It's why we had to leave New York," she admits. "We were too late to get her into any of our top schools." I suppress an eye roll that *this*—her child's rejection from a $48k-per-year preschool—is the moment that cleaved her world in two. It's not that I wish her pain, exactly, and more that I wish her the perspective to see what an ass she sounds like in this moment. But however hard this blow lands for me, I'm sure it lands twice as hard for Zoe and her empty uterus.

Feeling like I've overstayed my welcome in the motherhood conversation, I try my luck in the den, where David is having a drawn-out debate with his oldest brother Adam about whether Bitcoin is a good investment while they half watch the Giants game.

After two hours shuffling back and forth between the women in the living room and the men in the den, trying to picture how I might fit into this family, I feel wrung out. Even though everyone's been nice to me—in June's case, exhaustively so—I can't get myself to relax. And the effort is starting to take a toll. Frazzled and on edge, I wander upstairs to David's childhood bedroom to sneak a minute to myself.

I take a lap around the room running my fingers over the soccer trophies on the dresser and the framed photograph of David at his high school graduation bracketed by both brothers. I flip open a dog-eared copy of a Hardy Boys mystery from the bookshelf. On one of our early dates, David told me he almost became a detective, because of this book series.

"Why didn't you, then?" I asked.

"Because Adam wanted to be a lawyer, and most of all I wanted to be just like him."

"You're kind of like a detective," I told him. "Being a lawyer still means solving cases."

"That's generous," he replied, "I think I missed the installment about the rogue trademark infringer. Between the two of us, you're the one pursuing their dreams. And I think that's incredibly sexy."

Now, being in this room filled with relics of David's earlier selves stirs an illogical jealousy in me that I never witnessed these past versions of him. The elementary school soccer star, the high school honor society president, even the NYC club rat. The latter, a brief phase memorialized in a photo of him with gelled hair and a shiny shirt beside a crew of college friends tacked to the bulletin board above his desk.

I swiped right on David's Bumble profile because of the

combination of his singular dimple and the quote in his profile: *You be the DJ, I'll be the driver.* I didn't realize it was a John Mayer lyric until our fifth date, but by then I liked him too much to care about his questionable taste in music. And true to his profile's promise: he was happy to let me be the DJ.

I always pictured myself dating a musician, someone as passionate about music as I am. Not a frontman, but maybe a drummer or a bassist. Someone who wasn't in it for the girls or the glory, but the craft. David couldn't be further from that. Last week I heard him singing the Stanley Steamer jingle in the shower and he once asked me for a six-letter word to answer the crossword clue: *Former boybander heralding a "Sign of the Times."*

"He's Boy Scout cute," Priya remarked when she caught him sneaking out of my bedroom the morning after our second date. And she was right. He's the kind of boy next door handsome that has old ladies chatting him up in the grocery checkout line. I didn't think that would do it for me; I pictured myself with someone tattooed and broody. But, somehow, just about everything about David does it for me.

A knock on the doorframe startles me and I clutch the paperback I was leafing through to my chest. When I turn around, David's leaning against the wall with a small smile on his lips. "Hi," he says.

"Hi," I say back, feeling shy having been caught prowling around his bedroom.

"What are you doing up here?" he asks. "I looked all over the house for you."

"Just being a creep," I admit.

"Well, if we're admitting creepy things, is it weird that I like seeing you in here? I didn't exactly have any girls up here in high school. There's a real wish fulfillment to this." He looks me up and down.

I flush at his assessment. If his parents weren't downstairs, I'd think about pulling him down on the bed, but instead I settle for crossing the room and giving him a chaste kiss. Nothing we'd be embarrassed about if his parents walked in.

"Should we go back downstairs before we're missed?" I ask.

"No, let's stay a minute. I could use a breather, too. I know they can be a lot. It means so much to me that you're here today."

He pulls me into his chest and I let myself sag against him, resting my head on his shoulder. I inhale the smell of his deodorant and the sandalwood and leather scent of his cologne. That's all it takes for something in my chest to loosen. It feels like I can breathe for the first time all day. I might not have preschool recs to trade with Jen and Zoe or opinions on cryptocurrency or football, but I realize I'm glad to be here, too. Because this is where David is, and these are the people he loves most. And I want them to love me, too.

The dinner table is magazine spread worthy. After retiring as the local middle school's vice principal, June spent last summer taking an eight-week course at the Culinary Institute of America outside Poughkeepsie, and today is her recital. She flits around the table filling glasses and cutting turkey into bite-sized pieces for the grandchildren.

"So, David," Jen says once everyone is settled, "when are you going to put a ring on Hannah's finger?" She takes a sip of her wine to hide her self-satisfied smile as the side conversations grind to a halt so the rest of the family can hear his answer to the question they're all wondering, but only Jen is bold enough to ask.

"Well . . . ," David sputters as he glances around the table for someone to save him.

Nate claps him on the back. "C'mon, Jen, maybe he's waiting to do it at Christmas and now you've ruined the surprise."

"Mom *is* knitting Hannah her own stocking," Adam says with a knowing tone.

It's clear his older brothers are eager for David to join their ranks as husbands and fathers. It would be cute; except I suddenly feel like I'm in the midst of one of those dreams when you're called to the front of the class to give a speech you didn't prepare for, and, oh yeah, you're not wearing pants either, as everyone at the table looks back and forth between me and David. I briefly wonder if it would look suspicious if I excused myself for the bathroom and let the Becker clan sort this out among themselves.

"Leave him alone," David's father says in the tone he uses to quiet a classroom of rowdy high schoolers.

"You know I was teasing you, Davey," Jen says as she tops off her wineglass. "I'm just trying to help Hannah out! I'm sure she's getting impatient. I know I would be." She flashes me a wink like we're on the same team.

Jen reminds me of my own sister. Tanned, toned Jennifer with the perfect blond highlights was a corporate lawyer when she married Adam. Now she stays home with her two kids and brings the same competitive spirit to being the perfect wife and mother, as if she's on some elusive partner track at the firm of Mrs., Mom, and Homemaker.

For a while, it looked like Brooke was heading down a less conventional path. After the stock market crashed in 2008, and Lehman Brothers along with it, Brooke took her half of the money from the sale of our childhood home on some quarter-life Rumspringa, globetrotting and partying, probably relieved to be free of the responsibility of "taking care of me."

She returned a year later with Spencer, a fellow backpacker she met at a Full Moon Party in Phuket. I rolled my eyes when she insisted I come down from Boston the Thanksgiving of my junior year to meet him. I came, begrudgingly, when she pulled out the big guns: "You're the only family I have."

We ate turkey sandwiches from the deli downstairs from Brooke's Upper East Side apartment while Spencer lectured us on the superiority of Japanese sushi relative to its American counterpart and how I *must* get myself to Angkor Wat before it's ruined by tourism, like he was somehow exempt from tourist status.

There's no way he would stick, I thought after my trip.

But he did.

Spencer got a job at Citadel, and Brooke at Credit Suisse. They traded up for nicer and nicer apartments as their combined salaries ballooned. After two years together, they announced they were pregnant the same year I moved to the city. In quick succession, Brooke quit her job, they moved to a house in Highland Park—the town over from where we grew up—and Spencer put a diamond the size of a skating rink on Brooke's finger.

The next Thanksgiving, there were five of us: me, Finn, Brooke, Spencer, and baby Ella, who screamed her head off the entire dinner until she was a disconcerting shade of purple. After dinner, Brooke and I washed the dishes while Spencer and Finn strapped the baby into the car to drive her in circles around the neighborhood, the only thing that would make her stop crying.

It was the first time Brooke and I had been alone in years—there was always the buffer of Spencer, Finn, or the baby, sometimes all three—and I took the opportunity to ask something I'd always wondered. "Do you ever get sad thinking about Mom and Dad?" She never talked about them, but living in the town next door, she must drive past reminders of our childhood on a near daily basis. I imagined it would be like living in a museum of your own grief.

She heaved out a sigh as she swirled a bottle brush in one of Ella's dirty bottles. I couldn't tell if the sigh was due to the general exhaustion of being a new mom or exasperation with me. "You know what your problem is," Brooke answered, finally. "You need to stop living in the past."

"Jeez, I was just asking."

"I mean, sure, I get sad when I think about the fact that Ella will never meet her grandparents, or when I drive past Mom's old office—it's a Subway now, by the way. And god, I'd love Mom's advice on how to get Ella to sleep through the night, or just to hear some reassurance that parenting gets easier, or a hug or a homemade meal when I've gone a week without getting more than two hours of sleep at a clip . . ." Brooke trails off, seemingly lost in thought. "But you can't change the past, so what good does it do to dwell on it? It's not healthy, Hannah. In order to keep living, you need to move on."

In the intervening seven years, Brooke popped out two more baby girls and put even more distance between us, moving on with her own life so completely that I'm not sure I have a place in it anymore. When David invited me to Thanksgiving, I felt a mixture of victory and defeat as I declined Brooke's invitation. Here was proof I was moving on, too, just like she suggested, but doing so meant admitting that Brooke and I would never be close the way I hoped we would be.

After dinner, dessert, and three heated rounds of Pictionary, David and I are back in the car, the trunk loaded with Tupperware containers of leftovers. As David pulls onto I-95, he reaches over and puts a hand on my thigh. "My parents really love you, you know." He lets out a contented sigh.

"They're great," I say. "Jen, I could live without, but those gorgonzola mashed potatoes your mom cooked almost made up for her. Oh my god." I moan in ecstasy thinking about them.

"I'm sorry about Jen. You know that's just how she is. I said something to her about it after dinner. It wasn't fair of her to ambush you like that." He glances over at me, and I can tell he's nervous, his bottom lip caught between his teeth. "But, about what she said . . . would that be so crazy? If we got engaged, I mean."

I feel my throat tighten. "Not crazy, no. Just soon. Don't you think?" I only just checked off the milestone of spending a holiday with his family, and we're already hurtling toward the next one.

We've talked about marriage before, but always in the abstract. The same way we talk about taking a trip to Italy we can't really afford, and I don't have enough PTO for anyway. It's always *someday*.

And what do I know about being a wife—or fast-forwarding even further, a mother—with so many years without any family of my own? What if I fuck it up, and end up with nothing? My leg starts bouncing again as these thoughts dart through my mind.

"I don't think it's too soon. This is it for me, Han. I mean, we already live together; it wouldn't really change anything."

"So why rush, then?" I counter. "Weddings are expensive."

"I'd talk to my mom. I wouldn't let her force you into some froufy white wedding, if that's what you're worried about. I know that isn't you. We could get married at city hall and go to a diner afterward for all I care. It doesn't matter to me. I just want to be with you."

I look over at him and smile. I know David just wants a plan. He has five-year plans and ten-year plans and spreadsheets to project his retirement savings. Me, I try not to think too much about the future. Longevity doesn't exactly run in my family. It's not that I don't want to be with him, it's just that things are good right now, so why mess with that?

"Don't think I didn't notice that you didn't give me an answer," he says playfully. "So . . . ," he starts again, "if I proposed at Christmas, would you . . . say yes?" He asks the last part quietly, like he's afraid to hear the answer.

"Not to get sidetracked from the main point here, but we haven't even talked about Christmas yet. It's Finn's last Christmas in New York, and—"

"Wait," he glances over, his eyebrows knitted together in confusion, "you're not coming to Christmas at my parents'?"

"You know I always spend Christmas with my friends. I didn't come last year."

"But we live together this year," he says as if this solves everything. His confusion has been replaced by a wounded expression. "And I know Christmas is your favorite holiday. I was hoping we could build a new tradition this year. *Together.* I just thought after today—"

I cut him off because I don't want him to get the wrong idea. "Today was lovely! Your family is lovely! But Finn, Priya, and Theo, they're *my* family. And our Christmas tradition is a celebration of that. Christmas is important to me because *they're* important to me."

"I know they're important to you, but I want to be your family, too. My family could be your family," he says, and though his voice is soft and full of hope, his comment chafes.

"My family isn't in need of replacing, David. Just because it's nontraditional doesn't mean it's not real—"

"That's not what I—"

I feel myself getting heated. I need to get this out, to make him understand. "These people have been with me through thick and thin for the past ten years." I stare at the line of taillights unfurling ahead of us and take a deep breath. "There's part of me that will always miss my parents. It will never, ever be okay that they're gone. And for a while I was afraid I'd never find happiness, or safety, or comfort again. I was alone. But they were the ones who rallied around me, and gave me understanding, and love, and vitality. You call June or one of your brothers when you have a hard day, or when you have good news to share. Well, I call them. They're my family in all the ways that count."

For a moment, he's silent. He reaches over and takes my hand. "I should have chosen my words more carefully. I didn't mean to imply what you have with them is any less valid. I can't even begin to fathom what you've been through—you're truly the strongest person I know—and I'm so deeply glad you've found people who give this to you. But Hannah"—he pulls at my hand, trying to get me to look over at him, which I do—"can't you see that I want you to feel loved, and comforted, and alive because of *me*, too?"

"I do, David." I squeeze his hand for emphasis, and he takes his eyes away from traffic for a second, gauging if I really mean it. "But it's different. You have your parents and your brothers, and you don't see me trying to replace them. Family and a romantic partner aren't mutually exclusive. I mean, plenty of couples spend the holidays apart."

"But I don't want us to be one of those couples."

We're both silent for a few seconds, it feels like we've reached an impasse.

"It's just . . ." He hesitates.

"What?" I ask, never one to leave well-enough alone.

"Nothing, never mind. I hate that this one little thing is making us fight like this."

I know it isn't his intention, but my brain latches on to the word "little" and it bounces around inside my head like one of those Super Balls from a quarter vending machine. "Little?! Are you listening to what I just told you? These are my people. That's not little. That's everything. And you're one to talk. Your family is Jewish, David! It's not like Christmas is so important to your family either."

He scoffs.

This was the wrong thing to say. I've seen photos of him and his brothers as kids in matching red sweaters tearing into presents wrapped in Santa wrapping paper. While they may not be Christian, June fully bought into the commercialized version of Christmas. I know Christmas is important to him, but why should I be the one who has to compromise? Why can't he be the one to realize that my tradition is equally as important to me?

We drive for fifteen minutes in silence, both of us lost in our own thoughts.

Norwalk.

Darien.

Stamford.

I count ten exits before I try talking to him again.

"David," I say.

"Just tell me, Hannah, what kind of future do you want?" He glances over and I can see the mix of hurt and anger in his expression. "And what place do I have in it? Sometimes I wonder if it's always going to be like this—you're the most important person in my life, but I can't seem to fight my way to the top of your list."

"I love you, David. You know that."

"I do, and I love you, too. But what are we doing? Where is this going?"

As he lobs questions at me my head spins.

I stop myself from saying that I like how things are now, because clearly he doesn't feel the same way. "I don't know," I say, finally. Not to hurt him, which I fear it will, but because the world already feels off its axis with Finn leaving. When I try to picture the future, it's like looking into the murky blue of a Magic 8 Ball. *Ask again later.* I feel like the walls of our tiny rental sedan are closing in on me.

"Well, would you do me the favor of letting me know when you figure it out?"

"I . . . ," I begin, ready to protest, but realize I can't. It's not an unreasonable request.

"Sure."

We drive the rest of the way back to the city in silence.

Back in Tribeca, David drops me off at the apartment while he goes to return the rental car to the parking garage around the corner where we picked it up. I'm pretty sure we're both relieved to have a few minutes to cool off.

"Happy Thanksgiving," I say to Frank, the night doorman, on my way past his desk to the elevators. Before I can press the up button, I decide against it and walk back toward the front door.

"Did you forget something, Mrs. Becker?" Frank asks as I walk past his desk going the opposite direction. His honest mistake lands like a blow and I tamp down the urge to correct him that David and I aren't married. Right now, we're barely speaking.

Outside, I hang a right toward the West Side Highway. I have too much anxious energy to burn off, and I don't particularly want to continue our conversation when David gets home. Maybe a walk will help clear my head.

Except by the time I get to Hudson River Park, I'm more mixed up than when I left our building. Maybe talking would help. I pull out my phone and press Finn's name at the top of my favorites list.

NINE

Finn

This year, November 22

For a few seconds after I wake up, I don't know where I am. I blink at the navy blue wall in front of me. My apartment's walls are white. I wanted to paint them, but I couldn't. It says so in my lease. I glance down at the sheets. They're covered in tiny cursive *A*'s, the Atlanta Braves logo.

Oh, right, I'm in my childhood bedroom. Now I remember.

I sit up to get a better look at the room. It was dark when I got in last night after an endless day of delays at JFK. Waiting suited me just fine—I had the final installment of the Throne of Glass series on my iPad and a bag of Combos from Hudson News. The longer the flight was delayed, the less time I'd have to spend with my family.

By the time a Lyft dropped me at my mother's doorstep in Peachtree City, it was after midnight, and I barely had the fortitude to brush my teeth before falling into bed. Turning on the lights would only mean getting out of bed to turn them off again, so I used my phone's flashlight to navigate to the bed and collapsed into a dreamless sleep without bothering to plug in my phone. The battery is at twelve percent, I need to find a charger.

The room is a time capsule. There's a stack of paperback fantasy novels with cracked spines on the windowsill. My father hated those. "You're too old for those sissy books," he said. "Go outside with the other boys instead." The only books he read were Jack Ryan novels. If something didn't explode every twenty-five pages, by nature it was sissy. An ironic worldview for an accountant. But the allure of those "sissy" books was the hope that I might find a false back on an armoire or get a visit from an owl and find an escape hatch out of his house or, better yet, discover I was a changeling and not his son to begin with.

Instead of dealing with the unpleasant memories that are bubbling up, suppressed from the last time I was here, I take in the shrine to my younger self. On the walls are posters of Michael Johnson from the 1996 Olympics and the 1995 Braves World Series team. I was too young to remember either sporting event with any real clarity, but my father hyped both to near-mythic proportions to the point where his memories felt like my own. Later, Johnson was an inspiration, both the reason I tried out for the track team and the subject of many teen masturbatory fantasies.

The room hasn't changed at all. But I've changed a lot. Except I still want to sleep with Michael Johnson. Well, maybe. I'll have to Google him and see how he's aged.

I feel sad for the boy who lived in this room. The boy who was desperately trying to win everyone's approval, especially his father's, and hide that he was gay, something he'd known with a fair degree of certainty since Ashley King's twelfth birthday party when he spun the bottle and it landed on Billy Bradford. I leaned toward the center of the circle, counting my lucky stars. He was the cutest boy in our grade. Billy was less enthused. My classmates burst into peals of laughter at my gaffe. Boys weren't supposed to kiss other boys. Everyone knew if it landed on a boy, you spun again.

Billy spent the rest of middle school telling anyone who would listen I was gayer than a fruitcake. Even if it was true, I wasn't keen on another label to differentiate me from the mostly white student body in our affluent suburb.

When my father got wind of the rumors, he drove to Billy's house to have a word with his father, man to man. The next day, Billy showed up at our door with an apology letter and a sheepish look on his face. He was so upset I almost apologized to him. I wanted to tell him he wasn't wrong, but my dad was standing behind me in the foyer, supervising Billy's apology.

I throw back the covers and cross the room to the dresser to find something to pull on over my boxer briefs. I wind up with a pair of Falcons pajama pants and am pleased they still fit, even if they're snugger than I remember. I left my suitcase downstairs. Carrying it up felt like too much effort, plus I like knowing my packed bag is beside the door in case I need to make a quick getaway.

It's strange being home. I never thought I'd be back here, let alone twice in two years. *This isn't home*, I remind myself, *this is the house I grew up in*. My real home is a postage-stamp-sized apartment in the West Village above the third-best pizza place on the block, but not for long. I gave my landlord thirty days' notice and have to be out by December 15. But I can only handle one panic spiral at a time, so I head downstairs.

Aunt Carolyn is rolling out pie dough on the kitchen island. "Finn!" she announces with a mixture of excitement and trepidation, like a colonial sailor spotting land, when she spies me plodding down the stairs.

"Still not an early riser, I see" is my mother's warm welcome. She looks different. Her hair is shorter and she's wearing it natural in tightly coiled curls. I've never seen her without her hair pressed except in the grainy, yellowing photos of her childhood. She looks up from the enormous turkey she's basting and gives me an indulgent smile as I shuffle over to the ancient Mr. Coffee machine in the corner.

I open the cabinet above the coffeemaker in search of one of my mugs. My mother never worked. This house was her work, always dusted within an inch of its life and redecorated every five years, like she was on high alert for a drop-in from *Architectural Digest*. Legos, Barbies, and anything plastic weren't allowed outside our rooms. Her only concession to chaos was our family's clashing collection of mugs amassed from sports teams and charity fundraisers. I flinch as I push aside a #1 DAD mug (the irony!) to look in the deepest part of the cabinet for my favorite, a green mug from my senior year on the track team that says TRACK: IT'S BETTER THAN PLAYING WITH BALLS.

But there are no signs of any of my mugs. I pull down a purple mug from Amanda's Girl Scout troop and pour myself a cup of coffee.

"Can I help with anything?" I ask.

"We're all set in here," my mother says, not looking up from her basting.

"Do you want me to peel the potatoes?" This was my job when I was younger.

"Already done," Aunt Carolyn says, sounding pleased with their efficiency.

"Oh." I marvel at how completely I've been erased from this family over the past ten years. I wonder if they took down the school pictures of me on the photo wall in the living room. I wouldn't put it past my father.

"It's hotter than the devil's armpit in here. If you don't need anything, why don't you help Amanda polish the silverware," my mom says, and I realize that maybe she doesn't want to spend time with me any more than I do with her. Why did I even come?

I find Amanda at the dining room table. All the doors to the china cabinet are flung open like a poltergeist tore through the house before I woke up. Her elbows rest on the gleaming wood table, her face buried in her phone.

"What's up, doofus? Nice of you to finally join us. Mom never lets me sleep that late," she says without looking up from the novella-length text she's composing.

"She doesn't seem to care what I do. She kicked me out of the kitchen," I tell her as I slump into the upholstered chair beside her. They're new and decidedly more modern than the wooden chairs we had last time I was home.

"Must be nice. She's up my ass about what I'm going to do after graduation."

"Do you want help?" There's a mountain of unpolished silverware in front of her, the real kind with filigree rosettes on the handles that we only use for company. A wedding gift from Grandma Everett.

At least things aren't strained between me and Amanda. I worried our relationship wouldn't survive my leaving. She was eleven at the time. It's not like I could swoop in under the cover of darkness and hang out with her while she lived under my parents' roof. So I sent her emails: links to the announcement that the Jonas Brothers would be playing the Philips Arena or an article about the new bookstore they were putting in the outdoor shopping center downtown. I would have called, but she didn't have a cell phone and I was terrified my father might answer if I called the landline. But I wasn't going to lose my sister.

I was shocked but also elated when she made good on her promise to visit me in New York when she turned eighteen. She came over spring break with money saved from lifeguarding and various babysitting gigs, lying to our parents and telling them it was a senior class enrichment trip to job shadow notable alumni of the high school we both attended.

Hannah, Theo, Priya, and I took her to see *Wicked* and snuck her into the basement at Home Sweet Home to dance with a crappy fake ID purchased on St. Marks Place. When she left, I wasn't sure which she was more in love with, the city or Theo, who she followed around like a puppy, hanging on to his every word.

She's come every spring break since. There's only one more left before she graduates from Emory. I wonder if she'll come to LA for this one, but even if she does, I know it won't be the same without Hannah, Priya, and Theo.

Now that I'm awake, Mom and Aunt Carolyn have turned up the Whitney Houston in the kitchen. I recognize the album as Mom's favorite. The cassette had a permanent home in the tape deck of her Mercedes station wagon. We'd blast "How Will I Know" and sing along on the short drive to school. But the music was confined to the car, Dad didn't like it to be loud in the house.

A bark of Aunt Carolyn's laughter wafts out from the kitchen.

"Oh, you're bad," Mom says, also laughing.

"They've been like that all morning," Amanda informs me. "It's weird, right? I keep waiting for Dad to come out of his office and tell them to quiet down because he's on a work call. And then I remember."

"Yeah, it's super weird." This is true of the whole trip for me, not just the laughter. I'm not sure what qualifies as weird around here anymore. "She seems good, though?"

"She's happy to have you here."

"I don't know about that."

"She hasn't stopped talking about your visit all month. She's bringing back macaroni and cheese this year because she knows it's your favorite." I try to square this with the chilly reception I received in the kitchen, but can't. "She's just . . . adjusting," Amanda continues.

We all are. It's bizarre for me to be back in this house, too. Back at this table. Where it all went to shit. Where I told my parents I was gay and got expelled from my own family.

My father's response was an adamant "No."

Just *no.* Like the sheer force of his objection could change my sexuality.

And a year earlier, it might have. I would have said, "Yes, sir," and asked out one of my many female friends who were always leaning a little too close and touching my arm a little too long, like they were giving me a green light to kiss them.

But the summer after my freshman year of college was different because I'd been dating Sean Grady for most of spring semester. Sean was my first real boyfriend.

We met at a wine and cheese party thrown by his a capella group. The event was intended to be classier than the standard campus party with Busch Light and beer pong, but in practice the wine came from a bag. Sean had been out since high school, and he didn't like that I wasn't. I was out at school, but no one at home knew, especially my parents.

Out at school wasn't good enough for Sean. Before we left for summer break he gave me an ultimatum: tell my family while I was home or we'd have to reevaluate our relationship in the fall. In hindsight, this was super fucked up, but at the time I took his demand with the utmost seriousness.

I decided to make my announcement at dinner my first night home. Not because I expected it to go well, but I figured this would give my parents until the end of summer to adjust to my news, the same way Sean's parents had. "Trust me," he told me, "my parents are old-school Irish Catholic. If they can accept it, yours will be fine."

It was not fine.

After lodging his objection, my father stood up from the dinner table, poured a double bourbon from the decanter on the sideboard, which until that moment I thought was only for decoration, and locked himself in his office for the rest of the evening, slamming the door behind him for emphasis.

My mother's reaction was just an "Oh, Finn" before she got up to start the dishes even though she hadn't touched her salmon.

Oh, Finn, what, I wondered. *Oh Finn, how could you? Oh Finn, give him some time?*

That night, I sat in the shadows at the top of the stairs waiting to hear my parents' conversation when Dad emerged from his office.

"He'll change his mind real quick once I stop paying for that fruity-tutty liberal school of his. Just you watch, Suze," I overheard him tell my mother in the kitchen. He poured another bourbon and went back to the office.

I was shocked that she didn't stand up for me. I really thought she would. But she didn't say anything.

I'm jolted from the memory by the buzz of my phone against my leg. I pull it out of my pajama pants and see a text from Theo: How's it going at home?

Awful, I text back.

Last year, I went home with Priya for Thanksgiving. Usually, I'd spend the holiday at Hannah's sister's, but Hannah and I weren't speaking. Priya's mom cooked a feast of tandoori turkey for the meat eaters and a pumpkin and chickpea curry for the vegetarians, but my favorite thing was the masala mashed potatoes. The house was overflowing with people and Priya was treated like a returning hero back from the big city. Especially by her teenage cousins, who were dazzled by the duffel bag of beauty samples she brought for them, freebies sent to her by PR reps in hopes she would write about them. I was awed by how wonderful it must be to belong to so many people. I should have gone with her this year instead of coming here.

On my text thread with Theo, three dots appear and then disappear.

After two more starts and stops, all I get is a frowny face emoji. I wait to see if the dots appear again, but they don't.

I'm about to text Theo and ask what he's up to today, but my phone dies. Oh well, Theo doesn't need me bumming him out. He's in Napa with his boarding school friends, probably halfway into a case of cabernet even though it's only 9:00 a.m. there.

My mother and I have different definitions of a small dinner. This becomes clear when she asks me to put the leaf in the dining room table, which seats ten without it. A steady stream of aunts, cousins, and neighbors arrive throughout the afternoon. We sip sweet tea and mill around the formal living room we only use when company visits. I stay glued to Amanda's side so I don't have to explain my ten-year absence or sudden reappearance.

But I needn't have worried. Everyone is in their church clothes and on their best behavior. They were raised right; they won't say anything to my face, but I know I'll be the topic of gossip on everyone's ride home. The closest thing my absence gets to an acknowledgment is an "I've been praying on you," from my great-aunt Eunice.

By the time Aunt Carolyn calls everyone to the table at 2:55, the house is packed and the table is groaning under the weight of a dozen serving dishes, including three kinds of potato salad, every auntie convinced theirs is the best.

"Kids' table is in the kitchen," Aunt Carolyn scolds a child in a miniature Lacoste polo shirt when she catches him sidling up to a chair at the dining room table. I don't recognize him. He must be a cousin born during my exile.

I follow Amanda to the kitchen table. We'll be the oldest, but at least I'll be spared the adult table. We can filch extra wine from the pantry and gossip about the boys she has crushes on at school. There are always plenty of those.

"Not you." Aunt Carolyn holds her arm out like a militant crossing guard to block me from the kitchen. "You graduated college, you graduated to the adults' table!" She makes it sound like a reward, not a punishment.

"But I want to sit with Amanda," I protest.

"Nope." Her tone leaves no room for negotiation.

I end up seated between Aunt Ruthie, my mom's older sister, and my second cousin Travis, who I gather is Polo Shirt Kid's father. As a teenager, I assumed Aunt Ruthie was a lesbian, but had the good sense not to make a big production of it. She worked as a park ranger at Tallulah Gorge State Park and went on yearly trips to other national parks with an all-women's tour group. But maybe I was wrong and she just didn't want to be tied down by marriage like her younger sister. After all, Aunt Ruthie never lost her place at our family's holiday table, although maybe that's putting too much stock in the infallibility of my father's gaydar.

Dinner passes without incident. My mother is quick to interfere when Uncle Robert asks whether I have a girlfriend back in the city. "Did you know Finn got a new job at Netflix? We're so proud of him," she interrupts. A collective *ooooh* goes up from the table. I'm not sure whether to feel happy that I'm finally worthy of my mother's pride, or disgusted that she's still doing everything she can to hide my sexuality.

"Do you think you can get them to bring back *Bloodline* for another season?" Uncle Robert asks, taking the bait.

Aunt Ruthie and I are the only people availing ourselves of the wine. "It's good you made time for us," she tells me in a tipsy whisper after her third glass of Chardonnay, and the "us" sounds more like "ush." "I've heard all about how busy you are back in the city, but you've been away too long. Your mama missed you."

I choke back a bitter laugh at the implication that my absence was by choice.

Later, after the relatives have cleared out and the dishes have been scrubbed by hand—"The dishwasher doesn't get them clean enough," my mother argued—the three of us are installed in the den in front of the TV.

"Let's watch *Schitt's Creek*," Amanda suggests. "I think you'd like it, Mom, it's about a family."

"I don't want to watch anything with profanity in the title," she counters.

Amanda and I exchange a look, but neither of us argues. It feels too difficult to explain, so we settle on a Hallmark movie about an uptight city bitch who goes skiing with her best friend only to find their chalet double-booked with a pair of eligible bachelors. It doesn't matter that the movie is halfway over; the guide description makes it obvious where this is heading.

I have one eye on the TV and the other on my phone where I navigate to Theo's Instagram profile to see if he's posted from California, but there are no updates. My deep dive into the cast of boarding school friends he's traveling with is interrupted when my phone lights up with a call from Hannah.

"I'm gonna take this." I rocket off the couch, glad for any excuse to be saved from this movie and trot up to my bedroom.

"Thank god!" Hannah says when I answer. On her end cars whiz by in the background and she pants lightly, like she's power walking. This doesn't sound like Connecticut.

"What's wrong?" I ask.

"Everything."

"Could you narrow it down a bit?"

"David and I had a fight." She pauses like I'll know what it was about without her having to tell me, and at a different point in our friendship I might have. But right now, I have no clue. About kids? Does he want her to move to Connecticut? I wrack my brain trying to think about anything Hannah's said recently about their relationship, but come up blank.

"About Christmas," she adds.

"What about Christmas?" I ask.

"He doesn't get it. On the way home from Thanksgiving, we had this fight and he was all, 'How do you expect us to move forward if you won't spend Christmas with my family?'" I'll give it to her, she does a spot-on imitation of David, dropping her voice and adopting his clipped, precise way of speaking.

"You've been together almost two years. It's not completely unreasonable for him to want you to spend Christmas together."

"Finn! You're supposed to be on my side."

"I'm always on your side," I tell her, "but I'm saying that I can also see why he's upset."

"It's stupid that he's upset," she rants. "He's Jewish! Christmas isn't even his thing."

"Sure, and when was the last time you went to church?" I'm positive it was for the baccalaureate Mass that was part of graduation weekend, and only because it was mandatory. There's silence on her end and I can picture her trying to come up with a gotcha she can throw back at me.

"Seriously, Han, if you want to spend Christmas with David's family, I understand."

"That's not why I'm calling. I don't want to be let off the hook, I want you to be outraged, too. He doesn't understand that you guys *ARE* my family. He called our tradition *little*. How insulting is that? But what really grinds my gears is that we wouldn't even be having this fight if I wanted to spend Christmas with Brooke, and it's not my fault she's a complete narcissist."

Downstairs, the doorbell rings. Who on earth is ringing my mother's doorbell after nine? A horrifying thought pops into my head: *What if she has a secret boyfriend?* My stomach roils at the thought. That would be too weird.

"Finn," Mom yells from downstairs, "it's for you."

I bring the phone with me, holding it between my ear and shoulder as Hannah continues to vent, her rant seamlessly transitioning from David to Brooke. I know from experience this could go on a while. As I pad down the stairs a pair of leather driving moccasins come into view.

I take a few more steps and see dark jeans, rolled at the ankle.

A few more steps, a green sweater I recognize.

Theo's here? In my mother's foyer? And he looks exhausted. A battered brown leather duffel rests at his feet.

"Uh, Han, I have to call you back. *Theo's here*," I tell her, and with her permission, I end the call.

At the sound of my voice, he looks up at me and his face cracks into a shy smile.

"What are you doing here?" I wonder aloud.

Theo looks around to make sure no one else is in earshot. "Your text," he says. "You said it was awful, and then when I tried to call you your phone was off. So I came to save you. Or suffer along with you. Your pick, really."

"You came . . . here?" I ask, my brain still catching up to what is happening.

He nods.

"So, do you think we should make a run for it?" He points over his shoulder at the front door and flashes me a wink.

"No . . . I . . . ," I sputter. I can't believe he came all this way to save me from my family. Sure, this isn't my ideal weekend, but it's not that bad. I didn't need saving, I just wanted to complain. And now Theo cut his own trip short and hopped on a plane at a moment's notice to rescue me. I can't decide if I want to hug him or jump him or cry. My brain's still trying to process that he's even here.

"We're staying, right?" he asks after a minute. "Because your mum is heating me up a plate and I'm famished."

I tackle him with a hug. I'm glad my face is buried in his neck because I can feel tears prickling in the corners of my eyes. He rubs his hands up and down my back. "Hey, it's okay. You're okay."

And he's right. Now that he's here, I am okay. I bask in the sense of safety I feel in his arms. "Thank you," I whisper into his cashmere sweater.

"California was boring without you anyway."

I pick at a second slice of pie while Theo attacks a plate of leftovers, stopping every few bites to compliment my mother's cooking.

"My mum once burned a Tesco ready meal so badly the fire brigade had to come. It was a curry, I think, but by the time they put the flames out it was just charred plastic and rice. I think that's the only thing I ever saw her cook. I can't believe you made all of this, Mrs. Everett," Theo marvels.

"Oh, you're too kind," she says. I catch her smiling into her cup of decaf coffee at his compliment. "Finn didn't tell us he had a *friend* coming or we would have set aside a plate. I'm afraid it's just the odds and ends left." Her tone puts honking neon air quotes around the word "friend" to make it clear she suspects we're more.

"Nonsense, this is wonderful. I wouldn't want you to go out of your way," Theo says. He looks over at me and narrows his eyes, and the left side of his mouth quirks up in a mischievous smile. I don't like where this is going. "It's just that I didn't think I'd be able to make it. I was in California on some business, but the minute we wrapped up, I got myself on an earlier flight. I couldn't stand to be away from *my friend* a minute longer." He's ratcheted up his accent, the way he does when he's trying to charm someone, and by the look on my mom's face, it's working. He drapes his arm over my shoulder for emphasis.

I've dreamed about these moments so many times: being Theo's boyfriend, being home. I never dared to dream them together, but here I am.

And it's a joke.

I know this is a bit he's performing to cheer me up, to affirm we're in this together. *Us against the world!* But it's having the opposite effect. Instead, I feel unbearably sad. I should stop him. If I go along with this, it will only be a matter of time before we have to stage a pretend breakup or admit we lied.

"Well, isn't that nice," she tells him before I can object. "I'm glad Finn has someone like you in his life. It's so good to have you here again, and under happier circumstances this time. But Theo, you'll have to excuse me for being poor company. I was up before the sun to get this turkey in the oven and I'm exhausted. I'll leave you boys to it and head up to bed. But I'm so glad we'll get to spend the day together tomorrow."

"Me as well, Mrs. Everett."

"Call me Suzann, please," she tells him.

"Suzann, then," he basically purrs.

"Finn, you'll take care of the plates?" she says, an order masquerading as a question. "And leave a light on for your sister for when she gets home from wherever she went with her friends.

You know she'll come back drunk." She shakes her head as if to say, *Kids, what can you do?*

But I wouldn't know. I missed Amanda's high school years in this house. It's easier to agree anyway. "Yes, Mom."

As she walks out of the room, I remember something. "Mom, where are the sheets for the pullout in the basement?"

"Oh honey, I don't mind if you share your room. You know I'm more modern than your father. You boys sleep well."

Theo death grips my arm as she walks into the kitchen. He claps his other hand over his mouth as she rinses her coffee mug and puts it in the dishwasher. By the time she makes it up the stairs, he's convulsing with silent laughter.

"Admit it," he says between bursts of laughter after her bedroom door clicks shut. "That was cute!"

"That was not cute. It was weird, like she's campaigning for some kind of most-improved award. Earlier, she shoved me back in the closet when someone asked if I had a girlfriend. Let's not give her *too* much credit. I don't think she's getting a rainbow bumper sticker anytime soon."

"Does that mean you don't want to sleep with me tonight?"

I gulp down the lump that's formed in my throat. I want that more than anything, even though I know Theo only thinks of it as a continuation of his bit. "Really, if you'd rather sleep on the pullout, I can find the sheets. We should tell her we aren't together. She's got the wrong idea, and if we keep this going, we're going to need to stage some kind of fake breakup."

"You'd have to be the one to fake break up with me. I would

never break up with you, you're the best fake boyfriend I've ever had!" He ruffles my hair the way one would a little brother's.

"We're telling her in the morning," I say.

"Oh, come now, at least she's trying. Let her think whatever she wants. But, serious question, do you have another pair of those very handsome pants for me?" He gestures at the Falcons fleece pajama pants I put back on after company left. "I didn't bring any pajamas," he adds.

"These are one of a kind, unfortunately."

"Don't think I won't sleep in the nude . . ."

I feel myself blush.

Theo stacks his silverware on his plate and stands up from the table. "Are you going to show me your room?"

TEN

Finn

Christmas #8, 2015

Hannah peers into the Trader Joe's shopping bag and her reaction is immediate. "Oh, hell no."

"Either put it on or you can't come. I didn't make the rules."

She narrows her eyes at me like I'm personally punishing her. "I'm standing in a Starbucks bathroom dressed like a penguin, so it's not like this is ideal for me either," I remind her.

She gingerly pulls the green velvet elf costume out of the bag, gripping the fabric between her thumb and forefinger like she might catch crabs from it.

"It was dry cleaned if that's what you're worried about," I offer.

"I was more worried about my reputation." That's rich coming from Hannah, whose favorite sweater is brown and at least three sizes too large. I call her Mrs. Potato Head whenever she wears it.

"Don't worry, we won't tell *Vogue*."

She frowns into the bag.

"No one's going to see you. Take one for the team."

"No one's going to see me?! That's a blatant lie! This shit is televised!" she huffs. "Are you sure this is the only option?" She rifles through the bag like there might be a false bottom hiding other, better costumes.

"Priya got here before you and took the Mrs. Claus costume. So yeah, this is it. Also, why didn't you two come together?" Priya was on time, while Hannah was thirty minutes late. I sent Priya and Theo ahead to check in for us while I waited for Hannah. When she got here, I had to buy a second coffee because the bathroom code resets on the hour.

"Priya slept at Ben's last night."

"The travel photographer guy?"

"Yeah. Well, no. Same guy, but he's in med school somewhere in the Midwest now." She rolls her eyes. "He's here for Christmas, his parents live on the Upper East Side. She's been there every night this week."

Every six months or so, Ben comes through town and he and Priya crash together like magnets. It's all-consuming for the length of his visit and then she mopes around, flat and lifeless, for a month afterward. I dislike Ben without ever having met him.

There's an impatient knock at the bathroom door. It's the only one and it must see a lot of action judging by the overflowing trash can and the sheafs of paper towels littering the floor at 7:00 a.m. on Christmas.

"Just a minute," I yell, and flash Hannah a stern look. She groans and lifts her Bleachers sweatshirt over her head.

As she pulls on the synthetic-velvet elf costume, I think about how the heck I ended up here. After four years of failed auditions—I got close a few times, but never booked a part—it was clear I needed a plan B. Something creative, I thought. Even if I couldn't be onstage or in front of the camera, at least I could still be involved in making it happen. Hannah was the one who found the listing for my new job at ToonIn. She came to happy hour armed with a sheaf of printed job listings annotated with handwritten messages riddled with exclamation points like "This sounds cool!!" or "Fun perks!!!"

"Educational cartoons?" I mused aloud, less enthused by the prospect. That had to be the skid row of the entertainment industry.

"Think of it like a launchpad," she urged. "And it doesn't hurt to apply and get some experience interviewing." Much to my shock, I got the job. And I accepted on the spot, because after four years of "no," it felt exhilarating to finally hear "yes" for a change.

And while the job has many downsides—there's the always-burnt pot of Kirkland brand coffee, the glut of middle-aged suits obsessing over market research data on what the under-five demo deems "cool," and the elementary-school-themed free lunch Fridays (trust me: the square Ellio's pizza of your youth is worse than you remember)—one perk is the chance to ride on ToonIn's float in the Christmas Day parade.

A company-wide email went out two weeks ago, and I added my name in the first slot on the sign-up list. I grew up watching the parade on TV every Christmas morning. In my nine-year-old brain, watching the parade in person was something every New Yorker did on Christmas.

I'd bring Priya as my plus-one; she'd be the most game. Hannah and Theo could sleep in and meet us after. But when I checked the list again on Friday, my name was the first and only. How were people not more excited? This parade is an institution! Didn't they want to bring their kids? *Their loss is our gain*, I thought, as I added my cubemate Liam's name to the sheet in the second position. He wouldn't care, he was already in Breckenridge skiing with his aggressively WASPy family.

"Also, if anyone asks, Theo's name is Liam," I tell Hannah.

She looks up from putting on her pointed elf slippers to roll her eyes at me.

Three hours later, we're inching down Sixth Avenue so slowly I can only tell we're in motion if I mark our progress against a building and watch it gradually come closer. Hannah and I are stationed at the edge of the float waving and throwing candy into the crowd, while Theo and Priya are on a raised platform dressed as Santa and Mrs. Claus, flanking Chicky, the star of our network's top-rated cartoon and our float's guest of honor.

We met Keith, the paunchy guy in his late fifties assigned to wear the Chicky suit, in the staging area before he put on the head to his costume. Despite being dressed as a chicken—a female chicken, judging by Chicky's long eyelashes and pink-painted talons—Keith was overjoyed by his assignment.

Hannah and I are having a significantly less joyful experience. "My arm is so fucking tired," Hannah complains. "No wonder Michelle Obama has those biceps, it's probably from all the waving."

"The pain in my arms is a good distraction from how cold it is," I tell her.

"I forgot about how cold I am because of how badly I have to pee and now you reminded me."

"This sucks." I understand, now, why none of my colleagues signed up to come to the parade.

Up ahead, Bryant Park is on our left, which means we're somewhere in the lower forties. At this speed it will take an hour to get to the parade's end point in Herald Square. We are never doing this again.

"You need to give me something else to think about," Hannah whines. "I think my right pinky toe is about to fall off from frostbite. I'm considering peeing my pants because one, they're not my pants, and two, it would be warm. Is that totally nuts?"

"Totally disgusting," I tell her. "At least you have pants. I only have tights."

"Well, these elf slippers are not insulated!" she complains. "Okay, go! Entertain me."

"Entertain you how?"

"I don't know. Tell me a secret."

"You know all my secrets." Hannah and I keep up a near-constant stream of Gchat messages throughout the workday. I don't drink a LaCroix, take a pee break, or have a mean thought about Maureen in marketing that Hannah doesn't know about. But there is one thing I haven't told her. Maybe the cold is making me delirious because I feel the confession on the tip of my tongue.

She gives me a funny look while I debate whether I should say anything.

"I have a crush on Theo," I admit.

"I'm sorry, *that's* your secret?"

"Yeah?"

Her face splits into a gleeful grin, which in the elf costume makes her look like a horror movie villain. "That's not a secret. Everyone knows."

"Everyone knows?" Who is everyone? Does everyone include Theo? I thought Hannah believed the spark had passed. I'd been careful not to mention my crush since Theo and I became close friends.

Last Christmas—our second with Theo—was different from the one before. We left his apartment with plans to come back on New Year's Eve for the fireworks. It turned out the buildings surrounding his blocked the view, but we didn't mind. Instead, we killed six bottles of champagne and skinny-dipped in the building's rooftop hot tub that was supposed to be closed for the season.

In the new year, there were brunches that bled into dinners, and movie nights that ended with us all crashing on makeshift beds on Theo's living room floor. There were plenty of guest rooms, but we didn't want to miss a single second of one another's company, even to sleep. By the time the piles of gray snow lining the sidewalks had melted, the four of us had become inseparable. I didn't realize there was something missing in our group before, but Theo seamlessly filled in the gaps, acting like our grout.

One night in March, my phone rang while I was watching *Parks & Rec* for the zillionth time to stave off the Sunday scaries. "Did you know London is less rainy than Miami?" Theo asked when I answered. No preamble.

"I did not know that. Are you in London or Miami right now?" If it was nine on the East Coast, that would make it two in the morning in London.

"London. It's my father's birthday and he's hosting a massive celebration of himself. It's not even an important birthday. It's his sixty-ninth." I stifled a giggle.

"Is it raining there?" I asked.

I heard the rustle of blankets and imagined him getting out of bed to check. In my imagination he was naked, a vision I could readily conjure since the skinny-dipping on New Year's Eve.

"It is raining," he reported.

"My weather app says it's eighty-two and clear in Miami. I'd pick Miami."

"Me too," he answered.

I got these calls whenever Theo was away and couldn't sleep, which was often. Usually, he'd open with a fun fact that sounded like it was cribbed from a Snapple cap. *Did you know a male kangaroo is called a boomer? Today I learned that the Dallas Fort Worth airport is larger than the island of Manhattan. What's the only US state with a one-syllable name?* (Spoiler: it's Maine)

The calls lasted hours, sometimes until dawn wherever he was in the world. While our in-person conversations were frothy and fun, these late-night phone calls were more serious. Talking without seeing each other and the late hour made it easier to lay ourselves bare. He told me about his parents' very public and acrimonious divorce when he was ten, I told him about the summer I stopped speaking to mine. It felt like someone hit the fast-forward button on our friendship.

One night in May, when Theo was in Morocco, as our call ticked into its fourth hour my fatigue gave way to giddy delirium and I screwed up the courage to ask the question I'd been wondering. "What about the girls?"

"Are you asking if I call Hannah and Priya on our off nights? I regret to inform you that I'm a one-man man. And you're it. Purely monogamous with my insomnia, I'm afraid."

"No, I was asking about the girls you . . . you know . . . date? Do you still date girls?" I squinted my eyes shut as I braced for his answer. Maybe I was only a failed experiment.

"Do you ever have an incredible conversation with someone, like so good you're turned on by the way their brain works? Not because they're smart necessarily, though that's hot, too, but just the way they see the world?"

I thought of the conversation we were having and wondered if he was using coded language to talk to me about myself. "Mhmm," I said, not wanting to interrupt wherever this was going.

"To me, it's about that feeling. I'm attracted to the person, not the package."

"See, to me the package is very important." The words slipped out of my sleep-addled brain, and I cringed as my crude joke ruined the moment if he *had* been talking about me. Here was proof my brain worked like that of a horny seventh grader.

"So are you saying you're pansexual?" I asked to make sure I was clear.

"If you want to put a label on it, I suppose you could say that."

He changed the subject to the proprietary color blue of Yves Saint Laurent's house in Marrakech. It's called Majorelle blue, he told me, and I opened my eyes and blinked at the ceiling of my bedroom, both disappointed by the subject change and relieved because the conversation had been edging closer to the line in our friendship that we never discussed, but by mutual unspoken agreement never crossed either. Not since the first night we met.

Over the past year, I've gotten very little sleep, but I've learned in addition to being hot and mysterious, it turns out Theo is also kind, generous, funny, and functions on four hours of sleep a night, at best.

"Have you two really never talked about how you met?" Hannah asks.

"Of course we haven't!" I retort, horrified by the thought of that conversation, which could only result in my rejection.

"Well, this isn't exactly shocking news, Finn. Priya and I talk about your crush on Theo all the time," Hannah reports with a glance toward where he is stationed in his Santa costume beside Chicky's gilded throne. "We weren't sure if you knew or if it's a subconscious thing. But you know you talk about him nonstop, right?"

"Sure, because we're friends."

"No, you, like, gush about how great he is all the time."

I feel myself blush. "Does Theo know?" I hold my breath as I wait for Hannah's answer.

"I don't know," she says. "Probably."

This is so bad. If Theo knows, it means he doesn't reciprocate my feelings. Because if he knew and he felt the same way, we'd just . . . be together, right?

"Also, you haven't dated anyone since you met him," Hannah continues.

"Not true!" I snap back. "I went on a Hinge date last week."

"And how did it go?"

"He lived in Hoboken, so it would have been a long-distance relationship." Her look tells me she's not buying my excuse. "Nothing happened, but it could have if I wanted it to."

"But you didn't want it to, because you have a crush on Theo. I think you should tell him. Look, he's obviously attracted to you. You met because you went home together, so he doesn't think you're some hideous bridge troll."

"Right, but maybe he was only looking for a hookup."

"Sure, maybe, but the two of you are attached at the hip. He enjoys spending time with you, he was attracted to you enough to go home with you. I think you're being dumb."

I'm not being dumb. I'm being cautious. I remember how easily my father rescinded his love. If he taught me one thing it's that, no matter what people say, love is conditional. And what if Theo doesn't like the new terms I propose? Even the thought of a Theo-less life leaves me feeling hollow. It's better to have him as a friend than nothing at all.

"We're kind of in the middle of something here. I don't want to be stuck on a parade float with someone who rejected me."

"So, tell him after. Promise me you'll tell him today."

"Why today?"

"It's Christmas, and I kind of feel like Christmas is lucky for us. Don't you? I mean, it brought us together." Hannah has a dreamy look in her eye, and for a moment I let myself believe that maybe today is lucky for us. On the plus side, I can say with absolute certainty I'm not cold anymore. My body has broken out in a nervous sweat. Am I finally going to do this?

When the parade ends, we make our way to the nearest bar, an Irish pub between Penn Station and Herald Square. Our only criterion is that it has bathrooms, which we sprint to on entering.

Even though it's Christmas and the bar caters to the commuter crowd, it's doing solid post-parade business. There's a fireplace in back, and the warm, beer-tinged air has fogged the front windows creating an aura of coziness. It's so warm, in fact, Theo has stripped down to his Santa pants and suspenders and is holding court half-naked at the bar beside Priya, looking like the December page of a charity fireman's calendar.

Every ten minutes, someone interrupts their conversation and asks to pose with Theo for a photo. The first to ask is a middle-aged waitress. She shimmies into his lap, juts her chest into his face, and whispers what I can only imagine is a proposition into his ear. Theo throws his head back and laughs at whatever she said as the bartender snaps a picture.

I watch from the booth where Theo abandoned his Santa coat in a pile with the girls' purses and reusable shopping bags filled with everyone's street clothes. I'm being held captive by Keith, who changed out of his Chicky costume into a pair of too-wide jeans and a threadbare red flannel. Keith is a mechanic in Mount Kisco, which I learn is up in Westchester County.

"I didn't see myself becoming a parade person," he tells me. "But my wife liked it. She passed from ovarian cancer five years ago, and I keep coming back. It makes me feel close to her, I guess, and it's not like I have anything better to do on Christmas."

"I'm sorry about your wife," I tell him.

He waves off my sympathy and dives into a detailed history of his rise through the parade's ranks. We're on year seven, the year Keith held one of the Snoopy balloon's strings.

"It was windy that year. Terrible balloon weather," he says. I'm having trouble mustering any enthusiasm for his story. He's a nice guy, but I'm annoyed I'm stuck babysitting him. Hannah went to get us drinks, and has been flirting with the bartender, a tattooed guy with an Irish accent, for the past fifteen minutes. Knowing Hannah, he's in a band. I think about abandoning Keith, but I can hear my mother's voice in my head telling me to mind my manners and respect my elders.

While Keith continues his 1998 parade play-by-play, my gaze wanders to Theo's half-naked body at the bar. His broad, muscular chest is tanned from two weeks in Bondi Beach earlier in the month. I'm also keeping an eye on a trio of twinks further down the bar who showed up thirty minutes ago and are also eyeing Theo appreciatively. I'm not sure if they wandered in off the street or if Theo summoned them on Grindr, but either way my window to talk to him is closing.

I need to choose my moment wisely. I don't want to wait until the end of the night and risk either of us being drunk, but I could use some liquid courage before I'm ready to bare my soul. It's a delicate balance.

One of the twinks gets up from his seat and heads in Theo's direction. Fuck it. I have no choice but to be rude to Keith, plus I'm pretty sure I'll never see him again—I'm a one-time parader— so what does it matter if he thinks I'm a jerk?

"Keith, I'm so sorry, I've got to go over there and talk to Theo." I catch myself. "Wait, no, I mean Liam, about something real quick. Would that be okay?"

"Oh, you go on. I've been holding you captive with my silly memories for too long anyways. I should be making my way to Grand Central and getting a train home."

Over at the bar, the twink has his hand on Theo's forearm and points to his friends at the end of the bar. Theo waves at them.

"Your stories aren't silly. It's just . . ." I don't know what to tell Keith. Hell, I might as well tell him the truth seeing as my odds of running into him again are slim to none. "I'm in love with, um, Liam," I say, stumbling over Theo's fake name. "The guy dressed as Santa? And I need to tell him. Right now, ideally."

Keith's eyes bulge out, betraying his shock. He's probably some homophobe and now I'm in for a lecture. Instead, he says, "Did I tell you my wife and I got engaged on Christmas?" He smiles at me. Oh god, another story.

"You know what," Keith says, "that's a very long story and I should probably go tell it to that fellow over there." He points to the man talking to Theo and flashes me a wink.

Keith pops up from the booth and makes a beeline to the bar. He's sprier than he looks. He taps the man on the shoulder and launches into his story. The guy looks confused, but Keith doesn't give him an opening to object. Meanwhile, Theo looks around, bewildered by his abandonment. He spots me sitting alone in the booth and I give him a shrug.

Is this my moment?

Theo saunters over in his red velvet pants and suspenders. He should look ridiculous, but he looks good. Really good. Meanwhile, I'm wearing a penguin costume, which was not intended for sitting. All the fabric has bunched up in my crotch. Theo plops himself down in the seat across from me.

"I've barely seen you all day. I miss you." He draws out the word "miss" like he's a balloon deflating. He's well on his way to drunk.

"I've been here."

"With another man!" He waggles his eyebrows at me. "Do I have something to worry about with you and Keith?"

I laugh, but I can't tell if he's flirting or making fun of me. He has a dry sense of humor, and I haven't learned when I'm in on the joke or the butt of it.

I lock eyes with Theo, going for something between a smolder and a smize, but I don't think I'm pulling it off. "I was hoping to get to talk to you," I begin.

"Nothing bad, I hope?"

"No," I reassure him. Well, that depends on how he thinks about me. Maybe this will be bad to him, having to reject yet another person in what is surely a long line of suitors. I back-pedal, "Well, I don't think it's bad. Maybe? No."

Theo cocks his head and squints at me, trying to figure out what's going on. I'm already messing this up.

"Here goes," I begin again.

Theo's eyes light up. His lips purse into a smile.

This is good. Hannah's right, I haven't been as covert about my crush as I thought. Theo knows what's coming and from the looks of it, he looks . . . excited. Maybe I was being stupid. This is Theo. This isn't scary.

"So, you probably already know, and it's okay if you don't feel the same way, but I—"

I pause when I realize Theo's eyes aren't meeting mine. Is there someone behind me?

I look over my shoulder toward the door. A South Asian man in a camel overcoat is striding our way. He looks like he stepped out of a magazine ad, like one minute he was brooding into middle distance with his elbow on his knee selling watches or trench coats or really expensive whiskey, and he got bored and wandered off the page. His thick black hair is mussed in an intentional way, like after a team of stylists spent hours getting it absolutely perfect, they decided to run their hands through it because no one would believe that level of perfection, but somehow messing it up made it even better. I turn back to look at Theo, who is definitely looking at this man and not at me.

Shit, shit, shit.

When the Rolex model reaches our table, Theo says, "Raj, you made it!" He sounds delighted, like Raj is the Christmas gift he begged for all year. Theo scootches out of the booth and rises to standing.

"I told you I'd come," Raj replies as he beams at Theo with a gleaming smile. He takes off his overcoat to reveal a white dress shirt with the cuffs rolled to the elbows. He has sexy forearms, I notice as he hangs his coat on a hook at the end of the booth.

Also, who the hell is this guy?

"Raj?" Priya shouts from the bar and launches herself off her barstool and into his arms. For a second I wonder if maybe this is some never-mentioned cousin of Priya's before realizing how totally racist that is.

"I'm Priya. I've heard so much about you," she adds. There goes that theory.

Raj rests one hand possessively on Theo's bare chest, and I feel my heart sink into my stomach.

"Finn, meet Raj," Theo says, and they both look down at me in the booth, the sad penguin. "My new boyfriend," he adds. As if to demonstrate the point, Theo leans in and gives Raj a searing kiss that goes on a few seconds longer than is polite in public.

Since fucking when, I want to yell. And how does Priya know about it when Hannah and I don't? I'm suddenly very jealous of Keith, who spent the whole parade stationed between Priya and Theo. If only his chicken suit let him hear what they were saying and he could have warned me.

I'm furious. I have no right to be, but I am.

"You okay, mate?" Raj asks in a smooth British accent.

"Yeah, too much to drink," I lie. I haven't had a single drink. I stand and try to pick the moose knuckle the penguin costume is giving me as subtly as possible before shaking Raj's hand.

"Pleasure," Raj says, "I've heard so much about you."

"Pri, why don't you and Raj grab a drink. Finn was in the middle of telling me something important," Theo says.

Priya loops her arm through Raj's like they're old pals, but she throws a concerned look over her shoulder toward me, assessing how I'm taking the news.

"Sorry, what were you saying?" Theo asks as he sits back down across from me.

"Oh, um, I think we should do New Year's on your roof again."

"Bloody brilliant! Absolutely."

Theo gets up and claps me on the back before adding, "You should probably slow down on the drinks, you don't look so good." I nod, and he leaves to make his way to Raj at the bar. Once he's gone, I collapse my head onto my forearms on the table. Now I'll have to watch Theo kiss Raj at midnight. Perfect.

ELEVEN

Hannah

This year, December 1

David and I are on our way home from the Union Square farmers' market, his tote bag weighed down with stalks of Brussels sprouts, a bouquet of rainbow carrots, a carton of mushrooms, and a loaf of fresh sourdough. My only add was a bag of Martin's hard pretzels, which have become a minor addiction in the five months we've lived together and I've been accompanying him to the greenmarket on Saturday mornings.

He's telling me about the Melissa Clark coq au vin recipe from the *New York Times* cooking section he wants to try tonight when he interrupts himself. "Should we get one?" He points to a stand selling Christmas trees on the sidewalk of West Broadway.

We stop to survey the rows of trees, each wrapped in netting, so the only discernible difference is their height. "Didn't you say you've always wanted a real tree?" he asks.

My heart flutters at his thoughtfulness. The way he always

remembers my small comments. I did say that. I specifically said I wanted a tree from one of these sidewalk stands that pop up in late November and fill street corners with a sweet pine scent. At Orchard Street, there was no room for a tree. Our living room was like a game of furniture Tetris as we wedged in more and more sidewalk finds over the years: a pair of end tables Priya stripped and repainted, a vintage trunk, a tripod floor lamp. We set up a miniature artificial tree on the coffee table and made ornaments from back issues of Priya's *Us Weekly* subscription and tubes of glitter glue. Last year's tree-topper was a red carpet photo of Meryl Streep cut into a star shape.

"Okay, let's do it," I tell David. Maybe *this* can be our new Christmas tradition, something just for us.

Half an hour and four blocks later, I have misgivings about the tree as the pine needles stab my bare fingers like actual needles. "Can we stop for a second?" I ask between pants. "I need to adjust my grip."

"Do you want to switch sides?" He's bearing the brunt of the weight with the trunk, but I have the spiky top half, which is impossible to get a solid grasp on.

"Uh, not really," I say. "Why? Do you?"

"I think we should just power through the last two blocks. Get it over with," he suggests.

"Are you saying we should attempt to jog with this behemoth? Because I was half considering leaving it on the sidewalk. I know the book is called *A Tree Grows in Brooklyn,* but I think this tree could have a pretty nice life on the sidewalks of lower Manhattan, too. We live in a good school district," I pant.

"I can admit it's possible I was wrong to suggest we get the biggest tree," David says, his shoulders slumping forward slightly and his tote bag sliding down his arm.

My gut twists with guilt. "No. You were totally right!" I rush to tell him. "This is going to look amazing. Just wait until we get some lights on it. This was a great idea, truly." I hook my fingers into the netting, letting it cut off my circulation.

"I'm ready," I announce. "One . . . two . . . three . . . go." I take off in an awkward trot that makes us look like we stole the thing.

By the time we stagger out of the elevator we're both sweating, and the tree has lost at least twenty percent of its needles. "What if it has a bald spot?" David wonders aloud as we carry it down the hallway to our apartment, leaving a trail of pine droppings in our wake.

"We'll have to love it anyway because there's no way I can repeat this heroic act of strength. I'm sure Amazon sells tree toupees." We smile at each other with punch-drunk grins.

"Maybe we can get a second tree, a younger girlfriend to complete his midlife crisis," he says between laughs.

David goes to set up the stand while I head for the half bath to minister to the tiny cuts on my fingers. There are no bandages in the medicine cabinet, but I know David keeps some in his sock drawer, ready to use with his black dress shoes that give him blisters.

In the sock drawer, there aren't any Band-Aids, but there is a black velvet box nestled among his neatly organized selection of socks, all paired with their mates.

My heart rate ticks up.

This might not be what you think it is, I tell myself.

Even as a fluttery, nervous feeling takes up in my stomach, I cling to the idea that the box is a pair of cuff links or a Christmas gift for his mother. Maybe a nice pendant necklace or a pair of earrings. Just please don't be a ring. I don't feel ready for it to be a ring. I realize from years of rom-coms and women's magazines packed with recipes for "engagement chicken"—a roast chicken to make for your boyfriend in hopes of conjuring this exact moment—that this isn't the correct reaction. But it does shed some light on why things got so heated on Thanksgiving. Maybe it wasn't about Christmas at all. Maybe it was because David already bought a ring.

After a glance toward the door to make sure David is occupied—he's squatting in the corner of the living room trying to get the tree into the stand by himself—I flip open the lid to the box.

Inside is a pointy oval-shaped diamond on a simple gold band. The only thing I can think to compare the shape to is a vagina.

What the fuck?

For a second, my nervousness is replaced with sheer confusion. I've never been the type to fantasize about my dream engagement ring, but I'm positive this isn't it. What about this ring reminds David of me? If I wasn't sure David isn't the cheating type, I might think the ring was meant for someone else.

Suddenly, my breath grows quick and shallow. Doesn't he know me at all? How could he think *this* is the ring I'd want?

"Hannah? Can I get your help for a sec?" he yells from the living room. I clutch my chest as if he'd walked in on me wearing a wedding veil and waltzing with a photo of him. I pop the lid of the ring box closed and slam the drawer shut with my hip.

In the living room, he asks me to hold the tree straight while he screws it into the base. I do so while staring mutely at the wall trying to untangle my thoughts about the vagina ring from my thoughts about an engagement, but I can't.

David is so focused on the tree, he doesn't notice my withdrawal. After the stump is screwed in, he puts the Beach Boys Christmas album on the record player and sinks down next to me on the brown leather sectional. He wraps an arm around me and pulls me into his side. "This is my dad's favorite Christmas album." He gives a contented sigh as we stare at the slightly crooked tree that's noticeably sparser in the top left quadrant.

Our decorating has reached its anticlimactic conclusion since we don't own any Christmas ornaments. But after a minute, David hoists himself off the couch.

"Where are you going?" I ask accusingly. For a second I stop breathing, wondering if he's going to get the ring, but he passes the bedroom and heads for a seldom-used hall closet. The closet is a vertical junk drawer packed with ski gear, board games, plastic bins of loose charging cables whose purposes have been long forgotten, and the sleek white boxes from every Apple product we've ever owned, which we agree we don't need but also cannot bring ourselves to throw away. The only items of note in there are our suitcases, and my panic shifts from a proposal to a fear he's leaving. I don't want that either! Why can't things stay exactly as they are? Things are good how they are. Steady.

Instead, he pulls out a medium-sized cardboard box with *fragile* written on the side in his mother's looping cursive and two packages of string lights.

"My mom sent us some things to get us started," he tells me. "I've been nervous all week that you were going to find them and ruin the surprise."

"Nope, I had no idea," I tell him. But what I really want to know is when he plans to employ his other surprise, the one I did stumble on, and why he picked that particular—hideous—ring.

He sets the box down in front of me. Inside are a few sealed boxes of glittery red and gold balls; a selection of ornaments David made as a kid, including a photo of him and his brothers in a popsicle-stick frame; and, wrapped in tissue paper, a half dozen of June's beloved Christopher Radko ornaments. I recognize them because I scoffed at the price—$103 for Perfectly Plaid Santa—when we bought one for her as our joint gift last Christmas. Her willingness to part with them feels akin to an engraved invitation to the family.

"It was really nice of her to send these," I tell him, and lever myself off the couch to hang a sparkly snowman ornament on the tree, so he doesn't mistake this for his moment to propose.

Meanwhile, David methodically adds a hook to the photo ornament of him and his brothers—the three of them match in holiday sweater vests; he smiles with the crooked buck teeth he had before braces gave him the straight, even smile he has today. "I was wondering," he asks, then hesitates for a moment. "What kind of Christmas ornaments did you have as a kid?"

"Well, my mom always did all white ornaments. Sometimes a few gold ones, too, but nothing else," I tell him as I remove the tape sealing the package of glittery red ornaments.

"Should we get some white ornaments in her honor?" he asks.

I laugh. "Oh god, no! It's a nice suggestion, but definitely not. I was terrified of her tree. We weren't allowed to touch it, but I did anyway, and I was so scared Santa would find out. I always tried to wake up a little early on Christmas morning to sneak downstairs and make sure there were still presents for me and that I hadn't made the naughty list."

He sticks out his bottom lip in an exaggerated pout. "Sweet baby Hannah."

"I know," I say, laughing. Warmth spreads through me thinking about the Christmases of my youth. I hadn't thought about the fussy white trees in ages. I'm glad to be able to share this memory with David.

"Okay, here's an idea." He pauses for dramatic effect. "What if, instead, we become a kooky-tree family."

"I like it!" I tell him.

I try to hold on to the contented feeling while we decorate the tree to the sounds of Brian Wilson crooning that it will be a blue

Christmas without you, but the ring keeps popping into my mind. And telling myself not to think about the ring only makes me think about it more. Rings with cartoonishly large Disney character feet cha-cha through my brain, taunting me.

When we finish, we collapse back onto the couch to admire our handiwork. "Well, we definitely have our work cut out for us," David remarks. "This tree does not look kooky at all. In fact, it looks like the kind of tree that has a mortgage and drives a Honda Accord." I laugh, already excited about the prospect of hunting down more ornaments to make this tree *ours*.

"How about you pour some wine while I start dinner?" David asks.

"Sounds perfect," I say. Relief courses through me as he heads toward the kitchen. Braised chicken feels like a fairly unlikely place to hide a ring.

TWELVE

Hannah

This year, December 2

The next afternoon, Theo leads me through the designer women's wear floor at Saks, navigating us around displays of sequin-encrusted evening gowns. Behind a selection of pointy-shoulder blazers that remind me of "Vogue"-era Madonna, he rings a doorbell next to a plain wooden door.

After he invited me on this last-minute shopping trip, my next call was to Priya, ostensibly to invite her to join, but I also wanted her opinion on the ring. She knew David the best out of my friends. Even though David lived alone when we started dating and we easily could have holed up in his apartment, he made it a point to spend time at mine, too.

One rainy Sunday early in our relationship, Priya made chana masala—another of her mother's specialties—as we watched back-to-back showings of *Ocean's 11*, *12*, and *13* on cable. After licking his bowl clean, David insisted she teach him how to make the dish. For months, our minuscule kitchen became an off-license cooking school as the two held weekly Sunday cooking lessons. They only stopped when we reached the dog days of summer and the apartment was too stuffy to justify using the stove. Priya taught David to make saag paneer and malai kofta—the latter requiring a few FaceTimes with Priya's mom to perfect. I was happy to be the designated taste tester, and even happier to see David win Priya's enthusiastic stamp of approval.

But when I called her this morning, she brushed me off with vague excuses about work even though it's Sunday. "Maybe I can meet you later?"

"Also, I found a ring in David's sock drawer," I told her before she could hustle me off the phone.

"That's great, Hannah. Congratulations!" She sounded distracted and I could hear a man's voice in the background. I wondered where she was and who she was with. "But I gotta go. Let's plan drinks next week, okay? And I'll try to make it later if I can." Before I could protest that I wasn't sure this could wait until next week, she'd hung up.

As I waited for the E train to take me uptown to Theo, I couldn't shake the feeling of distance growing between me and Priya. I wondered if there was something going on, and if so, why she didn't want to talk about it with me. So it's just me and Theo on today's shopping trip, since Finn is apartment hunting in LA.

A woman with a blondish-gray bob opens the hidden-in-plain-sight door, and a cloud of Chanel N°5 wafts out along with her. I'd recognize the scent anywhere, the same one my mother wore.

"Miriam!" Theo exclaims, leaning in for a double cheek kiss.

"Theo!" she coos back at him in a similarly posh British accent. If we weren't in a department store, I might be fooled into thinking she's his mother by the affection in her voice.

"And who do we have here?" she asks, looking over his shoulder at me.

"This is Hannah." He shoves me in front of him so Miriam can kiss my cheeks, too.

"A pleasure to meet you," she says. "Come in, we have everything set up."

She leads us back to a sitting room with tall windows overlooking Fifth Avenue framed by gauzy white curtains that billow down to the floor. I feel like I'm in a Celine Dion music video.

Trays upon trays of printed silk scarves, statement earrings, and delicate gold watches are set up on the glass coffee table. On a console table off to the side are at least a dozen purses. Everything is beige or gold, including the furniture. It's like I'm in an I Spy book trying to spot the thing that doesn't belong in the sea of ecru, cream, and gold. Except the thing that doesn't belong is obviously me in my scuffed Doc Martens and eight-year-old jeans with a hole in the knee.

"Champagne?" Miriam asks. Even the beverage adheres to the color scheme.

Theo turns to me, deferring the decision, so I say, "Yes, please."

Miriam goes to fetch the champagne, leaving us alone with what I imagine is hundreds of thousands of dollars of merchandise.

We have two missions today: the first is to find Christmas gifts for Theo's two mother figures, and the second is to figure out what we should do for Finn's last Christmas. I'm equally overwhelmed by both tasks, but it feels good to have a distraction from the ring.

Annabelle, Theo's actual mother, married Theo's father at twenty-two and divorced him at the height of his net worth, of which she took a substantial chunk. Now she splits her time between a townhouse in London, a penthouse in Paris, and a spread in the South of France. We've never met her, but she sounds more like a fun aunt than a mother, nipping into town once a year and plying Theo with cocktails and shopping sprees.

"By the time I came along, they hated each other, but the divorce took a good decade because dear old dad knew it was going to be expensive," Theo explained once. He spent most of his childhood in an empty townhouse with Lourdes, his beloved governess, whom we're also shopping for today.

"So, what does your mother like?" I ask.

"Spending my father's money and almost nothing else." He holds up a pair of diamond earrings so they catch the light and refract rainbows on the walls around us.

Miriam returns with two flutes of champagne on a silver tray. "Miriam," Theo asks, "What's the most expensive thing in here?"

She picks up a clipboard from the console table and runs her index finger down the list. "That would be the Cartier tennis bracelet." She crosses the room to show him her list and spare us the embarrassment of hearing the price spoken aloud.

Theo nods. "That's sorted. Can you have it wrapped and sent to the London address?"

"Of course." Miriam remains cool even though she's likely earned an eye-watering commission. "If you'll allow me a moment, I can have the room switched over so you can select the other gift."

An army of shopgirls descend on the room with such speed it makes me wonder if Miriam is hiding a panic button up her sleeve to summon them. The women whisk away the trays of white scarves and diamond jewelry.

Miriam, looking like the world's chicest stewardess in her black pantsuit and pointy heels with a jaunty red scarf tied around her neck, wheels in a cart of new trays, except instead of mini cans of Diet Coke and ginger ale, the trays are filled with strands of gumball-sized pearls and candy-colored gemstone earrings. There are scarves as well, in electric blue and Barbie pink and orange. One of Miriam's helpers brings in an armful of handbags, all in bold colors. Another wheels in a rack of furs.

"Now this is the fun part," Theo says. "Lourdes likes things flashy."

He moves from the sofa to the console table to run his fingers over a fire-engine-red crocodile purse. It's certainly flashy. "That's limited edition. Five in the world," Miriam tells him.

He offers it to me to hold. When I take it from him, I almost drop it. It's so heavy it may come with its own gold bricks included.

"What do you think?" he asks me.

"I mean, I'm not the best judge." I have one black purse that I've had for years. "It's heavy?" I offer, unsure if that's good or bad. Theo smiles at my reply, he knows I'm clueless but wants to include me anyway.

"What about a fur coat?" he asks.

"Doesn't she live at the beach?"

"Right."

"Does she like scarves?" Miriam asks. "Scarves are the best friend of any woman of a certain age." She gestures at her own scarf-clad neck, and I wonder what's hiding underneath. Gills or a prison tattoo feel equally unlikely but make me giggle to myself all the same.

"I don't think I've ever seen Lourdes wear a scarf."

"What about something more personal?" I suggest.

"Like what?"

"I don't know." I sift through the roster of gifts Brooke and I gave our mother as kids: Color Me Mine pottery, Fimo clay bead necklaces, cheap plates screen printed with our school art that she proudly displayed in the kitchen. The Christmas before she died, I made her a photo album. I picked out an expensive pebbled leather album and used the photo kiosk at Walgreens to make copies of my favorite photos of the two of us. One time I found her asleep in the hospital bed in our living room, cuddling it to her chest like a stuffed animal.

"I made my mom a photo album one year and she liked it," I volunteer.

"Jay Strongwater does some lovely crystal and enamel picture frames," Miriam jumps in, "and Cristofle has some gorgeous platinum-plated ones. Would you like me to have a selection brought up?"

"Thanks, Miriam," Theo says.

I don't bother to correct either of them that this wasn't exactly what I had in mind. Miriam teeters off in her spindly heels to make it so.

"Do we have to get something for your dad, too?" I ask Theo, who's sunk back into the sofa.

"No, he doesn't value things, only experiences," Theo says, using exaggerated finger quotes to emphasize the word "experiences."

"I can't imagine what kind of experiences a billionaire would value," I reply. "A trip to space? Hunting endangered species? Bankrupting a small-town bookstore?"

Before I can come up with more ideas, Theo chimes in: "He already knows what he wants. He wants us to work together. He offered me a job."

"A job?" I say, confused. As far as I know, the only job Theo's had is when he tried to start a private members' club in London with some of his boarding school friends, a more exclusive Soho House with a younger clientele. It failed spectacularly; there weren't many twenty-four-year-olds who could afford the exorbitant membership fee. But even then, Theo was the money guy. He didn't have any operational role outside bankrolling the whims of his cofounders.

Since we've known him, he cochairs the Art Party at the Whitney every year and sits on the board of a handful of charities giving underprivileged students access to arts education programming, but I don't think he's ever had a meeting that wasn't accompanied by lunch or cocktails.

Theo drags his hands down his face, horrified by the prospect of working for his father.

"What did you tell him?"

"I asked if he'd broken Colin, his little business boy. I'm just the spare for the day when Colin finally has a nervous breakdown, but I hadn't expected it to happen until his fifties, at least."

"Are you thinking about accepting?" I can't stop a note of panic from creeping into my voice. I assume the job would mean a move to London and I don't have the stomach for another friend leaving.

"No." He waves this off like it's a ridiculous idea. "It's just some power play."

He takes a sip of champagne to cleanse his palate of this distasteful notion.

"What's new with you?" he asks. "You'll forgive me for saying it, but you seem . . . off."

"Off?" I echo.

He doesn't elaborate, just looks at me, waiting me out, and I almost blurt out everything going on with David—our fight on Thanksgiving, the weirdness that's persisted since, the ring in his sock drawer—but I can't bring myself to. The more people I tell, the more real it feels.

"Oh, I'm fine," I lie, but I feel like I need to give him something. "Just stressed about work, I guess. I keep pitching this music history podcast and getting shot down. It would be my first solo project, but I can't get my boss to see the potential I see."

It's especially frustrating given that Mitch has greenlit every flavor of two-dudes-talking show in his three-month tenure. Two dudes talking about cult eighties movies, two dudes talking about actual cults, two dudes talking about fantasy golf. Last week, he made his threat official: if I can't line up mutually agreeable talent for the pilot of *Aural History* by the end of the year, he'll shut the whole thing down. He alluded to needing a lead producer for *Porn Stache,* his newest two-dudes creation, where two comedians watch and dissect VHS tapes of eighties pornos.

"What's your show about?" he asks.

I tell him my idea for the podcast and he smiles when I reveal the name. "That's very clever," he says. "I think it sounds like a smash. What's the problem?"

"We can't agree on which song to use for the pilot. I had my boss sold on 'Candy' by Mandy Moore, but her people never got back to me. You don't happen to know her, do you?"

"Can't say that I do. But what about Clementine?"

"What about her?"

"I'm sure she'd love to help!"

"That seems like a stretch. I can't imagine she even remembers me."

"Of course she remembers you. Didn't you see her on Fallon last month? She taught him how to play sheet game and the whole thing went bloody viral." I must have missed that. "Do you want me to call her for you?"

"Are you in touch?"

"Not really." He shrugs.

As much as I want to say yes, to get the story behind her moody new album and clinch my own podcast—Mitch would go bonkers for this; the album has already gone platinum—I hesitate. It feels disloyal to Finn to bring Clementine back into the mix, just when Finn and Theo are both single. What if he calls and it rekindles their old spark? This is unequivocally against the best friend code. "I'll think about it," I tell him, but I already know I won't take him up on his offer.

I take a sip of my champagne. It's perfectly dry and tastes like a really good croissant. I don't know anything about wine, and even I can tell this is the good stuff. "You keep taking me to all these fancy places," I muse.

"You're welcome?"

"I feel like it's my turn to take you somewhere."

"Where would you have us go?" he asks, and I can hear a hint of fear in his voice.

An hour later we're installed in a brown patterned booth in the Times Square Olive Garden, when Priya joins us.

"This is the actual last place on earth I expected to find you two," she announces as she slides into my side of the booth. Theo has two matte black Saks shopping bags on his side, one with a bejeweled photo frame and the second with the two-ton limited-edition red handbag. He couldn't decide which Lourdes would like more, so he bought them both.

"Trust me, I'm equally shocked." Theo locks eyes with me, uncharacteristically serious. "Of all the restaurants in Manhattan, *this* is where you wanted to bring me?"

"Well, there isn't a Chili's in Manhattan, or we would have gone there," I tell him.

"I'm more of a Taco Bell gal myself." Priya's eyes go dreamy at the mention of the fast-food chain.

"I'm sure I'm sorry to have missed both of those," Theo drawls.

"Make fun of it all you want, but we used to go to Olive Garden or Chili's every Friday night when I was a kid. You're never too old for soup, salad, and breadsticks. You took me to shop for things your parents would like, now I'm taking you somewhere that mine would like."

"Now I feel bad for making fun of it," he says with a sigh.

A waiter arrives at the table, interrupting our play-bickering. "One Tour of Italy," he announces as he places my meal in front of me.

"And your Zuppa Toscana, sir. Flag me down when you're ready for more. Or if you want to try a different kind of soup, that's fine, too. However you want to make the most of it," he says, oblivious to the disdainful glare Theo's giving his bowl of soup.

"And should I bring you a menu?" he asks Priya.

"No, thanks, I'm good. I already ate." It doesn't slip by me that Priya doesn't volunteer any details about where she's coming from, but I decide not to press the issue. I'm just glad she came.

"But we are definitely going to need to get a photo of this for Finn," she says. "He won't believe Theo stepped foot in here without photographic evidence. Smile," she tells Theo. And reluctantly, he obliges.

As Priya takes the photo, I'm struck with a realization. "This is so weird," I say aloud.

"I know," Theo agrees. "I can't believe they use iceberg lettuce."

"No, you snob, not that. It's weird that it's just the three of us. This is how it's going to be next year. Us sending photos to Finn because he's not here."

"Shit, you're right," Theo says. A silence settles over the table as we process the imminent reconfiguration of our friend group. Suddenly, it feels so much more real.

"Speaking of Finn, have you two figured out what we're doing for Christmas this year?" Priya asks.

Theo and I both shake our heads.

"I don't have any ideas," I say. "I've been wracking my brain all week, and nothing feels big enough for Finn's last Christmas."

"Wait a second," Theo says, "The Tour of Italy. Is that what that's called?" He gestures at my plate with his spoon.

"Yeah, so?" I say as I twirl my fork in the supersized helping of fettuccine alfredo, ready to savor the taste of my suburban childhood.

"What if we did a trip for Christmas? We could actually go to

Italy, because I regret to inform you that the food there looks nothing like this."

"I don't know . . ." Priya plucks one of Theo's breadsticks out of its basket.

"It would be something different," Theo prods.

"I feel like whatever we do has to be in New York, right?" I ask. "Isn't that the point? Finn's leaving, so we give him one last New York Christmas?"

"I suppose you're right," Theo concedes. "What about Bobby Flay? I met him at a charity gala a few years ago, something about hungry children. He does much better Italian than this. Should I ask if he'd cater?"

"Right," Priya says, "because Bobby Flay wants to spend Christmas making dinner for four randos instead of with his own family?"

"I think he's divorced. Maybe he trades off holidays with his ex and it's not his year. Maybe he's a bit of a Christmas orphan as well?"

"So, you're saying we'd be doing him a favor?" I ask.

"Is that a no, then?"

"Oh, I'm totally game," I say. "I just think we might want a backup plan."

"Well, do you have any better ideas?" Theo asks, his tone a bit huffy.

I have zero ideas. Nothing feels special enough to top our past Christmases. We need a grand finale, something worthy of the decade of Christmases Finn has given me.

Mid-bite of chicken parm, it hits me. "What if we didn't need a new idea?" I ask.

Theo looks intrigued. "That would be excellent because all of ours are rubbish. In fact, I think they're getting worse. What do you have in mind?"

"What if we re-created our first Christmas together?"

The proposal hangs in the air between us as we mull it over.

"Bloody brilliant!" Theo bangs his hand on the table for emphasis. Some soup sloshes onto the paper place mat.

THIRTEEN

Hannah

Christmas #9, 2016

"Finn, thank you!" Priya says, holding up a glittery lilac travel mug.

Finn beams at her reaction. "It keeps your tea warm for five hours." This is a nod to their tradition of "tea time." I often come home from work to find Priya and Finn curled up on our couch partaking in their sacred tradition of drinking mugs of actual tea while gossiping about an array of D-list celebrities I've never heard of, but they share an outsized knowledge of thanks to their mutual obsession with the celebrity gossip podcast *Who? Weekly.* At some point the gossip transitions to the minor players in their own lives: Finn's cubemate, Priya's nephews, Theo's doormen. I've thought of starting to listen to the podcast just so I could participate in these recaps.

Theo's living room floor is littered with wrapping paper. Cartoon penguins wearing scarves from Priya, classic brown Kraft paper from Theo (but he went all out on bows), and tiny red station wagons with trees strapped to the top from Finn. In the corner, a ten-foot Christmas tree—this year a silver tree with a disco theme—presides over our gift exchange. Framed photos of each of our last three Christmases have earned a place of pride on Theo's otherwise austere shelves.

My knee bounces as I wait for my turn. I did so much better.

This year we put a $50 price limit on gifts after Theo got us all iPads last year. It's not that I didn't appreciate his gift. In fact, I love mine, especially since I found out the New York Public Library has an app that lets me borrow e-books. But I felt like an idiot when he gave me an iPad and I gave him sweatpants as a joke. I'd never seen him wear anything less formal than jeans and thought he'd be grateful I introduced him to athleisure, but they haven't made an appearance since. They're probably buried in a drawer with the tags still on.

Even with the price limit, I'm positive I nailed it. The gift, not the wrapping paper. My wrapping paper blows. It's a cheesy cartoon Santa motif, the only gift wrap left in stock at Duane Reade at 11:00 p.m. on Christmas Eve.

Priya rips the last of the paper off the second part of Finn's gift and shows off a mint-green tin of Fortnum & Mason tea. "Oooh, the Royal Blend," she announces before taking the lid off and burying her nose in it. She makes that satisfied humming noise people make in Folgers commercials after they have their first sip of coffee.

"Jeremy helped pick it out," Finn tells her. "He prefers tea, too."

"Tell Jeremy thank you from me," Priya says.

Finn whips out his phone to relay the message. By my count, this is the third time Finn's brought him up this morning. The most positive thing I can say about Jeremy is he exists. He's the Flat Stanley of boyfriends: good for a picture, doesn't add much to the conversation. But he's all Finn can talk about: *Jeremy prefers tea to coffee. Did you know Jeremy went to Princeton? Jeremy has a blue sweater just like that.* Even facts about Jeremy are boring. But Jeremy's blandness aside, it's cute how smitten Finn is.

It's also, frankly, a relief.

After last Christmas, Finn spent January and February moping about Raj. Even after Raj's dismissal around Valentine's Day, Finn's mood didn't improve. "Why don't you tell him now?" I urged once Theo was single.

"I don't need to hear the words to know. I've had as much rejection from Theo as I can take."

"But he's never rejected you."

"Not outright, but tacitly. If he wanted to be together, we'd be together by now."

"I think you're being dumb," I told him, because he was.

Spring was better. After almost a year working at ToonIn, Finn saved enough to move to a studio apartment in the West Village—his first without roommates—declaring it perfect because it's halfway between me and Priya on the Lower East Side and Theo on the Upper West Side. But Theo spent most of the spring in Paris, consoling his mother after the end of her third marriage, which clocked in at a mere eighteen months. In his absence, Finn downloaded every dating app in the app store and committed to dating like it was a second job and he was gunning for a promotion. Early drinks and a dozen oysters at Mermaid Oyster Bar with one guy and a nightcap at Dante up the street with another.

"No one is looking for anything serious," Finn complained.

"Are *you* looking for something serious?" The way I saw it, he needed a palate cleanser, maybe a slutty phase.

"Of course I want something serious! There hasn't been anyone serious since college. I've wasted all this time hung up on Theo and now I'm behind. I have a gay wedding this summer. It's not just the breeders who are getting married, even the gays are starting. Can you believe it?"

I could believe it. Priya and I had so many save the dates and invitations to bridal showers and weddings on our fridge that we ran out of magnets and were posting them in overlapping layers based on date. I didn't realize I liked enough people to be invited to so many life events. Though, to be fair, more than half of them were for events celebrating Priya's family members. But I was happy to fill in as her plus-one as needed. I'd learned Hindu weddings were much superior in both food and spectacle to the American ones I was invited to. At her cousin's wedding last summer, the groom entered riding an elephant.

After six months of frenzied dating, Finn met Jeremy. I see why Finn swiped right. Jeremy has a mop of sandy blond hair and Abercrombie model looks, but his thick black Warby Parker glasses and dopey *who, me?* grin take the edge off his attractiveness and make him approachable. The first time we met, over happy hour Narragansetts in the backyard of a low-key bar off Bowery, Jeremy showed up in spandex and a cycling jersey and spent the first five minutes explaining his cycling conditioning schedule before transitioning into a ten-minute set about the feeding habits of the sea anemone he breeds in the lab where he works at NYU. By my second beer I was drowning in an ocean of useless factoids.

"He's nervous," Finn whispered when Jeremy went to the bathroom.

After our first meeting, I wondered if Finn was settling because he was worn out, not to mention dead broke, from his dating spree. Surely Jeremy was a rest stop on the highway to true love. But here we are, three months later, Finn gushing about Jeremy's taste in tea bags.

"Okay, it's my turn," I announce, unable to wait a single second longer to give everyone my gifts. I pass out medium-sized boxes to each of them. "They're all the same. You can open them at the same time."

Finn and Priya rip into their presents, while Theo meticulously unwraps his like he plans to save the crappy drugstore wrapping paper for a second use. Finn is the first to lift the lid off the box inside. He pushes aside the tissue paper and holds up a jean jacket in front of him with a confused look on his face.

"No, turn it around!"

He does, but his baffled expression remains.

Priya has her jacket in her lap. "You made these? How neat!" she says with faux cheer, the way you talk to a four-year-old who hands you a crayon drawing of yourself that's just a green blob.

I did make the jackets. Well, not the jackets themselves. For those, I spent weeks scouring Buffalo Exchange and Beacon's Closet to find ones that would fit each of them in the same medium-blue wash. From there, I special ordered iron-on letters from Etsy. Not the ones from Joann they use for kids' soccer jerseys, nice ones. I even found a bedazzling gun on eBay and used it to add studs and rhinestones across the back. There's no denying the jackets look homemade, but they also look cool.

Theo has his out of the box now, too, and is pursing his lips together. His shoulders twitch like he's holding in laughter.

"C'mon, guys, I worked hard on these! They're our members' jackets. For the Christmas Orphans Club!"

Christmas Orphans Club has too many letters, so instead, I abbreviated the club's initials: COC.

"Say it out loud, Han," Finn urges.

"Cee. Oh. Cee," I spell aloud.

Priya circles her hand in front of her, urging me to put it together.

"The jackets say 'cock,' Hannah." Theo bursts out laughing, doubling over his jacket.

"We'll look like a gay biker gang that can't spell," Finn adds. He's laughing so hard he wipes tears from the corner of his eyes.

"A crafty gay biker gang." Priya fingers the rhinestones edging the collar of her jacket.

I pout, but a sardonic laugh slips out, too. So much for my perfect presents.

Finn steals a glance my way. "Well, we have to wear them out today!" he announces. "There is literally no one I'd rather be in a semiliterate gay biker gang with." He drapes his jacket over his shoulders without putting his arms through the arm holes and glares at Theo.

Theo puts on his jacket, too, and gives a twirl to show it off. It's a few inches too short and he looks ridiculous. Now I'm laughing in earnest. "I'm wearing mine everywhere. Not just today!" he says.

"I wrote an article about these best-friend leather jackets last year. These are way cooler," Priya adds as she slips hers on. The four of us are verging on hysterics.

I put mine on, too. Even though the jackets' message is hornier than intended, I love what they represent. We may not look like siblings, but now we have an outward signifier of what we mean to one another. I want people to see us in a crowded room and know that *these* are my people. When I look around the circle, I feel lucky. I can't imagine needing more than this.

"Now that we're outfitted for the day, it's time for Toaster Wars," Theo says.

I don't have time to question the two seemingly disparate words that came out of Theo's mouth because Priya says, "Not for me, I'm going over to Ben's parents' apartment for a few hours."

"What?" This is the first I'm hearing about it.

"I'll meet up with you guys tonight. I'm only going for lunch."

"But we always spend Christmas together," I tell her.

"And we're still spending Christmas together. I'm here now, and I'll meet back up later," she says. At my wounded expression, she adds, "Seriously, this is not a big deal. From everything I've gathered about this holiday, lunch is like the least important meal. I'll be back before you know it." Finn and Theo's eyes ping-pong back and forth between us as we negotiate the terms of Priya's departure.

I bite my tongue to keep from pointing out that she and Ben aren't even together. They might have been at one point back in college, but now Ben is in his third year of med school at the University of Wisconsin. He keeps her on his bench for when he passes through town.

"Whatever," I say. If she doesn't get why this is important, I can't force her to understand. Finn rests a hand on the middle of my back, which I interpret as his solidarity. Our Christmas isn't a stopover, it's the main event.

Priya slips away, still wearing her jacket, while Theo leads us into the dining room.

At each place setting there's a plate, a mug, a champagne flute, and an individual toaster. In the center of the table are plates heaped with a dozen varieties of Eggos, Pop-Tarts, and Toaster Strudels. I smile at the mental image of Theo in the frozen food aisle at Gristedes, filling his cart with box after box of frozen waffles.

"I've never had a Pop-Tart," Theo announces, "and all the American sitcoms I watched as a child made them look so good, so I figured we may as well remedy that together." He takes a pink frosted Pop-Tart and deposits it in his personal toaster.

"Dig in!" he urges.

This is my ten-year-old self's dream come true, but I can't muster the right level of enthusiasm. Priya leaving dampened the magic.

After a lazy afternoon of mimosas and Monopoly (something else American Theo missed in childhood—not because they didn't have it in the UK, but because his brother was so much older, there was no one to play it with), we head downtown to the West Village. Finn forces everyone to wear their jackets knowing no one will bat a false eyelash at a gang of thirsty gays with a poor aptitude for spelling where we're going, a Christmas-themed drag show billed as *The Ladies of the North Pole*.

When we arrive, we separate. We each know our jobs. Theo heads to the bar to change twenties for singles for tips and Priya, reunited with us after lunch at Ben's parents', follows to order a round of dangerously strong vodka sodas in Dixie cups. Finn and I claim a sticky cocktail table by the stage. In here, it feels more like Halloween than Christmas. There's a crew of shirtless boys wearing butterfly wings and body glitter at the table next to us, and across the room is a graying bear in a red latex catsuit straight out of the "Oops, I Did It Again" music video. A buzz of tipsy chatter complements the soundtrack of pop divas.

Across the table, Finn's absorbed in his phone. I reach over and give his thigh a squeeze to bring him back to the moment, annoyed he's not giving our festivities his full attention. He looks up with a guilty expression, and when his phone inadvertently tips toward me, I catch a glimpse of a shirtless selfie of Jeremy. His cycling conditioning routine is working for him.

The show is fantastic. Halfway through, Theo runs out of singles and starts tipping with fives, then tens, then twenties, making our table the center of attention. Afterward, two burly bouncers push aside the tables to make room for a dance floor. Priya and I are breathless and sweaty after an hour of dancing to remixes of early Madonna and late Cher. I'm also more than a little drunk after tequila shots with the butterfly boys and a drag of a cigarette and a Jack and Coke in the back alley with the show's emcee, a drag queen dressed like a sexy Grinch. This is on top of the steady stream of vodka sodas in kiddie cups Theo keeps passing my way. I've lost track of how many drinks I've had, which is probably for the best because the number is alarmingly high.

Finn and Theo have each been off on their own since the show ended. Finn is on his phone at the bar, probably texting Jeremy, while Theo hit it off with a drag queen dressed as "All I Want for Christmas Is You" Mariah Carey. Fauxriah Carey is grinding up on Theo, who has the top four buttons of his shirt undone. It's gaping open like a *Romeo + Juliet*-era Leonardo DiCaprio.

Theo dances his way over to me and Priya.

"Hey," he yells to be heard over Donna Summer. He rakes a hand through his sweaty curls and leans in like he's about to tell us a secret. "Do you want some molly? I bought it off Mariah Scary." He flashes a miniature plastic bag with four pills in it from the front pocket of his jeans.

"I don't know," I say, "I've never—"

"Absolutely!" Priya shrieks with glee. She grabs the baggie of pills from Theo. Her excitement washes away my hesitance and I find myself holding my palm out for a pill. If there was ever a time to try molly, tonight is the perfect night. I'm with my friends, I have a week to recover from what is already sure to be an epic hangover, and I'm in a tinsel-covered gay bar full of happy people. Hell, most of them are probably rolling, too. I take a swig of vodka soda to wash down the small yellow tablet stamped with a smiley face.

"Don't worry, I've got you," Theo says and grabs my hand. "I'll be your trip chaperone. You're in good hands."

True to his word, Theo stays glued to my side and keeps checking to make sure I'm okay. The drugs kick in after thirty minutes, but it's not scary at all. I feel like a melting strawberry Popsicle, warm and happy. Everything's a bit prettier, too, like someone's applied an Instagram filter over reality. I know I'm feeling something when one of the butterfly boys dances into my periphery and I reach out to run a finger through the glitter on his hairless chest. He laughs and twirls before dancing off in another direction.

It turns out Theo is a great dancer. How is it possible that in all our years of friendship I've never seen him dance? We went dancing at China Chalet our first Christmas with Theo, but I mostly remember him and Finn talking by the bar. Theo's dancing is surprisingly sexual. There's a lot of hip gyrating, and I try to mirror his moves.

We make eye contact and both dissolve into a fit of giggles.

Tonight is the best!

Theo reaches for my hand and spins me away from him and then back in. I land with a thud against his chest. He puts his other hand on my shoulder to steady me. Then his hands are reaching up into my hair. Gross, my hair is soaked with sweat. I reach up and run a hand through his hair to see if it's as sweaty as mine.

He pulls his hand out of my hair and cups my cheek. His other hand, the one on my shoulder, skates down my arm before coming to rest on my hip. I look up at him and smile. I'm having so much fun. I want to tell him. But then we're kissing.

This is hilarious. Theo and I are kissing.

I feel him smile against my lips like we're both in on the joke. I still have a hand in his hair and use it to pull him closer, like maybe we can melt into a single person. For a moment, I'm lost in the delightful idea that Finn, Theo, Priya, and I could merge into one being. That way I could keep them as close to my heart as possible, because their heart would be my heart, too.

Now Theo's tongue is in my mouth. His fingertips dig into my hips. I haven't kissed anyone in a long time. I forgot how much fun it is. Theo's a good kisser.

We break apart, both of us out of breath. I think only a few seconds passed, but I can't be sure. Time feels bendy.

Wow, I kissed Theo. How funny! I start laughing again and can't stop. I'm doubled over laughing. This is so funny.

"Are you okay?" Priya's at my side with her hand on my back. I arch into her touch like a cat, it feels so good.

"I'm great. I'm—" I can't get my words out, I'm laughing too hard.

"Oh, I thought you were crying," she says.

"Crying? No. Why would I be crying? Tonight's the best." I straighten up and look her in the eye. She's so beautiful. I look around for Finn. He was at the bar but now he's missing. Why isn't he dancing with us?

"Where's Finn?" I ask.

"He's been on his phone all night," Theo says. "Booorrrring!"

"I think he left?" Priya's answer comes out like a question.

"Left?" I mimic her words back at her in confusion. "Why would he leave? We're having so much fun."

Priya squints one eye shut like trying to remember is physically painful. "I think he looked mad when he left."

"When did he leave?" I'm instantly sober, like someone dumped a bucket of ice water over my head. Is Finn okay?

"A few minutes ago, while you were making out," Priya says.

"We weren't making out," I protest.

"No, I'm pretty sure we were making out," Theo says.

Shit. Did Finn see? Is that why he left? I have to find him and explain. I turn around mid-conversation and head for the door.

"Hey, wait!" Theo calls from behind me. "Wait for us."

I ignore him.

I stumble up a flight of wooden stairs using the wall for balance and out the front door. The minute I'm outside, my skin prickles with goose bumps. I had a sweater earlier, plus my jean jacket and a winter coat. I'm not sure where any of them went. But it doesn't matter, that's not important right now.

I look both ways down the side street the bar is on for any sign of Finn, but there isn't any. His apartment is a few blocks from here. It's 3:00 a.m. Where else would he have gone? I need to find him and make sure he's alright. He's probably not even mad. If he's as drunk as the rest of us, maybe he Irish exited to go home to bed.

We're fine. We have to be fine.

Oh god, what have I done?

FOURTEEN

Finn

Christmas #9, 2016

Can you talk? reads Jeremy's text.

I'm still out. Everything OK? I write back.

Are you having fun? he asks.

Good question. I'm not having fun, even though I should be. I feel off for some reason. Something about being here at this drag club is making me sad. The place is packed like it's a regular Saturday night and not Christmas, and part of me wonders why these people aren't with their families. How many are like me and can't go home? Being here tonight makes me feel like a gay cliché.

No one else seems too worried about it, though, so I take a pull of my drink and try to wash away the unsettled feeling. I think about going outside and calling Jeremy, but his texts have gotten more frequent and desperate as the night's worn on and I'm not in the mood to hear about his idyllic nuclear-family Christmas. Part of me thought maybe he would invite me, even though we've only been dating three months. It's too soon, but maybe there's a special exception because I don't have family to go home to. But no matter how many hints I dropped, no invitation materialized.

The bartender places another vodka soda in front of me. I didn't order it, but he's taken a liking to me ever since I complimented his sweater and it's paid dividends. The sweater is red and covered in a garish hodgepodge of bows, garland, and ornaments. Definitely homemade. It would kill at an ugly sweater party, but I don't think he's wearing it ironically.

Over on the dance floor my friends are off their faces. Theo and Hannah are dancing together under the glow of a janky disco ball that looks like it might detach from the ceiling at any moment. It's endearing how awful a dancer Theo is, since he's so poised in every other way. It's like he learned all his moves from studying *Magic Mike*. There's a lot of gratuitous hip gyrating and running his hands through his hair and down his chest. Inexplicably, there's also a lot of pointing. The fact that his shirt is mostly unbuttoned only adds to the faux stripper vibe.

Hannah is half dancing with him, but every thirty seconds she gets distracted by one of the hot pink laser lights and stops to track it with her finger. Those two are going to be so hungover tomorrow. Priya's nowhere to be seen. I hope she's not puking in the bathroom. Maybe we can all sleep at Theo's tonight, and I'll make pancakes in the morning.

I'd be having more fun if you were here, I text Jeremy. It's not his fault I'm in a bad mood or that he has a supportive family who loves him.

His text back is immediate. It's after 2:00 a.m., so he must be in bed. I can't imagine there's much to do in Scranton, Pennsylvania, this time of night. Same. I wanted to tell you what I'd be doing to you if I was there, but you can't talk :(:(:(

Oh, wow. Sweet, reserved Jeremy is also blotto. I get half hard thinking about having phone sex with him while he's in his childhood bedroom with his parents asleep down the hall. I consider going to the bathroom to call him until I play out the scenario in my head and realize that would make me the creepy guy jerking off in the only stall in the men's room. Will you be up in an hour? I text. I don't think anyone here's going to last much longer.

Three dots appear, then disappear.

I look back over at Hannah and Theo on the dance floor. And . . .

WHAT THE HELL?

No.

It can't be.

But it is.

They're kissing?

They are definitely kissing. And they look into it.

I don't have a good angle from my barstool, but I'm pretty sure there's tongue. I count in my head as I watch.

Thirteen . . . fourteen . . . fifteen.

This isn't a friendly peck. This is an *I want to rip your clothes off* make-out.

Maybe I'm drunker than I realized. Maybe I'm hallucinating. This can't be right.

"Excuse me," I call to the bartender, who's wiping down a bottle of well vodka at the other end of the bar, and signal for the check. When he returns with my card and receipt, I add a hefty tip and scrawl an illegible signature.

I take a final glance over my shoulder as I head up the stairs to the street. They're still kissing. Hannah's hands are in Theo's hair, his are on her ass.

Upstairs, I push the door open with so much force it bounces off the brick wall of the building and comes flying back at my face. Of course it does.

On my third lap around my block, I realize I left my coat at the bar. That's okay, my rage will keep me warm. I'm too keyed up to go inside my apartment. I want to scream or punch a wall or send an eviscerating text to Hannah and Theo letting them know what awful people they are. I'm workshopping the wording in my head as I storm up Seventh Avenue and hang a right on Leroy.

By the time I make a right on Bleecker, I'm back to considering screaming to see if it will make me feel any better. My rage feels like a teakettle set to a full boil. I've seen far stranger things than a man shouting at the sky on the streets of New York at two in the morning, but then I spot a middle-aged man in a parka up ahead, coaxing his corgi puppy to pee, and decide to scrap the screaming so he doesn't think I'm crazy or, worse, ask if I'm alright. Then I'd have to explain that my best friend kissed my other best friend who I'm in love with even though I have a boy-friend, and I don't think I could make anyone understand that.

It sounds like petty bullshit, but it's not. It's fucking betrayal.

On my fourth lap around the block, I see Hannah sitting in the doorway to my building as I approach my stoop. She's in a tank top with her arms wrapped around herself. My first thought is *She must be freezing*. But then I remember her heart is made of ice so she's probably plenty comfortable out here.

I consider walking the other way and pretending I didn't see her, but I'm starting to get cold, and I want to go inside. Maybe I'll try punching a wall in my apartment and see if that works—straight bros seem to love that move. Maybe I'll leave the city and move back to Boston and the hole I punch in the wall can be someone else's problem. My friends are the only thing keeping me here and clearly they don't give a crap about me.

"I don't want to talk to you," I announce when I'm a few yards away. She can sit out here all night and freeze for all I care. I note that Theo hasn't even bothered to show up.

"Well, too bad. I'm not leaving," she yells back. Her voice is too loud and betrays how drunk she is.

"Suit yourself. I don't care if you stay out here all night. I'm going inside."

She stands up and puts herself between me and the front door. You know what, if she wants to make a scene on the street, that's fine with me. We can have it out and end things. Right here, right now. There's no coming back from this. There's no explanation that makes this acceptable.

"I'm sorry."

The fact that she thinks she can fix this with a simple apology makes blood ring in my ears. "I don't care."

"But clearly you do care."

Ugh, fighting with drunk people is the absolute worst. "I don't care that you're sorry," I clarify. "Let me save you the time because there's nothing you can say to make this alright."

She tries again anyway. "I shouldn't have done it. We were drunk and on molly, but we still shouldn't have done it." She pauses, probably waiting for me to forgive her.

"You're right. You shouldn't have done it," I say. "There. Are we done? Can I go upstairs, please?"

"No, we're not done here, Finn. I'm trying to apologize, which, let me say, is ridiculous. You have a boyfriend. One you haven't stopped talking about all day. *Jeremy looooves tea. Did you know Jeremy's parents have a German shepherd? Have you seen Jeremy's dumb bubble butt from his dumb bike he never shuts up about?*" she says in a whiny voice that's supposed to be an imitation of me. World's worst apology. "So, yeah, it shouldn't matter who Theo kisses. You have no claim on him, plus you know it didn't mean anything. It was a stupid drunk kiss."

Mentally I am shouting at full volume off the side of a canyon. Physically I am standing on my stoop trying not to slap my ex–best friend, who would definitely deserve it. "You should have known better! This isn't some rando, this is Theo. It's . . . I . . ."

"Oh, you love him? Maybe you should tell him instead of

telling *me* over and over and over. Then maybe you'd be with him instead of with this boyfriend you clearly don't even like and are only with to prove a point to yourself. Or maybe to Theo? I can't decide which is more pathetic."

"Well, you'd know about pathetic," I yell. "You're so obsessed with Christmas. You moped around all afternoon when Priya left for two whole hours, you hate it whenever any of us have lives outside this group that don't involve you, and you've always been jealous of Theo."

"Oh, *I'm jealous*? Do tell!" She crosses her arms over her chest and shifts her weight to one side.

"You've been jealous of Theo since the first day I brought him around. You're threatened by him, terrified that I'll get closer to him than I am to you. So now you went and kissed him. To what? Steal him from me? Make me jealous? Just because you're content living this sexless loner lifestyle doesn't mean the rest of us are. You know I'm not your boyfriend, right?! You know what, Hannah, this was too far. You should have known better."

"Oh? Just like Theo should have known you're in love with him even though you've never told him? And you probably never will? That's not how it works, Finn. We're not freaking mind readers. You're never going to be with Theo because you're a coward. And I'm sorry you went out and got yourself a new boyfriend you don't love, but that's your shit to deal with."

For a minute we stare at each other, both of us out of breath from screaming, waiting to see if the other one cracks.

I'm prepared to wait all night, but Hannah caves first. Her tone is softened. "I think we should talk about this in the morning, once we've both sobered up and cooled off."

"I've said everything I need to say."

"Well, I haven't," she says and stomps her foot like a petulant toddler.

"Can I go inside now?"

"Fine." She moves aside to unblock the door. "I'll text you in the morning. Late breakfast at Waverly Diner? This is nothing hash browns can't solve. I'm, uh, going to go back to the bar and get my jacket. I can get yours, too. I'll bring it for you in the morning."

I scoff. Like I give two shits about the dumb, bedazzled jackets she made us. "Frankly, Hannah, I don't want to be part of any club that would have you as a member."

I open the door and pull it closed behind me so she can't follow me in.

That's the last time we speak for a year.

FIFTEEN

Finn

This year, December 14

My cab pulls up to Theo's building and I swipe my credit card while the driver wrangles my bags from the trunk. Two hard-shell suitcases, a shopping bag of gifts, and my beat-up old back-pack are all that's left of my life in New York. Everything else I own is on a moving truck heading for LA.

Until the truck's slatted rolling door slammed shut, the move didn't feel real.

It didn't feel real when I signed my job offer or when I told my friends. It certainly didn't feel real when I flew to LA two weeks ago to find an apartment. That felt like playing the Game of Life, picking a place to live for a fictional version of myself. My little blue peg is moving up in the world!

But it is real. An hour ago, I closed the door to my newly empty apartment and left the keys under the super's doormat. It's weird to think I'll never see the inside of the place I called home for the past three years ever again. I snapped a few pictures on my way out as a keepsake, but they already look like nothing. The kind of photos you take when the camera app opens by accident.

"Are you excited?" my sister asked when she called last night, and I didn't know how to answer.

On the one hand, my new apartment—a two-bedroom in a West Hollywood high-rise—is way nicer than my old studio. The real estate agent regaled me with lists of amenities: new chrome appliances, central air, and a walk-in closet, but what impressed me most were the clean, freshly painted walls that weren't pock-marked with dozens of tiny holes, hastily spackled over by scores of former tenants. This apartment was shiny and new. It even smelled like a fresh start, although that was probably the linen-scented candle the real estate agent was burning on the kitchen island.

The problem is, I can't picture what my life in LA will look like. I can picture myself driving to work, sitting in traffic listening to one of Hannah's podcasts. I can picture my office, mostly because it was shown to me when I stopped by for a tour. But I can't picture my life outside of work.

Whenever I try, I can only conjure scenes from TV shows, and I'm pretty sure my life won't look like *New Girl*—unfortunately, I'm not moving into a loft with three built-in best friends—or *The Hills* with their rowdy pre-games. The clubs they went to don't exist anymore, and I don't think I'd get in if they did.

The biggest blank is who I'll hang out with. Sean Grady, my college boyfriend, lives in LA, but according to a quick Instagram stalk, he's married with two pugs he gushes about in lengthy monthly birthday posts about their evolving likes and dislikes as if they're actual children. A girl I went to high school with is trying to make it as an actress in LA. I know because she posts braggy status updates on Facebook about how lucky she is every time she books a commercial for IBS medication or car insurance.

This is the part of moving that scares the shit out of me: I have to make new friends. What if I'm too old to make new friends? Will I even have time? And I already know if I do manage to make new friends, they'll never be as close as the ones I already have.

A member of the building's army of doormen rushes out to help me with my bags, breaking me out of my impending side-walk panic spiral. "My man." He offers me a fist bump.

It's a point of pride that I've won over the doormen at Theo's. I've even made strides with Dwayne, the head doorman. When I pass his desk, he offers me a two-finger salute. I don't need to stop because for the last year, I've been on Theo's list—the list of approved guests who don't need to be checked and can be let right up. But I'm tempted to stop and explain myself to Dwayne anyway. Make sure he knows I'm not using Theo for his money or his apartment. That I'm not like Elliot or the others. I actually care about Theo. But that feels like a weird thing to explain to a doorman who, at best, tolerates my presence in exchange for a paycheck.

The thrill of the fanciness of Theo's apartment has dulled

over the years, and now when the elevator doors open, the only thing I can think is: *Home.* For the next two weeks, at least.

Theo saunters into the foyer, drawn by the ding of the elevator. "Hello, roomie!"

I don't try to hide the shy smile that blooms at his welcome.

"I have the blue guest room all ready for you." He turns on his heel and I trail him through the living room to the guest room across from his office. The one with the best view. Even though it's illogical, I'm slightly disappointed. On the ride over, I'd allowed myself to fantasize that I'd be sharing with Theo.

On Wednesday, I return to our newly shared apartment after using the building's gym. Theo goes to Equinox even though there's a gym on the second floor. He says it's because he likes to use the steam room after he lifts, but I suspect he likes the pickup scene even more.

I leave a trail of sweat droplets on the floors as I make my way from the elevator to the kitchen. My quick treadmill 5K turned into an hour-long run. When I push open the swinging door to the kitchen, I'm surprised to find Theo unpacking reusable totes of groceries. I assumed there were people to do that for him.

Theo pauses and sweeps his eyes over my sweat-soaked body. My workout tank is stuck to me like second skin. "Good run?" he asks.

My arms break out in goose bumps at his assessment. "Uh,

yeah," I answer. "I got in seven miles. I think unemployment is getting to me. I felt guilty about not doing anything all day."

It's a lie. I've only been unemployed for four days. What's getting to me is living with Theo. After a restless night's sleep, I emerged from my room this morning to find him sprawled on the couch watching *Live with Kelly and Ryan* in nothing but Christmas plaid boxers and a pair of horn-rimmed glasses that look so good on him they make me question why he bothers with contacts. His curls stood up at odd angles from sleep.

There's a surprising intimacy to living with someone, I realized, bearing witness to their in-between moments before they ready themselves for the world. I never thought about what Theo did while he was home alone, but if I'd been forced to speculate, watching daytime talk shows in his underwear would have been near the bottom of the list. I'd have found it easier to believe he was hosting a Magic: The Gathering circle with the building's school-aged residents or doing old Jane Fonda workout tapes.

We sat on opposite ends of the couch for three hours watching *Live!* followed by the fourth hour of the *Today* show followed by *The View* until I announced I was going for a run. In truth, sitting next to a half-naked Theo was making me uncomfortable. Or horny. Or uncomfortably horny. I couldn't decide because I was distracted by the line of hair running from his chest down his stomach and into the waistband of his boxers.

It was all too much to take on four hours of sleep. Last night, as I tossed and turned in Theo's absurdly comfortable guest bed,

I played Hannah's words from our fight on a loop. *You'll never be with Theo because you're a coward.* No one can hurt you like the people you love most, because they know your squishiest parts. Worst of all, I recognize the kernel of truth at the heart of her words. And so, off to the gym I went to pound my feelings into the treadmill.

Now, dressed in a pair of dark-wash jeans and a sky-blue crew-neck sweater, his curls tamed into momentary submission, Theo is transferring packages of sugar and flour into glass jars with chalkboard labels. The scene is oddly domestic. A thought flits through my brain about wanting to share more of Theo's boring bits. The mundane moments that make up a life.

I cross the galley kitchen, easily the least impressive part of Theo's apartment, toward the glass-fronted fridge for a bottle of water. I accidentally graze his butt with my hip as I pass, an inevitable accident in a kitchen this narrow. It was designed with the assumption someone other than the owner was the one doing the cooking. I open the door and let the refrigerated air cool me down, part from my run and part from the look Theo gave me.

Before I can move, Theo turns and hovers his head over my right shoulder looking past me into the fridge. "Can you see, is there butter in there?" he asks.

"Uh, yeah, there's a whole box."

"Salted or unsalted?" Theo is so close I feel his breath on my neck when he asks. How is such an incredibly unsexy question such a turn-on?

I bend over, not thinking, so I can read the label on the box of butter. My ass bumps Theo's crotch and I hear his breath hitch in his throat.

Is this? No, it couldn't be.

This is an embarrassing accident caused by his narrow kitchen and my overactive imagination. I've been fantasizing about this moment for years. Actual years. In plenty of my fantasies, things started with me sweaty after a run. Imagining such a scenario is what kept me on the treadmill downstairs pounding out mile after mile, way past my initial goal of three.

But I never imagined it would start with butter.

"The butter is unsalted," I announce, my voice hoarse and croaky.

I straighten up, unsure what to do next. Do I lean back into Theo? Do I turn around? If I turn around, will he kiss me? Am I completely misreading what's happening here? And if this is Theo making a move, why the hell has it taken so long? Why has he waited until two weeks before I move? The last two questions make me angry.

I swing around to face him, unsure if I want to kiss him or yell at him. I expect him to step back, restoring my bubble of personal space. But he doesn't. He moves forward, backing me against a shelf in the still open fridge. He leans against me, pushing his cashmere-clad chest to my sweaty one.

"Sorry," he says. "Trying to see what brand it is."

How on earth are we still talking about butter?!

Is he waiting for me to kiss him? For a second, I consider it before the too familiar line rattles through my brain. *You're never going to be with Theo because you're a coward.*

Instead of making me brave to prove her wrong, Hannah's words from our fight invite reality to come crashing in.

What do I have to lose? For starters, a place to stay. I could probably stay with Hannah and David for the two weeks before I leave, but from what I've heard about their current Christmas standoff, that doesn't sound too appealing. And then, worse, I could lose one of my best friends. I'm not willing to chance that for a kiss. Not if I'm not positive.

And just like that, the moment evaporates. Theo takes a step back and leans against the counter, watching me with his forest-green eyes to see what I'll do next.

"I'm going to take a shower," I sputter out. Apparently, what I do next is chicken out. I scurry toward the kitchen door, my shoulders slouching forward in defeat.

"Wait!" Theo calls.

I feel my heart jump into my throat as I turn around. He hesitates, one finger held aloft in the air between us. Finally, he says, "Do you want to watch *Ellen* with me after your shower? Clementine's the guest."

"Uh, sure."

It's going to be a very long, very cold shower.

SIXTEEN

Hannah

Christmas #10, 2017

"Oh man, I'm so late." David makes his way from the bathroom to the closet. His light brown hair is still damp from the shower.

On the nightstand, his phone lights up with a flurry of incoming texts. "Someone keeps texting you," I say as messages ping in one after the other.

"Adam is so pissed. The kids are having a meltdown because my mom won't let them open presents until I get there."

He reappears at the closet door in a white Oxford shirt neatly tucked into jeans, looking every inch the goody-two-shoes honor society president his yearbooks confirmed him to be. He was voted Most Likely to Succeed while I was voted Most Likely to Never Be Heard from Again, a superlative that proved spot-on if you were one of my high school classmates. Being with him *almost* makes me want to go to one of my high school reunions, if only to show him off and back-door brag about my job working in podcasting. Show them that for the weird girl everyone pitied, I turned out okay.

He smirks at me; the reason he's late is fresh in both our minds. "Are you sure you don't want to come?"

"Oh, I already came. Twice," I answer from where I lie naked under the sheets.

After coffee and presents—a John Mayer album on vinyl from me as a nod to his dating-app bio, and tickets to see the National at Forest Hills Stadium from him—he dragged me back to bed, where he gave me what he claimed was the other part of my Christmas present and went down on me for half an hour. Not that I'd taken much convincing.

"I'm being serious. Come to Connecticut. It's our first Christmas. Shouldn't we spend it, you know, together?"

"I don't want to be the stranger who crashes Christmas. I've only met your parents once."

"And they adored you!"

"Next year," I tell him.

"Next year," he echoes back with a shy grin.

He comes over to the bed and gives me a final kiss before he leaves. "Call me if you change your mind or things get too awkward with Finn. I'm just saying there's a twelve forty-five train from Grand Central. I can pick you up at the station in Fairfield."

"It's going to be fine. We're all adults," I say with more certainty than I feel. A minute later I hear the door close behind him.

Finn has become a ghost haunting our relationship. Heard about, but never seen.

Once, in our early days of dating, I brought David to Lucky's for the first time. The *Friends* had Central Perk, the *How I Met Your Mother* gang had McLaren's, and we had Lucky's. A few years ago, we tried switching to Bar Belly down the street with their $1 oysters and happy-hour craft cocktails, but it didn't feel right. Lucky's is a dive, but it's our dive.

The minute we opened the door we were assaulted by a blast of air-conditioning and the scent of stale beer. Michelle, our favorite bartender, looked up from where she was mixing a screwdriver for the lone patron at the end of the bar and said, "Oh hey, girlie! Long time no see. Where's your other half?"

She meant Finn. I hadn't been there since our fight. I gave her a shrug and hoped David interpreted her comment as referring to a nonexistent ex-boyfriend, not a very real ex–best friend.

It was inevitable that David would hear bits and pieces about Finn, him being so omnipresent in my memories, but I hadn't exactly been forthright about our fight. I'd only started going number two at David's apartment the previous week; it felt too soon to tell him I wasn't speaking to my best friend. I feared it would make me look like an unfeeling monster.

I led David to one of the tall wooden booths and slid into one side of the banquette. When he settled into his side, he eyed me warily across the booth. "Should we go somewhere else? Schiller's is right around here, isn't it?"

"No!" I was crestfallen he'd written this place off. But I got it: Lucky's didn't look like much on the surface. The walls were plastered with signed headshots of famous patrons—exactly zero of whom we recognized; Finn was convinced it was a prank and they were photos of the owner's friends—and the tables had a sticky patina that had become permanent. In the four months we'd been dating David had taken me on a tour of his personal landmarks in the city. Eating and drinking our way through "his spots." This was the only place in the city I had the audacity to claim as mine. "This is *our* spot. Let's at least have one drink."

"*Our* spot?" he asked, confused, thinking I meant me and him.

"Me and Finn's spot. We started coming here right after we moved to the city."

"Ah, the infamous Finn," he mused. "I feel like he's your imaginary friend. When am I finally going to meet him?"

"Well . . . ," I stumbled, wondering about the ethics of inventing a glamorous job abroad for Finn. Maybe he was in Barcelona, or better yet, Shanghai, where the time difference made FaceTiming difficult. But in the end, I opted for the truth. I didn't want to lie to David. "We're not exactly speaking right now."

He drew his head back in shock, eyes wide, before he could school his expression into one of mild curiosity. "Why's that?" he asked finally.

"What's my girlie having today?" Michelle interrupted.

"Can you tell me what beers you have on draft?" I asked, grateful to draw out the distraction even though I knew I was getting a frozen margarita. The only good part about Finn not being there was that he couldn't roll his eyes at my order and speculate about the last time they washed the margarita machine.

As Michelle ticked off the draft options, my shoulders inched down from my ears. When she left with our orders, I changed the subject to David's softball league, giving him an opening to rattle off statistics about his teammates' batting averages.

It feels inconceivable that Finn, my most important person, has never met David. Since then, information about Finn has been meted out in small doses. One Sunday in September, over bagels at David's apartment, a crossword clue caused a chink in my armor. "What's a nine-letter word for 'Phantom's love interest'?"

"Christine," I answered without looking up from the book on my iPad, *Eleanor Oliphant Is Completely Fine.*

"How did you know that?"

"Finn played Raoul in a production of *Phantom* our sophomore year. He wanted to play the Phantom, but he didn't get it." I went on to tell him about the costumes we wore on our first Christmas and the winter break of adventures that followed.

"I know you miss Finn, but you and I could go on adventures, you know?" he said shyly. It was sweet, so I kept it to myself that the Finn-sized hole in my heart was not one in want of filling. My love for David occupied a separate but equally important compartment, but they weren't interchangeable, as much as some days I wished they were.

"I'd love that," I told David, because it was still a sweet offer.

And David excelled at planning adventures. He sent me event

listings from *Time Out* and write-ups of secret dumpling kiosks hidden in shopping malls in Queens with notes that said: This weekend? We went to Storm King and the Met Cloisters and a secret bar hidden behind a telephone booth in a hot dog restaurant. The adventures were a good distraction from missing Finn. So were the early days of falling in love.

After David leaves for Christmas Day at his parents' house, I spend the morning scrolling Instagram in his bed, trying to distract myself from my anxiety over seeing Finn for the first time in a year. I show up at 2:05, as casually late as I can stand, to the address on Canal Street Priya gave us. She's already here, dressed in a plum-colored coat that stands out against the gray stucco building behind her. The nondescript building gives zero clues about what she has planned for today.

When I'm in arm's reach, she pulls me into a hug and squeezes me for a solid thirty seconds, even though we saw each other yesterday morning before I left for David's and her for Ben's. "Merry Christmas!" she squeals directly in my ear. Her excitement verges on manic, like if she's done a good enough job planning, she might be able to repair the rift in our friend group, and I desperately hope she's right.

"Where is everyone?" I ask.

"Running late, I guess." Priya shrugs.

Over the past year, while Theo became a ghost, Priya became our glue, going the extra mile to spend time with each of us. Making sure there was a friend group to come back to if Finn and I finally mended fences. She was the one who vetted and blessed David. She had a standing Friday lunch date with Theo whenever he was in New York, which had become rarer, his travel schedule picking up as the year—and my and Finn's fight—dragged on.

Theo and I never talked about the fight; we didn't talk at all except for a handful of polite texts on our respective birthdays. But it's as if he thought by removing himself from the equation— or at least my side of it—Finn and I, and by extension our group, might go back to how things were.

And I knew Priya spent time with Finn, too, even if she refused to tell me about it. "If you want to know what's going on with him, you can talk to him yourself," she said when she got sick of my less-than-subtle questions. The only exception she made was to clue me in that Finn had fibbed and told Theo our fight was about Jeremy, which, to Finn's credit, it partly was. Having our story straight apparently superseded her refusal to play middleman.

Priya cheerfully took on the burden of planning this year's Christmas festivities, but she's kept the details a surprise. All month I've watched her sneak away to take furtive phone calls and hustle shopping bags into her bedroom.

"Will you at least tell me if Finn is coming?" I asked last week.

"He's coming, but it wasn't easy to get him to agree."

While Priya and I wait for the others, I babble nervously about my gift exchange with David. The enormity of seeing Finn has

me on edge. In April, I floated him a text to test the waters. A
link to an article about the demolition of BC's gym, affectionately
called the Plex, with its weird-looking circus-tent roof, to make
way for a new state-of-the-art athletic facility. Nothing personal,
which gave me plausible deniability that the text wasn't meant for
him if he didn't respond, which he didn't. Two hours later, I
couldn't stand the idea of the text floating in the ether, and I sent
a see-through excuse: Sorry, meant to send to someone else.

I know our fight is stupid. At this point, I'm mostly angry at
him because he's still angry at me. It's the kind of fighting I did
with Brooke when we were kids and she'd catch me listening in
on her calls or I'd borrow her favorite tube top from the dELia*s
catalog without asking. Eventually, our mom would say, "This
house is too small for half its residents to be fighting," and force
us to say one nice thing about the other person, hug, and make
up. But Finn and I don't have any parents between us to inter-
vene. And of the bystanders we do have, Priya is way too nice to
tell us off and Theo is keeping his distance.

While I hope today ends with us burying the hatchet, I'm terrified it will only make things worse, and we'll burn the bridge
for good.

Ten minutes later, Finn rounds the corner from Bowery pulling a wheeled suitcase with one hand and Jeremy with the other.
I didn't realize they were still together. I have a momentary flash
of anger at Priya for not telling me Jeremy would be here and
letting someone new into our tradition without asking. I tamp
down my annoyance because I already have enough grudges

among today's company, but I can't shake the feeling that this Christmas is already getting away from me.

"Jere," Priya squeals, "you came!" Another jab of annoyance, this one mixed with jealousy, that Priya's spent enough time with Finn and Jeremy to be on a nickname basis.

"Sorry we're so late," Finn says. "We got the bus back from Scranton after breakfast and presents with Jeremy's family and there was traffic."

"I lied and told you to get here an hour earlier than you needed to." Priya rolls her eyes at him and Jeremy hiccups out a nervous laugh. Still awkward as ever, I see.

"Hannah, you remember Jeremy?" Priya asks in an attempt to break the ice.

Jeremy scrapes his blond mop away from his forehead and smiles at the sidewalk instead of at me. Finn stares me down, and I want to blurt out a million apologies and beg for his forgiveness, but it doesn't feel like the time or place. Not with Jeremy here. I wonder what Finn told *him* about why we're not speaking. Not the truth. I can't imagine they'd be together if Finn told him I made out with the man he's in love with and he lost his mind over it.

I'm saved from figuring out the correct thing to say when a black Escalade pulls up to the curb, depositing Theo onto the sidewalk. "I thought I'd at least beat Finn here!" Theo slings an arm around Finn's shoulder.

The knot in my stomach pulls even tighter. It seems there were no repercussions for Theo over last Christmas's debacle; the two of them appear tight as ever.

"So will you tell us what we're doing?" I ask now that the whole group is here.

Priya bounces on her toes as she looks around the circle, milking the big reveal. "It's a Christmas-themed escape room," she says finally.

A chorus of groans travels around the circle.

"What?" she asks, like she doesn't see anything wrong with locking this group in a room for ninety minutes. She's either completely clueless or an evil genius. From the challenging look she flashes my way, I'm leaning toward evil genius. "It got a write-up in *New York* magazine in October," she explains. "It's been sold out for months. Do you know the strings I had to pull to get these tickets? We're doing it." Her tone leaves no room for argument.

"Are there teams?" Finn asks as he inches closer to Jeremy.

"No. Why would there be teams? The whole point is to spend Christmas together." Definitely an evil genius. At least we'll have an activity to focus on.

Fifteen minutes later, Brian, a man with a pitifully sparse goatee in a Zelda T-shirt who introduced himself as our "puzzle master" without a hint of irony, leads us to our red-and-green prison.

Our room, one of three on the premises according to the plastic sign on the front desk, is themed "Seventies Grandma Christmas." The room is the size of my and Priya's apartment, meaning small. It looks like Brian hit up the estate sale of a tacky Long Island grandma and dumped all his loot in here, the former offices of a now-defunct startup. In one corner is a floral couch with a crocheted red-and-green afghan draped over the top, and in another is an artificial silver Christmas tree decorated to the max with its lights set to blink. I can already feel a headache building behind my eyes.

It even smells like an old lady in here, something cloying and floral with mildewy undertones, like maybe the previous owners' perfume soaked into the couch over the years and their scents merged, or worse, they died on this couch.

"You have ninety minutes," Brian explains, "but if for any reason you need to leave, I have a camera feed set up to the front desk. So just wave and let me know. I have to say that for insurance purposes, but you're not gonna want to leave. This room is sick! It's our hardest room. Built it myself."

I cough to cover a laugh, embarrassed for his earnest excitement about this hideous room. Across the room, I catch Finn smirking, too.

You'd think being locked in a room with someone you're not speaking to would be plenty of motivation to race to find clues and get out, but as soon as Brian takes his leave, Finn begins monologuing to the room at large about his Christmas Eve with Jeremy's family in Pennsylvania even though no one asked. He does a solid five minutes on the eggnog alone. As he delivers his soliloquy, a blotchy rash climbs the side of Jeremy's neck, creeping higher with every passing minute. I guess I'm not the only one attuned to the tense vibe in here.

I roam the room running my hands over the walls, each

covered with a different wrapping paper motif, with the dim hope I might stumble on a hidden latch that will open the door and end our misery.

The only person who shows any enthusiasm or aptitude for the escape room is Theo, who's taking this way too seriously. "I found a map of the North Pole, but it's ripped." He holds up a page that looks like it's torn out of a kids' coloring book. "I think I need a decoder? Or maybe there are more pieces somewhere in the room. Look for map pages!" he urges us with the seriousness of a man coaching his wife through labor.

"I found a key!" Priya exclaims. "It was in the Christmas tree like an ornament." She proffers a massive old-fashioned key that looks like it would unlock a crumbling stone mansion in the Scottish Highlands.

"Does it open the front door?" Finn asks under his breath. "Maybe we can leave?"

A sardonic chuckle escapes me before I can catch myself. I wish it were that easy.

Then my fingers skim over a button on the wall that's been wrapping-papered over and is invisible to the naked eye. I press it and a creepy-looking Santa pops out of an imposing grandfather clock across the room shouting, "Ho! Ho! Ho!"

"Holy shit, that thing scared the crap out of me," I say. Even though I'm the one who pressed the button, my heart races. "Is he a clue? How do we make him stop?"

The answer is . . . we don't. The deranged Santa cuckoo clock is a fresh layer of hell here in Brian's torture chamber. Three minutes later, Santa pops out of the clock and yells, "Ho! Ho! Ho!," and once again I jump out of my skin. "Fuck, he got me again. Is he going to keep doing this? Can someone stop him? Or maim him?"

"Priya, give me that key you found. Does it fit in the clock?" Finn asks. This is the closest we've gotten to speaking since we arrived.

Finn tries the key in the front compartment of the clock even though it's comically too large to fit. "Ho! Ho! Ho!" Santa pops out and bellows directly into Finn's face like he's aware he has the upper hand.

"We have to make that thing stop. I can't take another"—he looks at the countdown clock above the door—"hour and twenty minutes of this!"

How have we only been in here for ten minutes?

"Does this go with your map, Theo?" Jeremy squeaks, holding up another kids' coloring book page between his thumb and pointer finger like it's a delicate artifact that must be handled with care, as opposed to the likely reality that it was purchased in a ten-pack on Amazon.

"Fantastic work!" Theo says, and does a fist pump above his head. The two of them hover over the desk trying to piece the two pages together or see if one decodes the other.

"Jeremy is really good at puzzles," Finn announces to the room. "He does the *Times* crossword every morning." It's unclear if Finn is bragging about Jeremy for my benefit or Theo's. If we were on better terms, I'd tell him that David does the crossword every morning, too.

Someone's phone starts ringing.

"No phones!" Theo snaps. "No cheating either!"

"Jeez, I wasn't going to answer it," Finn says. "And how would I even cheat? I don't think there are cheat codes for this on Reddit."

"Who was it?" Jeremy asks over his shoulder.

"No one, just my sister," Finn answers.

"Oh, you didn't get to talk to Amanda this morning. We've gotta remember to call her back later." Jeremy's use of "we" doesn't escape me. He must have met Amanda on her annual spring break trip, and I feel another twinge of jealousy that Jeremy was there and I wasn't. I wonder what else have I missed out on in Finn's life over the past year.

"I think we're missing two more map pieces that go below these," Theo mumbles to himself.

Finn's phone starts ringing again.

"Ho! Ho! Ho!" Jack-in-the-Box Santa roars. He's definitely possessed—there, I said it.

"Does anyone see any locks this could fit into?" Priya holds up the key again.

"I found a blacklight flashlight!" Jeremy announces.

"Maybe it will work on the map!" Theo is obsessed with the stupid map.

Jeremy weaves around me and Priya in the center of the

too-crowded room and scans the black light over the map. "I don't think this works on the map," he tells Theo after a few seconds.

"I bet you can use it on the wall." Priya hits the light switch and plunges the room into darkness.

"Hey! Turn that back on, I was looking at the map!" Theo protests.

"Ho! Ho! Ho!" Santa chimes in.

Finn's phone starts ringing again.

"Can you get that? Or turn off the ringer? Or something?" I snap at him, forgetting for a second we're not speaking. I think I might have a panic attack if I'm trapped in this room for one more second.

He rolls his eyes and picks up the phone. "Hey! Can I call you back in—" He stops short and turns toward the corner, plugging his other ear with a finger to hear better.

"Slow down, I can't understand you," he says.

After a few more seconds he says, "Wait, what?"

Then he's banging on the door.

"Let me out of this room right the fuck now," Finn shouts.

"Ho! Ho! Ho!" Santa answers in response.

"Oh, c'mon, Finn, don't do that. We've gotta finish," Theo says from where he's hunched over his precious map.

"Brian, don't let him out," Priya says into the camera in the corner.

"I'm not joking, Brian. Let me out of here!" Finn yells, banging on the door some more.

Finn takes a step back and turns his face up to the camera. There are tears streaming down his cheeks. Oh, this isn't about the terrible escape room. This is real.

Jeremy rushes to him and puts an arm around his shoulder. "What's wrong? What happened?"

Finn opens and closes his mouth like a fish, more tears rushing down his cheeks, but no sound comes out. For the first time since we entered, the room is silent.

When he finds the words, he says them so quietly they're barely audible: "My dad died."

SEVENTEEN

Hannah

This year, December 25

It's a steel-gray morning that hints at the possibility of snow. Maybe it will be a white Christmas. Despite my best effort to sleep in, I gave up just after seven and came out to the living room to read in the glow of the Christmas tree's light.

The tree has gone from spartan to flamboyant as David and I spent the last month one-upping each other with increasingly eccentric ornaments. A David Bowie one from him, Santa riding a unicorn from me. A bust of Ruth Bader Ginsburg from me (the closest thing I could find to a lawyerly decoration), a glittery pickle from him.

On a normal morning, I'd be checking emails, but my laptop is packed away in my work tote until next year. The time away from my job is a relief, a weeklong détente in my losing battle with Mitch about my podcast pitch. Last week I caved and listened to an episode of *Porn Stache,* and it was somehow even more repulsive than I imagined. Not because I have a problem with porn, but because it's a wall-to-wall block of misogyny. Sixty minutes of objectifying women's bodies interspersed with ad breaks to sell supplements and meal-kit delivery services. If it comes to that, I'll be job hunting in January. But for now, I push work out of my mind.

My body hums with excitement. I can't wait to see how Finn reacts to the day we planned for him. I wish life had a 0.5× speed button, the same way my podcast app does, so I could sit in this day and savor it for as long as possible, especially since it might be the final year of our Christmas tradition.

I also can't wait to give David his gift. I splurged on a gift certificate for dinner at Blue Hill at Stone Barns just outside the city after we saw it on an episode of *Chef's Table*, his favorite Netflix series. I still can't believe I spent that much on a single meal. For the $350-per-person price tag (excluding tip), we could each have sixty-six Shack Burgers or eighty-eight perfectly greasy square slices of Prince Street Pizza, but I know how happy this experience will make David. Admittedly, I went overboard in hopes that it might smooth over my missing Christmas with his family. I even snuck out to his favorite bakery yesterday afternoon for croissants under the guise of needing to call Finn. At least we can still have a perfect Christmas morning.

I've only made it to page five when David emerges from our bedroom, stretching his arms overhead as he autopilots to the coffee maker. "Merry Christmas!" I say from the couch.

"Morning," he mumbles back. He's cute when he's sleepy, like a grumpy toddler. David doesn't fully become human until after his first cup of coffee.

I read two more pages while he busies himself making coffee. When he finishes, he traces his steps back to the bedroom, mug in hand. I glance over to the coffee machine and notice he only made enough for himself.

Shit. He's really mad. Last night, we had another not-quite-fight. One that has become all too familiar. "So you're really not coming tomorrow?" he asked as I got dressed to go to Theo's.

"I don't know what else you want me to say." We've had this conversation once a week for the past month and I've been perfectly clear: I can't come to Christmas. Not this year, not Finn's last. But he's remained willfully obtuse, asking me again and again like the answer might suddenly be different. "But please come to Theo's tonight, everyone would love to see you. Or I can stay here and we can order takeout and watch Christmas movies if you'd rather." Couldn't he see that I really am trying?

"I'll just be the odd man out," he said. He didn't seem mad, exactly, just resigned.

As excited as I am for today, a small part of me is also looking forward to tomorrow so David and I can put this argument behind us and go back to normal.

Now I follow David into the bedroom, where I find him in the attached bathroom lathering his face with shaving cream. "Are you okay?"

"I'm fine." He doesn't look at me as he answers. He stays focused on the task at hand, picking up his razor and sweeping it down one cheek.

"I thought we could do presents and breakfast before you go," I try again.

"I'm late."

"Is the baby mine?" I ask, trying to joke him out of his sour mood. He doesn't even crack a smile. I look over my shoulder at the digital clock on the nightstand next to the rumpled bed. "It's only seven forty-five," I tell him.

"My mom's making brunch. They want to eat at ten."

"Oh," I say, careful to mask my disappointment. "Maybe we can do presents tonight when you're back. We're doing a lunch thing, so I shouldn't be late. What time do you think you'll be home?"

"I don't know. I might stay over."

This is the first I'm hearing about this plan. "Oh, I didn't realize."

"I need to clear my head," he says, dragging the razor more roughly down his chin. A prickle of blood blooms where he nicks himself. "Damnit!"

"What's got your head so unclear?" I venture.

"Us."

"Us?" I feel sick to my stomach. "What about us?"

"I think we should talk when I'm not in a hurry."

Alarm bells go off in my head. Nothing good has ever followed someone saying they need to talk. A talk means breaking up. But we can't break up. We have a lease together, we have concert tickets to see Maggie Rogers in March and a trip to Charleston planned in May. But most importantly, I love him. I trust him. He makes me feel safe. I think about trading confidences with him in the dark, wrapped in his arms in our bed. Me telling him that I'm afraid I wouldn't be a good mother, not without parents of my own for so long. Him telling me that he's scared he's wasting his life in a job he doesn't even like, just because it pays well. I couldn't bear to lose him. I told him about my parents, and even though the memories were small, it felt huge to me. I don't talk about my parents with anyone, not even with Finn.

I feel my heart rate pick up. I know he's upset I'm not coming to Christmas, but I didn't think we were in breakup territory.

"Let's talk now," I urge.

"I told you, I'm late."

"You can't drop that bomb on me and leave." He must realize this will ruin my day, maybe multiple days if he's not planning to come home tonight. "Are you trying to break up with me?"

"I don't know, Hannah. I just don't know what kind of future we can have if you won't commit to this. To us."

"I am committed," I argue. "We have a joint checking account for household expenses, we co-own a set of dishware, I shared stories with you about my parents, about my past. You're everything to me. How is that not commitment?"

He puts his razor down, bracing his hands on the edge of the vanity and stares at my reflection in the mirror, his eyes filled with hurt. "Then why are we spending Christmas apart? Do you realize that when you refused to come to mine, you never even invited me to yours? Wouldn't that have been the obvious compromise?"

His comment takes me by surprise. I'd been so wrapped up in the planning, and in my worries about our Thanksgiving fight, that I didn't even realize he was waiting for an invitation this whole month. "I mean, ordinarily, sure. But this is the last year of our tradition—"

"Right. I can have you when there are no better offers?" He huffs out an exasperated breath. "Honestly, I'm not sure you need me or even want me now that you have Finn back."

"That's not true!" My voice edges on a yell. How could he possibly think that?

"Like I said, I think this is a longer discussion." He reaches a hand into the shower and turns on the tap. "Can you close the door? I'm getting in the shower," he says like I'm a stranger he doesn't want to see him naked.

After I close the door behind me, I run breathlessly to his sock drawer. When I open it, the only thing inside is socks. With shaking hands, I rifle through them in case the ring box is hidden beneath them or pushed to the back of the drawer, but it's not there.

I turn on my heel and head back to the living room. I snatch the creamy gray envelope containing the Blue Hill gift certificate off the couch cushion and stash it in my work tote. I knew things weren't great between us, but I didn't realize they were this bad. It feels like everyone I love is slipping away from me.

EIGHTEEN

Finn

This year, December 25

There's a light knock at the door. "Finn?" Theo calls from the hallway, "Are you awake? It's Christmas."

"I'm awake," I reply, my voice still froggy from disuse. I've been awake for hours, too keyed up to sleep. I wish there were auspicious words to say to make sure today turns out perfectly, the way you say *rabbit, rabbit* on the first of the month for luck. After two dud Christmases in a row, I feel like I've been waiting three times as long for this day to roll around on the calendar.

"Do you want coffee?" Theo asks from the hallway.

"Yes, please."

The doorknob turns and Theo pokes his head into the room with a mug in hand. I didn't realize he meant immediately. I feel around the bed for the T-shirt I peeled off when I got too warm in the middle of the night and pull it on while Theo watches from the doorway.

When I'm clothed, he offers me a Spode mug with a Christmas tree on the side. I recognize the China pattern from Grandma Everett's house, but I've never seen these mugs here. He must have bought them special for today.

"Are we late?" I ask.

"Our call time is ten."

"Call time?" I echo, noting the strange word choice that makes it sound like we're actors reporting to set. "Are we making a Christmas movie? Because if so, I hope it's the kind where I meet a rugged blue-collar man with a heart of gold who can teach me the true meaning of Christmas. I'm hoping for a furniture maker, but I'd settle for a lighthouse keeper if that's all you can find on short notice."

"Are you looking to get married and move to a small town?" Theo asks. "Because I've got some bad news for you: everything you own is on its way to LA."

"Maybe my dream furniture maker will have to move out west. Aiden Shaw did well for himself whittling chairs in the big city," I tell him as I throw back the covers. I swear I catch his eyes traveling down my body as I do. "Well, I've gotta get in the shower. I want to look my best in case I meet a curmudgeonly widower who needs to be banged back into the Christmas spirit," I tease as I brush past him into the hall.

We're in gridlocked traffic in Times Square, the worst five-block radius of Manhattan. The blinding light coming off the fifty-foot billboards for *Aquaman* and Swatch watches has me wishing for sunglasses even though it's an otherwise cloudy morning.

Theo's been tight-lipped about our destination, going so far as to tilt his phone away from me so I couldn't see the pin on the map when he called a car. But everything we pass is closed, from the M&M's store to the three-story Olive Garden to the TKTS booth.

Fifteen minutes and six blocks later, we pull up to a tan brick building on Forty-Fourth Street. It would have been faster to walk.

"Follow me," Theo urges as he heads for an unmarked metal door. I trail him through a maze of cinder-block-lined hallways until we reach another metal door, this one decorated with a homemade gold star caked in glitter with my name written in the center in Hannah's wonky cursive.

"Ta-da!" Theo announces with a flourish as he opens the door and reveals Hannah and Priya sitting in folding canvas director chairs in front of mirrored vanities. A woman with coarse gray hair held back with a pair of chopsticks stands in front of Hannah with a palette of rhinestones she's applying to Hannah's already intense eye makeup look.

"Is that Finn?" Hannah asks with her eyes closed, reaching one hand out to grasp at the air beside her.

"Don't even think about opening your eyes," the makeup artist warns as she aims a pair of tweezers holding a rhinestone at Hannah's face.

"Well, merry Christmas, whoever you are!" Hannah says, earning herself a glare from the makeup woman.

"Finn, this is Paula," Theo says. "If there was a Tony for theater makeup, she would have won it for *Hello, Dolly* last year." I stick out my hand, in shock I'm about to touch someone who's touched Bette Midler. Paula looks down at my hand with distaste and waves her tweezers at me instead. Guess not.

"And this is Anton," Theo points to a petite man in a leopard-print kimono squatting in the corner to steam the hemline of a red silk gown. "He was the assistant costume designer for *Hamilton*."

Anton looks up from his steaming and says, "Charmed," in a gruff Eastern European accent.

"And what are we doing here?" I ask, trying to catch up to what the hell is going on, and how and why Theo roped these talented people into spending their Christmas morning with us.

"We're re-creating our first Christmas!" Hannah says. She flings an arm out to the side, almost knocking away Paula's palette.

"But better, obviously!" Theo adds. "We couldn't figure out what we should do this year until we realized, what better way to spend your last Christmas than paying homage to your first?"

"This has very Make-A-Wish fund vibes. You know I'm not dying, right?" The assumption that this is my last Christmas with them stings, even though the same thought crossed my mind this morning. I prefer the vision of future me as a guest star, returning each Christmas much to the studio audience's delight, or like a college student taking a time out from their full and exciting social calendar to head home for the holidays.

Paula uses a tissue to blot the bright red lipstick she applied to Hannah's lips and stands back to consider her work. "You're a masterpiece," she declares. "Don't eat anything. Don't even think about crying. It would be best if you don't talk either." Paula counts off rules on her fingers.

Hannah flashes her a thumbs up and leans closer to the mirror to inspect herself. I've never seen her wear this much makeup.

"Who's next?" Paula asks.

"Finn, you go!" Priya urges from the director's chair at the station beside Hannah's. She's lounging in a pink velour tracksuit with her legs draped over the chair's arm.

It's been years since I've worn stage makeup, and I forgot how uncomfortable it is. I feel like someone accosted my face with an entire can of Aqua Net. My skin feels simultaneously tight and sticky, and the experience gives me a whole new respect for Trixie Mattel.

"Stop it. Don't ruin my masterpiece," Paula scolds as I open and close my mouth, trying to crack through the stiff feeling while she attacks my eyes with even more makeup. Paula has been at it for forty-five minutes. The only hint at what she's doing came in the form of a curious "Oooh!" from Priya fifteen minutes ago.

When she finishes, half an eternity later, I open my eyes to survey what she's done. She's given me a rainbow ombre smokey eye, just one. It fans out onto my forehead and cheek, like a colorful wink to the Phantom's half mask. It's the most beautiful and intricate thing I've ever seen.

"Do you like it?" she asks shyly, a 180 from her militant orders of earlier. "They told me you were the guest of honor, so I wanted to give you something special."

"I love it," I tell her and then startle at the sight of the false eyelashes fluttering like bats in my peripheral vision.

After makeup, Anton puts me in a pair of slim tailored pants and a crisp white dress shirt. The cape he adds is more Joseph's technicolor dream coat than the Phantom's staid black number, and it's heavier than the cheap drama department one I wore our first Christmas.

While Priya and Theo take their turns in the makeup chair, I wander to the stage. I assume a generous donation from Theo bought us the run of the place for the day.

When I walk out from the wings, I'm surprised to find Hannah already sitting there with her legs dangling over the edge of the stage, eating a bagel with cream cheese. My pulse skyrockets thinking about how not allowed this is, even though there's no one here to yell at us.

"Paula's going to kill you," I tell her.

She startles and looks up at me. "I'll give you a bite if you don't tell on me." She holds out half of her bagel sandwich. "I ran to the deli on Seventh while you were getting your makeup done. I got some real weird looks on the street. Who am I supposed to be anyway?"

She's in a floor-length red gown, the one Anton was so carefully steaming, with a red feathered headpiece. "You're Dolly Levi from *Hello, Dolly*," I tell her.

"Never seen it." She shrugs. "For red dresses it was either this or orphan Annie, and that felt a little too on the nose."

"Would that make David Daddy Warbucks?" I ask, taking a seat next to her.

"I'm not the expert here, but I'm pretty sure there was no sexual relationship between Annie and Daddy Warbucks."

"Oh, so you didn't see Annie Two. It was dark."

She looks at me with narrowed eyes, trying to tell if I'm kidding.

"I probably would have auditioned for it if it existed," I tell her. "Not that I would have gotten the part." *Like always*, I add in my head. Back in my auditioning days I had a pocket-sized Moleskine notebook I brought with me everywhere. In it, I tracked the auditions I went to, the directors I auditioned for, and the results—a few callbacks, but mostly radio silence. I told myself when I hit a hundred auditions, if I hadn't landed a role, I'd find a different job. *A real job*, I could hear my father's disapproving voice say in my head.

On my ninety-ninth audition, I got a callback. This was it! In bed the night before the callback, I rehearsed how I'd tell my story of perseverance when I accepted the Tony award I'd undoubtedly earn even though the role was for an unnamed ensemble member.

I didn't get the ninety-ninth role, and on my hundredth audition my voice cracked during my audition song, and I knew as soon as it happened I wasn't getting the part. I threw the notebook in a trash bin outside the theater and haven't been on a stage since. I've barely even been in a theater. When Theo brought me to see *Hamilton* for my birthday last year, I was queasy from the very first song. I feigned a migraine at intermission so we could leave.

"From where I'm sitting, I think you dodged a bullet," Hannah says as we gaze out at the rows of crimson velvet seats. "I'd be terrified to do anything with this many people watching."

My eyes scan up to the mezzanine and then the balcony. Performing in front of this many people would have been my dream.

I wipe at my eyes, embarrassed they're starting to well. I thought this was going to be my life: performing in front of an adoring crowd. I wonder where the *Sliding Doors* moment in my life was that I took a left instead of a right and it all went so completely wrong.

Hannah shoves a wad of napkins in my direction. "Paula's going to have a double homicide on her hands if you don't stop," she says around a mouthful of bagel.

"I really tried to make it work here," I tell her.

"You make it sound like your life in New York was awful. It hasn't been that bad, has it?" she asks.

"Nothing worked out the way I thought it would." I dab at my eyes and the napkin comes away streaked with orange and purple splotches.

"I don't think that's how life works, Finn. If life worked out how I thought it would, I would have been a teacher slash ballerina slash astronaut, and you know I'd be terrible at all of those things."

I laugh at the mental image of her trying to control a room of screaming eight-year-olds while wearing a tutu and a space helmet. "But that's different. That's kindergarten career-day stuff. I could see this. I didn't change my mind, but then . . . no one would let me."

"Do you remember the night we met? You told me you were going to be famous."

"Oh god, I was so obnoxious!" I hang my head and cringe at my nineteen-year-old self, so sure this would happen for him. What would he think of me now? "I feel like I wasted all my time in New York on dreams that didn't come true."

"So what? So you didn't ever get cast. Sounds like a crappy life to me anyway. Eight shows a week? No free weekends? No social life? Cater waitering between roles for cash? Only so . . . what? You can *make it* and schlep around the country on a coach bus playing regional shows in Des Moines and Phoenix? You'd hate that."

"How do you even know all of that?"

"I googled it when you quit. I wanted to be prepared to talk shit about your path not taken."

I nudge her with my shoulder, touched by her willingness to hate my enemies, real or imagined. "But it's not just that." I stand up and pace a track from one end of the stage to the other to burn off some of the anxiety this conversation is creating.

"Enlighten me."

"It's theater, it's Jeremy—" She scoffs at the mention of his name. "Hell, it's Theo, too. I wasted so much of my time here."

"I think you're focusing on all the wrong things," she says, a hint of defensiveness creeping into her voice. "We had fun, didn't we? To me, New York is that time we went to a Yankees game before remembering that neither of us give a shit about baseball, so we bought hats and hot dogs and left. It's slices of Artichoke pizza in the Village at four in the morning, and biking across the bridge to Dumbo on summer weekends so we could stare back at New York across the river. It's the eight million dinners, and brunches, and nights out, even the ones that kind of sucked because those would be the best to laugh at over bagels the next morning. Not to mention the Christmases. Well, just the good ones. To me, New York is *us*, and that wasn't time wasted. Not to me, anyway."

"I'm sorry, have you seen my best friend? I think aliens might have abducted her because that was sappy as hell." But then I lean my head on her shoulder because she's right—there were lots of good parts, too. She leans her head against mine and we stare out into the theater.

"I'm proud of you, you know," she says after a minute, and I nod. "I'm sad for me, though. It feels like I just got you back, but I know you need to go." I understand because I feel the exact same way.

"I think a fresh start will be good for me. But we can have video calls—maybe we can do a monthly virtual movie night, all four of us? And you have David now. You'll be okay."

She lifts her head and stares down at the remnants of her bagel in its foil wrapper in her lap. "I don't know. He's pretty mad at me right now." She says it casually, but when I turn to look at her, her teeth are gritted, like she's trying hard not to cry.

I squeeze her arm and try to make my voice light, pushing aside the toll this conversation has had on me, too, and say, "Let's get back to everyone before Paula kills us for all this eating and crying."

As we stand up, I add, "You know I'm always here for you if you need to talk, right? Even when I'm not physically here, here."

After a short drive from the theater, our taxi pulls to a stop amid a stretch of luxury stores on Fifty-Fifth Street, all closed for the holiday. We must look like a clown car as we exit: Hannah in her red gown; me in the technicolor dream cape; Theo in King George's shiny red-and-gold suit, complete with a powdered wig, crown, and dalmatian-spotted capelet; and Priya in a black beaded flapper dress giving her best Velma Kelly. Across the street, a family of tourists in matching blue puffy coats stops to gawk. The dad pulls out his phone to snap a photo of the spectacle.

Theo leads the way to a gold door beside a planter box of hedgerows while Priya brings up the rear, toddling behind us on her pin-thin stilettos. Her range of motion is constrained by the dress, which is tight around her knees before splitting off into a curtain of beaded fringe.

When we enter, a maître d' in a plaid sport coat looks up from his iPad. "Ah! Mr. Benson, perfect! Welcome to the Polo Bar." He shakes hands with Theo, clapping him on the shoulder like they're old pals. "Would you like to have a cocktail before heading downstairs?" he offers.

After a round of dirty martinis served alongside silver bowls filled with perfectly salted chips, mixed nuts, and little fried balls that turn out to be olives stuffed with morsels of sausage, the maître d' leads us downstairs. The windowless dining room resembles the end-of-days bunker of an equestrian-obsessed member of the landed gentry. We're seated in a cognac leather booth along one wall. Each seat has a plaid pillow, for decoration or lumbar support, I'm not sure. As I survey the wood-paneled dining room, I can't help but grin at how we've upgraded from the dining hall pancakes of our first Christmas.

The moment we're settled, another waiter in a plaid bow tie and vest descends on our table with a bottle of champagne. The sound of the cork popping echoes around the deserted dining room.

"I'd like to make a toast," Theo says, clinking his knife on the side of his champagne flute.

"Finn," he begins, "did you know I consider the night I met you to be one of the best nights of my life?"

Even though my memories of the evening are hazy, at best, my cheeks flame at the mention of that night. The only night we were more than friends.

"Because that night brought you all to me, and you've become more like family than my actual family." Of course we cherish that night for wholly different reasons. I feel myself deflating, like a squeaky balloon giving its loud, flatulent death rattle. "I know today might be the end of a tradition, but it's not the end of my love for each of you. Our kinship is tattooed onto my heart. Not literally, obviously, but if we have a few more bottles of this"—he points at the bottle of Perrier-Jouet in the ice bucket beside our table—"I could be convinced."

A titter of laughter circles the table.

"I'm rubbish at talking about my feelings, but I wanted you to know how much being a part of this group has meant to me. So let's raise a glass to Finn and possibly our last, but hopefully our very best, Christmas."

"Hear! Hear!" Priya holds out her glass.

"Cheers!" Hannah adds her glass to the scrum.

I wordlessly lift my glass to meet theirs. Theo offers me a wink across the table. We all take a sip of our drinks to seal his words to fate.

There are no menus for lunch. Our bow-tied waiter returns with a two-tiered tea tray, the bottom filled with miniature pancakes and the top with a tin of caviar and a ramekin of crème fraîche. The caviar service is followed by a platter of pigs in a blanket with both beef hot dogs and vegetarian alt-meat ones for Priya, both kinds wrapped in a cocoon of pancake. Next there are miniature breakfast sandwich sliders—a runny egg, sausage patty, and slice of melted cheese sandwiched between two silver dollar pancakes. After that four waiters descend on our table simultaneously, each carrying a plate with a domed silver lid. They remove the lids with choreographed precision to reveal plates of obscenely fluffy Japanese-style pancakes in three stacks, the first drizzled with a berry compote, the second dotted with chocolate chips and topped with a cloud of whipped cream, and the third garnished with apple chutney.

A laugh escapes me when the plate is revealed. "Wait, did you get a restaurant to make us a meal that's entirely pancakes?" The staff, who outnumber us two to one, must be so confused by our bizarre holiday meal.

"Historical accuracy is important," Theo replies with a rakish tilt of his head, which sends his crown sloping to one side.

"Believe me, I was there, and there was no caviar at our first Christmas," I tell him.

"No champagne either," Hannah adds, "but I don't see you complaining about that!"

"So, we gave it a little upgrade," Theo says with a jaunty shrug.

We're so full that we barely touch our dessert—rich chocolate pancakes that taste like flattened molten chocolate cakes. When the fifth and final course is cleared, we sit with coffees served in porcelain teacups and finish the dregs of our champagne. "So, what's next?" I ask.

"Well . . ." Hannah hesitates. "This was kind of all we had planned."

"I honestly thought it would take longer." Theo looks down at his watch.

"We could head across the street to the King Cole Bar for another round?" Priya suggests.

"I think I'll explode if I put anything else in my stomach," Hannah begins, punctuating her statement with a sip of champagne. We're onto a second bottle. "Plus, we'll be sloshed and maudlin by sunset if we keep drinking. And David and I were maybe going to do gifts tonight."

At the mention of David's name, Priya flashes an approving smile at Hannah.

"I have an idea," I say. "We're right by Rockefeller Center and I've never been skating there. It feels like a New York Christmas rite of passage. Should we go? Mix in some new with the old?"

"Your wish is our command," Theo says as Priya and Hannah nod their assent. "Lead on."

There's a chance I miscalculated with my suggestion. The line of kids, hopped up on sugar and bouncing beside exhausted parents, starts at the sidewalk on Fifth Avenue and snakes back and forth on itself as far as the eye can see. Probably all tourists.

"Maybe this is the wrong line?" Hannah offers. "Maybe this is the line for Santa? Or Al Roker could be giving something away on the plaza?"

"Excuse me." Priya taps the man in front of us on the shoulder. "Is this the line for skating?"

"You have to wait your turn like everyone else, weirdos," he sneers back.

"Jeez, okay. I was just asking."

It takes us an hour to reach the front, rent skates, and get them on, which requires some maneuvering because my fingers froze into icicles during the wait.

"I don't know if this is a good idea." Priya stands unsteadily in a pair of bright orange rental skates. "I can barely walk in this dress, never mind skate."

"Maybe you can pull it up above your knees to get more range of motion?" I suggest.

"Or just hold onto the railing," Theo offers.

"We waited in that huge ass line. We're going skating. All of us," Hannah shuts down her complaints.

Our group ventures onto the ice. The famous Rockefeller tree looms over the rink and pop music blares through the speakers. When the song changes to "Merry Christmas, Happy Holidays" by *NSYNC, I whip around to face the group so I can lip-sync the lyrics at them while skating backward. "This song was my jam as a kid."

"Oh, you think you're the only one with moves," Hannah teases, "I took skating lessons as a kid. Watch this!" She lifts one skate off the ice, bringing her leg back into a low arabesque. She wobbles on her standing leg before putting her foot down. The whole thing lasts about three seconds.

"I used to be more flexible and remember that being much more impressive," she admits.

From my new angle skating backwards, facing the group, I see Priya hugging the wall a few yards behind us. I feel partially

responsible for forcing her into this, and now she's clearly struggling. I skate back to her and offer my arm.

"Hang onto me instead," I tell her. "I'll make sure you
don't fall."

"I think I'm getting off after this lap."

"Don't do that! Seriously, I've got you. I'm a great skater." I
speed up ahead of her and execute a quick circle, doing the fancy
crossovers I taught myself at the roller rink as a kid. "See!"

I skate back to her side and grab her arm, pulling us forward
to catch up with the group. The song changes to "Mistletoe" by
Justin Bieber and I steer us to avoid a group of young kids pushing traffic cones around the ice for balance, all but dragging
Priya along.

"You're going too fast," she complains.

"All you have to do is hang on. Trust me!"

"Finn, I'm going to—"

Before she can finish her sentence, her skate catches on a divot
in the ice and she step-step-steps trying to find her balance.
There's the sound of fabric ripping and silver beads spray over
the ice. "Motherfucker," Priya swears under her breath, but at
least she's regained her footing.

"That's bad language," a pigtailed girl in a pink coat stops
short to chastise Priya.

Time slows down as Priya crashes into the tattletale kid. I feel
her arm unlink with mine and watch with horror as she falls.
Hard.

NINETEEN

Hannah

Christmas #10, 2017

My dad died.

The minute Finn says those three words, our fight is forgotten. I rush to him and wrap my arms around his middle. His face crumples into the top of my head, tears soaking into my hair, while Theo yells at the video camera in the corner.

"Brian, we've got a real emergency in here!" He waves his arms overhead like he's signaling a plane on a desert island.

"C'mon, Brian, don't be a wanker," he tries again, and slams his palm against the door for emphasis. I've never seen Theo lose his temper, but all signs point to us being close.

After the longest two minutes of my life, Brian opens the door. "Sorry!" He's out of breath and red-faced. "I was in the bathroom. I didn't see you. I thought it would be fine. No one finishes in less than an hour. It's our hardest room!"

The five of us brush past him into the cramped lobby without acknowledging his apology.

"Please don't leave us a bad review," he pleads, hovering on the outskirts of the circle we've formed around Finn, who has collapsed onto a shabby olive-green couch with his head in his hands.

Jeremy crouches in front of him, placing one hand on each of Finn's knees. "What do you need?" he asks helplessly.

The rest of us don't wait to be told what he needs and spring into action. I feel desperate to do something, anything to take his pain away, but I don't know how, so I settle for getting him a glass of water while Priya conscripts a box of tissues from the check-in desk.

"There's a five o'clock flight out of JFK," Theo says as he scrolls through flights on his phone. "And a six p.m. out of La-Guardia."

"Wait a second," I interrupt. Four sets of eyes swivel toward me, even Finn's. "Do you actually want to go?" This is directed at Finn, the first words I've spoken to him in a year. "You don't have to, you know."

"I don't know," he answers. His eyes dart around the circle like one of us might have the answer. "I probably should, right?"

"Fuck 'should.'" I sit down on the couch next to him and press my shoulder into his. "I asked, do you want to? Because you don't have to."

Finn takes a beat to deliberate. My heart breaks as I watch him. What an impossible position his father has put him in. If he wasn't dead, I'd leave him a scathing voicemail right now. How dare he leave his son—his wonderful, warm, caring son—to be the bigger person. How dare he leave this world without making things right with him.

"I think I want to go," Finn says. "Or, I don't want to go so much as I'm afraid that, if I don't, I'll regret it."

"So it's a yes, then?" Theo asks. He has his credit card out, poised to enter it into whatever travel app he's using. He looks at me for approval.

Finn nods at me.

"It's a yes," I confirm with the gravitas of a five-star general choreographing a military operation.

"Four seats or five?" Theo asks. "Jeremy, are you coming?"

Jeremy looks up from where he's squatting in front of Finn. He looks like a deer caught in headlights. "Me? I can't . . . ," he says to Theo instead of Finn, like he knows enough to be embarrassed by his refusal.

"Are you fucking kidding me right now, Jeremy?" I snap.

"I have to work tomorrow. I need to feed my sea anemones or else I'll have to start my experiment all over again." This is undoubtedly the lamest excuse of all time.

Theo, Priya, and I are all in middle seats on the six o'clock flight out of LaGuardia. When the airline upgraded Theo to first class on account of his frequent-flier status, he insisted Finn take his seat.

Before the flight, Theo and Priya ran home to pack a bag, while I went with Finn to his apartment to help him pack. I didn't notice Jeremy had slinked away until the taxi pulled away from the curb at the escape room and it was only the two of us in the back seat, Finn clutching my hand in a vise grip on the cracked vinyl bench between us. I considered telling the driver to stop so I could go back and yell at Jeremy for his cowardice, but it's probably better this way, just the four of us.

At his apartment, Finn sat on the couch catatonic, while I threw open drawers and closets and cabinets doing my best to round up everything he might need for the next few days. Boxer briefs, razor, toothbrush, pajamas. I threw in a worn copy of *The Magicians* from his bookshelf in case he couldn't sleep on the plane. I know it's his favorite and figured he could use some comfort right now.

"Do you have a garment bag for your suit?" I asked him.

He shook his head. Tears began to well in his eyes again, threatening to spill over.

"No problem, I've got this," I reassured him.

An hour later, I stood in the boarding line with Finn's suit wrapped in an upside-down garbage bag as my carry-on. When the man in front of us side-eyed my choice of luggage, I stared back with open disgust until he looked away first. Today was not the day to cross me.

As soon as the seat-belt sign turns off, Finn shuffles to the back of the plane and taps the man next to Theo on the shoulder. I can't hear what he says from my seat in the last row, but watch

Finn point to his seat at the front of the plane. The older man gathers his belongings in a rush before Finn can take back his offer.

When I use the bathroom mid-flight—walking to the one in the center of the cabin instead of the one beside my seat—I'm relieved to find Finn sleeping with his head on Theo's shoulder. Theo gives me a sad smile as I walk by his row. I'm glad Finn's not alone.

In Atlanta, there's a handwritten sign on the desk of the Alamo counter. The message, written with a Sharpie in blocky capital letters, says: MERRY CHRISTMAS. WE'RE OUT OF CARS. GOD BLESS. We make our way down the row of abandoned rental car counters until we find the lone open kiosk. "It's your lucky day," the woman behind the counter tells us in a syrupy southern accent, "we have one car left."

She may have oversold our luck, because the last car turns out to be a bright yellow Hummer. In the parking lot, we stand a few yards away from the car, giving it a wide berth, like it might turn sentient and take offense if it hears us talking shit.

"Who's driving?" Theo asks.

"Aren't you driving?" I ask Theo. He paid for the rental and put his name on the insurance form.

"I'm not used to driving on the right side of the road. Even in, erm, more modestly sized vehicles. I'm afraid I'd run us off the road," he says as he eyes our monstrosity of a ride.

"I don't have a license," I offer. I let it lapse after four years in the city. It seemed like too much of a hassle to go to the DMV for a license I wasn't planning to use for anything other than getting into bars, and I could use my passport for that. Until tonight, it's never been an issue.

No one looks at Finn.

"Fine, I'll do it," Priya says. Theo tosses her the keys and she fumbles them. They skid underneath the car, and she has to get on her hands and knees on the asphalt to retrieve them. Not a fortuitous omen for the drive ahead.

In the car, Priya looks like a child, dwarfed by the massive red leather driver's seat. She adjusts it as far forward as it will go before turning the key in the ignition. When she does, "I Did It All for the Nookie" blares from the speakers at full volume. I jab at the buttons on the dashboard trying to get it to stop. Not the time, Fred Durst.

The Hummer roars to the curb in front of Finn's childhood home just after eleven. "You have arrived at your destination," the GPS lady announces.

Priya slams the breaks and the car jerks forward before settling to a stop on the quiet cul-de-sac. Once in park, Priya sighs with relief. Her shoulders ease down from where they've been hunched up by her ears for the forty-five-minute drive on a five-lane highway to Peachtree City, a leafy suburb south of Atlanta.

I stare out the passenger window at the house. I've never

pictured what kind of house Finn grew up in. I always thought of us as the same—lacking in parents, lacking a home, rootless—but the stately two-story white brick colonial in front of us is proof that Finn does have a family. And they rejected him. My hands ball into fists in my lap as I survey the house. There's a light on in the front room.

"I don't know if I can go in," Finn says from the back seat. His voice is shaky. "Maybe this was a mistake."

"Do you want me to make a loop around the neighborhood while you decide?" Priya offers. Her shoulders creep up at the prospect of turning the car back on.

"Can we just sit here for a minute?" Finn asks.

"We can sit here all night if you want," Theo offers. "You don't have to do anything you don't want to do."

TWENTY

Finn

Christmas #10, 2017

I wake with my head on Theo's shoulder. There's a crusted track of drool down my chin and my neck screams from sleeping at a weird angle.

My phone says it's 6:04. I didn't mean to stay outside all night; I only wanted a few minutes to compose myself, because once I go inside it will be real. My father will be dead, and I'll be face-to-face with my mother for the first time in nine years.

I open and close the car door as gently as I can, so I don't wake anyone. Up front, Priya is reclined in the driver's seat with her wrinkled purple coat draped over herself like a blanket, while Hannah's face is squished against the passenger window. Gratitude surges through me. No matter what happens inside, these people, the ones sleeping uncomfortably in this monstrosity of a car, are my real family.

For a moment, I stare at the house. To the right of the walkway is the happy willow. Willow trees only weep near water, so ours stands tall and broad, casting the front of the house in a welcome shade from Georgia's sweltering sun. The tree was always base when I played tag with the other neighborhood kids. It's taller since I left.

At the door, I freeze. I don't have a key—mine was abandoned in a junk drawer two apartments ago. I didn't think to keep it because I never expected to come back. It's not rational, but I never considered the possibility my dad could die. I assumed he might live forever; the bad guys always do. When I lived here, he ran five miles every weekday morning, even in the hottest part of summer, and hadn't touched bread since the Atkin's craze in the nineties.

I don't want to wake anyone with the bell, so I try the door-knob. To my surprise, it's unlocked. I step into the foyer and breathe in the smell of Pine Sol and the white gardenia candles my mother favors. It smells like home.

"Finn, is that you?" my mother calls from closer than I expected, not upstairs in her bedroom. She's in the living room, the one we only use for company, lying on the slipcovered white couch underneath a hand-crocheted blanket made by her own mother, who died when I was eleven. My grandmother's was the first and only funeral I've ever been to. Until now, I guess.

"Hi. It's me." I stand in the doorway to the living room sur-veying my mother. Her hair has started to go gray, I notice. I'm surprised she doesn't color it. She always cared so much about appearances. I wonder if I should give her a hug. I realize, too late, that when Amanda called with the news it wasn't accompanied by an invitation. I just showed up. Maybe my mother doesn't want me here.

At the sight of me, tears start streaming down her cheeks. I don't know the protocol for this situation. "I'm sorry about Dad," I say. This loss feels more hers than mine.

"I'm not crying about your father. It still doesn't feel real. I'm crying because you're finally home where you belong. Now come here." She beckons me to the couch. "I need to hug my boy."

I sit down next to her, and she wraps me in her arms, my head automatically nestles into her shoulder. I can smell her Jo Malone perfume, the same kind she's always worn.

"What are you doing down here?" I ask.

"I could ask you the same question. I heard you pull up in that monster truck out there last night and I've been waiting for you to come in ever since."

"I needed a minute. And then, I guess I fell asleep."

"I did, too," she says, and I'm not sure if she means that she needed a minute or fell asleep.

"How about I make us some coffee?" she offers.

I'm sitting on a stool at the kitchen island with my second cup of coffee as my mother dictates a list of everyone we need to call with the news. When to call is an etiquette quandary she doesn't have an answer for. After ten, she decides. People will sleep in the day after a holiday, and she wouldn't want to inconvenience anyone with the untimely death of her husband.

The list is going on three pages: co-workers, golf partners, distant relatives, college roommates, credit card companies, and the insurance broker. I never realized death required so much admin. I naively assumed you placed an obituary and the funeral home did the rest. My heart breaks for Hannah who had to do this as a teenager, not once, but twice.

"What do I say if they ask how he died?" Amanda didn't give any specifics between tearful gasps when she called with the news.

"Holiday heart," she says, like it should mean something to me. It sounds like the name of a Hallmark movie she'd probably enjoy.

"What's that?"

"The doctor said it's common, fifth one he saw yesterday."

"That's a pretty callous way to break the news," I interject.

"He said people eat and drink more than usual over the holidays and their hearts can't take it and it leads to heart attacks. Amanda googled it in the car, Christmas Day and New Year's Day have the highest incidence of heart attacks out of the whole year." She sounds numb, like she's relaying the plotline on an episode of *Grey's Anatomy* and not discussing something that happened to her husband of thirty-five years. At her lack of emotion, I wonder what their marriage was like during the decade of my exile. I wonder if she'll miss him, or if, like me, maybe she's the tiniest bit relieved to be free of him.

"But Dad was so healthy," I counter.

"He was getting older." She reaches for her cell phone and pulls up a picture of Dad with Amanda. "This was Thanksgiving."

I pull the phone closer to inspect the photo. His Georgia Tech polo strains across his bulging belly, and his hair is thinning. He adopted a bad comb-over to try and hide it. This man, who is obviously my father, looks nothing like the image I've been carrying around in my head. It's not like he was on Facebook, and no one sent me any family photos to update my mental image. He looks old, like exactly the sort of person who might drop dead of a heart attack.

A knock at the door interrupts our conversation.

"I think it's one of my friends." I've been inside for over an hour and failed to mention I didn't come alone.

"I'm not ready for company." She pats her hair, trying to smooth it down, and pulls her bathrobe even tighter over her already modest nightgown.

"Don't worry, they're staying at a hotel. They probably want to make sure I'm alright before heading over there. They'll only be here a minute."

Hannah is on my mother's doorstep, mascara smudged beneath her eyes, still in yesterday's clothes. "Hi," she croaks when I open the door. "I've really gotta pee."

I lead Hannah to the downstairs powder room, and wait outside the door while she relieves herself. Even though things have been going well with my mother, a knot in my stomach loosens knowing Hannah is here as backup.

"Do Theo and Priya want to come in, too?" I ask when she emerges from the bathroom, wiping her wet hands on her day-old jeans.

"We were going to go over to the hotel and check in so we can shower and change." Of course they already missed their reservation last night because I made them sleep in the car.

Ignoring my mother's wishes I ask, "Maybe you could . . . stay?" I don't know when she and I might run out of death admin to talk about, and then what?

"We could stay," Hannah confirms. "I'll get Theo and Priya."

Amanda makes an appearance at ten thirty, trudging downstairs on leaden feet. She whines from the kitchen that there's no coffee left. When no one answers she makes her way back to the family room. "Mom, did you hear me? There's no coffee."

When she spots Theo sitting on the overstuffed brown leather sofa, her posture snaps to attention and she whips a hand up to snatch the silk bonnet out of her hair, trying to cover by fluffing her curls.

"I didn't know you were here," she says to me in an accusing tone.

"Wow, what a warm welcome," I quip back.

I stand to go make a fresh pot of coffee so my mother doesn't have to. As I move to cross the room, Amanda launches herself into my arms and wraps me in a hug so tight I can't breathe. "I'm glad you came," she whispers in my ear, her voice thick with emotion. "I wasn't sure you would. But I hoped."

After we begin making calls, word must spread around town because by two o'clock, the house is full of visitors. An army of older women in pastel slacks and floral blouses descend on the house bearing casseroles and baked goods. I wonder if they have freezers full of them, ready and waiting in case anyone dies, or if they had to drop everything this morning to bake a consolation coffee cake. Or, in the case of the lady bearing a lime Jell-O mold with raspberries and marshmallows suspended inside of it, if we're being subjected to the worst of their Christmas leftovers.

When I offer to make what must be the tenth pot of coffee of the day, my mother shoos me away. "You'll mess it up," she protests, and I realize she still thinks of me as the nineteen-year-old who last lived under this roof.

"Mom, I've been making my own coffee for a decade. Trust me, I can do it." My tone telegraphs my annoyance. I take the coffee filter out of her hand before she can object, but immediately feel guilty for snapping at her. "Why don't you go sit down for a bit."

By late afternoon, the stream of visitors slows to a trickle, and by dinner we pack Aunt Carolyn and Aunt Ruthie into their cars, too. My mother collapses onto a stool at the kitchen island like an animatronic toy that's run out of batteries while the rest of us pick at slices of Partners Pizza that Theo ordered.

"I'm bone tired, but I doubt I'll be able to sleep tonight," she says as she blots a piece of pepperoni pizza with a napkin. When she finishes, she pushes it away without taking a bite.

"Do you want me to make some sleepytime tea?" Amanda offers.

"That won't do anything." My mother waves her off.

Theo goes into the hallway and returns with an orange pill bottle and offers it to my mom. "These might help."

"What kind of pills are you giving my mother?!" I ask. The last time Theo offered someone pills Hannah and I didn't speak for a year. We still haven't addressed that, just slipped back into our old groove.

"It's Ambien, but maybe only take half."

I don't expect her to accept them, but she pockets the pill bottle in her black linen pants. "Can't hurt," she concedes.

After Mom retires upstairs, the rest of us clean the kitchen. "Do you need anything before we go to the hotel?" Priya asks as she finishes wiping down the counters. She's still wearing the silver sweater threaded with tinsel she wore at the escape room. It was only yesterday, but it feels like a lifetime ago. Her hair is slicked back in a limp, greasy ponytail.

"Unless you want us to stay?" Theo offers.

I should let them go. They've already gone above and beyond. First the flights, which reminds me I owe Theo money for my ticket, then the car, and then spending the day making polite conversation with a house full of strangers. It would be unfair to ask them to stay.

"Because we're happy to stay," Hannah offers.

"You are?" I ask, trying to leave them an out if they want it.

"Of course we are," Hannah confirms. I let out a breath I didn't realize I was holding.

"It's pretty uncomfortable," I apologize as I make up the pullout couch with spare sheets. "Whoever gets stuck sleeping on it is going to wake up with a sore back. The air mattress is probably more comfortable, but it tends to deflate overnight." I keep up a constant narration of the less ideal points of their sleeping arrangements as I set up beds for them in the basement. The last time I had friends stay the night was for a track team sleepover I hosted junior year of high school. I should have let them go to the hotel.

"We don't care," Theo says with a hand on my back. "We're here for you, not the amenities. We won't be leaving a Tripadvisor review."

Thirty minutes later, I'm tossing and turning in bed. I should be exhausted after the past twenty-four hours, but sleep won't come. It's strange to be back in my childhood bedroom after all this time.

Just as I find a comfortable position and begin to drift off, footsteps on the stairs jolt me awake. It's probably Mom. I've heard stories about people sleepwalking and doing all sorts of regrettable things after taking Ambien. I should make sure she doesn't go wandering our subdevelopment in her nightgown or get on the desktop computer in the den and buy the entire Neiman Marcus website.

Before I can rouse myself from bed there's a light knock at the door. Then the doorknob turns. "Mom?" I ask, sitting up to see what she needs.

"Sorry, it's me." Me turns out to be Hannah. She's wearing a pair of Priya's pajamas: shorts and a button-up top printed with unicorns. I almost crack a joke about how off-brand they are until I remember—she didn't get to pack a bag of her own because she was packing for me, even after a year of not speaking.

"Did you need something?" I showed them where the thermostat was in case it got stuffy and left enough towels for everyone to shower. My brain cycles trying to figure out what I must have forgotten.

"No, I'm just checking on you. You've been taking care of your mom and sister all day. I wanted to make sure someone was taking care of you." She hovers in the doorway. "So, uh, how are you feeling?"

"I don't think it's sunk in yet." I pull back the blankets on the bed, an invitation. She crosses the room without hesitation and climbs in. Strands of her still-damp hair tickle my arm as she finds a comfortable position. We automatically arrange ourselves face-to-face, the way we've done so many times before in her bed at Orchard Street.

"How did it feel to see your mom again?"

"It feels weird. Like, is this forever or a weekend pass? We haven't talked about anything except logistics. Honestly, I'm more relieved to be speaking to you again than her."

Hannah touches my arm tentatively. "I'm sorry, you know. I didn't mean any of it, I only said those things because I was angry."

"I know," I say. "I'm sorry, too. We never should have let it go on so long."

Ironically, when I heard my father was dead, I didn't have regrets about what was left unsaid between us. Fuck him. I'm here for my mother and for Amanda. Sure, I was shocked by the news, but the leaden feeling in my stomach was for Hannah. What if something happened to her and we never got to make up? She at least tried to reach out; I remember her text in the spring that I left on read. How could I have been so cavalier, wasting a year not speaking, assuming there was an endless string of years ahead to make things right? How could I have taken one of the most special relationships in my life for granted? She was the who donned the mantle of loving me when the people who raised me weren't up to the job.

"We don't have to talk about our fight right now if you don't want to. You have enough going on," she offers. We lie in silence for a minute, and it feels more comfortable than awkward.

"Can I admit something embarrassing?" she asks out of nowhere.

"Always."

"Every time I had something to tell you and I went to call you and realized I couldn't, I recorded a voice memo to you on my phone instead."

"Oh my god." A laugh bubbles up in my throat.

"I know, it's so dorky."

"That's not why I'm laughing. I'm laughing because I started a journal where I wrote down everything I wanted to tell you, but couldn't because we were fighting. I went to McNally Jackson and got a new notebook especially for it."

Now we're both laughing. "Wow, we're officially the biggest nerds on the planet," she declares.

"I want to listen to those voice memos, you know?" I tell her. "I need to catch up on everything I missed."

"Good, because I want to read that journal."

"It's going to be so embarrassing."

"Don't worry, I probably won't be able to read most of it because your handwriting is atrocious."

I swat her shoulder.

"Do you know David calls you my imaginary friend because I talk about you so much, but he's never met you?"

"The infamous David—"

"He's infamous?"

"To me he is. Or maybe mysterious is more like it. Priya put a moratorium on asking about him. She said I could talk to you if I wanted to know more."

"She told me the same thing about you. She said I was annoying her with all my questions." The bed shakes with our giggles. I'm awash in comfort knowing she felt my absence as acutely as I felt hers. I'd started to wonder if she put me out of her mind and moved on. Or if she didn't need me anymore now that she was in a relationship.

"I can't believe you went and got a boyfriend when we weren't talking." There were a smattering of hookups in college, and the occasional first or second date, but I'd never seen Hannah serious about a guy.

"I had a lot of extra time on my hands."

"Oh, so are you going to dump him now that we're talking again?"

"No!" she snaps defensively. Then her voice goes quiet, "He wants us to move in together. Things are kind of serious." Her nose scrunches at her own earnestness.

"What? That's huge."

"It's terrifying."

"Will I like him?"

"Yeah, I think you will. He's a good guy. He's a lawyer. He hates most of my music—"

"Same," I interrupt. She bats my hand away when I shove it in her face for a high five.

"He can cook, which is nice." She pauses. "And I don't know. I just . . . love him." She covers her face with her hands like this is embarrassing to her.

Love, wow. I've never seen Hannah in love before, and I feel a pang of regret that I've missed so much change in her life. She sounds certain about him. If I'm honest, more certain than I feel about Jeremy after a year and a half together. It stings that Hannah, who was not speaking to me yesterday, is here, and Jeremy, whose bed I woke up in yesterday morning, is not.

But maybe I'm not all that surprised. My relationship with Jeremy was built on a foundation of relief. Relief to find someone who liked me back. Relief to not have to date anymore. Relief that I was no longer lagging behind on the life milestone checklist. And there was sexual compatibility, maybe even passion, but the passion never flourished into need. Not the same way I need Hannah or Theo. I can't imagine buying a journal to write down everything I wanted to tell Jeremy if he was away on a long trip with no cell phone service. That's probably not a great sign.

"Maybe we can go on a double date before I dump Jeremy," I suggest.

"Oh yeah, we didn't even talk about that. He was the worst yesterday."

I wince at her words, embarrassed that my boyfriend chose his sea plants over me.

"What a cop-out!" Hannah goes on. "You deserve better, you know. You deserve everything." Her hand finds mine in between us.

"Yeah . . ." I trail off, letting her think I'm dumping him because of yesterday and not because she was right about what she said when we fought: I don't love him, and I'm not sure I ever did.

After that we go silent, Hannah makes no move to leave, and I don't try to make her. A few minutes later her breathing slows. Even more than I relish being welcomed back into my childhood home and the nostalgic comfort of this room I grew up in, my true source of comfort is Hannah. The person that has stood by my side and witnessed my life when my biological family wouldn't. And even though I didn't think I could sleep, with her here, my eyes flutter closed, too.

TWENTY-ONE

Hannah

This year, December 25

"You sure you want to go to the hospital, lady? It's a zoo over there today," the barely legal paramedic teases Priya in a thick Long Island accent, like on second thought she might prefer to self-treat her leg, which is bent at an unnatural angle, with essential oils and prayer.

"Pretty sure," she tells him, her voice dripping in sarcasm. At least the crowd of spectators has dissipated. For a while, a swarm of tourists watched on while a pair of paramedics strapped Priya to a gurney, like this was a vital part of the New York City tourism experience.

"Well, be prepared to wait is all I'm saying." The paramedic offers his parting words before slamming shut the ambulance's double doors and slapping a flat palm against the door twice to signal his partner in the driver's seat.

Finn tried to ride with Priya, but she shut him down, so I'm in the back with her. "I'm not saying it's your fault, Finn, but if you listened to me, this never would have happened," Priya said skyward, her neck cradled in a head immobilizer in case of spinal injuries.

The emergency room at NYU Langone is more crowded than a sold-out show at Irving Plaza and the door policy is twice as tight. After Priya's X-rays a nurse deposits us in a curtained-off cubicle to wait for a doctor to tell us what we already know: her leg is broken.

"Does anyone want more coffee?" I ask from my perch at the foot of Priya's bed. A graveyard of takeout coffee cups litters the C-shaped rolling table beside us. If I have any more coffee I might need a hospital bed of my own, but the act of getting it from the vending machine in the lobby is something to do to pass the time.

"Not unless you have a flask to spike it," Theo replies. "2014 Finn would have had a flask."

"2014 Finn also would've had a hangover," I add. Theo gives a knowing laugh.

Finn ignores us, instead beginning what has become a familiar call-and-response over the past couple of hours. "Are you in pain?" he asks Priya.

"Yes," she answers through gritted teeth, though I'm guessing her harsh tone is more annoyance than pain.

"Is there anything I can do?"

The first few times he asked, she simply said no, there was

nothing he could do, but this time she snaps back at him: "Not unless you have a time machine and can go back in time and attend medical school."

This is getting uncomfortable. I grapple for anything to say to lighten the mood. "Finn failed Biology 101 twice," I offer. "He had to take geology for his science credit instead. They dumb it down so much they call it Rocks for Jocks. It's the class all the football players take to fulfill their core requirement. Trust me, you would not want Finn as your doctor."

Priya gives a grim nod. "Yeah, hard pass."

"So I guess it's gang-up-on-Finn day. I thought that's usually in April." Finn does not sound amused. He scrubs a hand through his hair. "Also, not to be a dick, but this was supposed to be one last special Christmas before I go to LA."

"Do not make this about yourself," Priya warns.

Before things can escalate, a staggeringly handsome doctor with a day's worth of stubble and coif of messy brown hair pulls aside the curtain to our cubicle. He looks like he was plucked from central casting of a network medical drama.

"Priya Patel?" he reads off the chart in his hands.

Priya smooths a hand over her own hair. Paula used so much gel to set her finger curls that there's not a single strand out of place despite a fall, an ambulance ride, and two hours in bed. I can't fault her for the vanity, though—the doctor is easily six feet tall and is surveying the room with a pair of ice-blue eyes.

"Ben?" Priya asks, her kohl-rimmed eyes wide with shock.

Ben? Like Ben, Ben?

Priya's Ben? Her ex-something, Ben?

It's true what they say that sometimes New York is like a small town, but if there's ever a time to run into an ex, doing it with professional hair and makeup might be the best possible option.

"Priya?" He looks down at his chart and then back up at her, equally shocked, like he's waking up from autopilot mode and didn't register her name when he read it.

"Erm . . ." He stumbles before stalling out.

The three of us swivel our heads back and forth between Ben and Priya.

"I can get you another doctor if you want," he says eventually, "but you'd probably have to wait."

"No, it's fine," she tells him. "Nothing you haven't seen before."

"Maybe your friends could step out for a moment so I can perform an exam?"

Over Ben's shoulder, I give Priya a questioning look, and she returns a subtle nod. "We'll be in the waiting room when you're done," I tell them.

We're lucky to find three chairs together, probably because everyone in the ER waiting room is avoiding the man sitting next to me, his finger wrapped in a blood-stained dishtowel. When he catches me looking, he confides, "Mandolin accident. That Ina makes everything look so easy, but I think I'm purely a Jeffrey from here on out."

Twenty minutes later a nurse beelines toward us. My body

tenses as I take in her panicked expression. Are things with Priya more serious than we thought? The paramedic insisted the head stabilizer was only a precaution, and they didn't truly suspect spinal injuries.

"What are you doing out here?" the nurse asks. She crosses her arms over her chest while she waits for our answer.

I look from side to side to see if there's anyone else she could be talking to. When she doesn't budge, I point at myself. "Me? Us?"

"Yes, you. Who else would I be talking to?" She cocks a hand on her hip like a stern schoolmarm. "You were supposed to be here at six. You're late."

"Excuse me?" Unless she's psychic, there's no way she was expecting us.

"You are the theater troupe, right?" she asks in an annoyed tone. "You're supposed to be on the children's wing, not down here. Your show was supposed to start after dinner. The kids are on a strict schedule and need to start getting ready for bed."

"What?" I ask, confused. Beside me, Finn and Theo have their heads tipped together and have dissolved in a fit of church giggles. When I look over at them, it hits me. I completely forgot what we're wearing. Finn in his rainbow eye makeup and matching cape, Theo with his powdered wig, his crown resting in his lap, and me in my ball gown. I snort-laugh imagining how we must look to everyone else in the waiting room; no wonder everyone is giving us a wide berth.

"Contrary to what our outfits might lead you to believe, we are not the theater troupe. Just some stylish citizens." Theo pops out of his chair to explain. He offers her a mock bow and his wig comes sliding off his head.

"I mean, we could be the theater troupe . . . ," Finn counters.

I elbow him in the side. "We're waiting for Priya."

"Fine, we're not the theater troupe," he corrects himself.

The nurse narrows her eyes, trying to figure out if this is some weird "Who's on First" bit. Before she can decide, Dr. Ben swoops in and offers to bring us back to see Priya. Theo throws the confused nurse a wave over his shoulder as we follow Ben out of the waiting area.

"It's broken," Priya announces when we walk into her cubicle. "We need to wait for ortho to come and put on a cast and then we can go. I'm going to be in it for at least eight weeks."

"That sucks," I offer.

"Maybe Dr. Ben will give you some private care to nurse you back to health," Theo suggests, waggling his eyebrows.

"Yeah, what's Dr. Ben's deal? I didn't know he was back in the city." Finn plops himself at the foot of the bed, ready for a gossip session.

"His deal is he broke up with me two weeks ago. Again. That's his deal."

"Wait, what? Why didn't we hear about this?" I ask. "I didn't know you started things up again, never mind that you broke up." If we never heard about it, it couldn't have been that serious. Embarrassing to run into him given the circumstances, sure. But not that serious.

"You didn't hear about it because none of you ever ask me

about my life!" she explodes, her face reddening as she throws her arms up to emphasize her point, accidentally causing a cascade of empty coffee cups to tumble off the side table.

"That's not true," I shoot back. Even with everything else in my life up in the air—my relationship with David, my job, maybe even my apartment—there's one thing I'm certain of, and it's that I'm a great friend. These are *my people* and I pride myself on being there for them. According to David, to the detriment of our relationship. How could Priya even *think* to accuse me of being a bad friend?

"You don't! All month it's been Christmas *this* and Christmas *that*. How can we make this stupid day perfect for Finn?" Priya swings her attention to Finn at the end of the bed. "And you!"

"Me?" he asks in a small voice. He's right to be scared. It's like a dam has broken in Priya and an entire friendship's worth of anger is seeping out the crack.

"You're as bad as she is. 'Is Hannah mad at me for moving?' 'I don't want to leave Hannah alone on Christmas.' You're all so obsessed with this stupid holiday."

"It's not stupid!" I'm so surprised by this ambush that my brain isn't firing quickly enough to refute anything but the last, least-serious accusation.

A hush settles over the room.

"What are we even doing here?" Priya asks after a minute.

Theo rushes to her side. "You fell, don't you remember?" He looks at me with panic in his eyes. "Should I get Dr. Ben? I googled it in the cab and memory loss could be a sign of a concussion. Did you hit your head when you fell?"

"Oh my god, calm down!" Priya says, shoving his hands off her shoulder. "I don't have memory loss. I'm just saying, we shouldn't have done Christmas in the first place this year."

I wonder if she has a point. This is the third year in a row that Christmas has ended in disaster. But my brain keeps cycling back to something she said a minute ago. "We never ask about your life?"

"Literally never," she confirms.

"If that's true, which I still don't think it is, it's only because you're so normal and . . . happy?" Finn adds the last word like it tastes strange in his mouth.

"That doesn't mean I don't have any problems! I'm sorry I can't compete with you in the trauma Olympics, but sometimes my life sucks, too. Ben dumped me for the millionth time, and oh yeah, last week I got fired."

"You got fired?" I'm shocked. Priya has talked about her job at Glossier nonstop since starting in April. Who wouldn't want someone as passionate and experienced as Priya on their team? I feel a surge of rage on her behalf.

"Yep. A pretty shitty month on all fronts." She flops her head back against the pillow and stares at the ceiling. The fire's gone out of her after her tirade. She looks exhausted and resigned, and completely at odds with her surroundings because she's still wearing an intricately beaded flapper costume.

"Why didn't you tell us?" I ask.

"Because you didn't ask. And it's embarrassing. How do I bring that up? 'Oh hey, guys, you know the job that I keep bragging about? The one that I love? Yeah, turns out they didn't feel the same way."

Theo perches on the bed beside Priya and clasps his hand with hers.

"I'm sorry," I tell her from where I'm standing frozen beside her bed. "Finn's right, you're always so happy. I guess sometimes we forget to ask about you."

"Well, it's bullshit," she snaps with a second wind of rage. "I'm 'happy.' You say that like it's a mythical island you're not invited to. You don't want to be happy. It's like you're allergic to happiness. Why aren't you with David right now? Or why isn't he here? I mean, how dare he have a family who loves him! Who loves you, too!"

My hackles rise at her accusation. "I'm not with David because this is our tradition and it's important to me. You're my chosen family. That means something to me. But apparently it doesn't mean anything to you."

"Hannah, we're together all year long. This one-day-a-year tradition isn't what makes us a family," she scoffs. "This is just a way to pass the time on a day that would otherwise be a real bummer for the three of you." She pauses. "I'm sorry, I know that was harsh, but—"

"She's kind of right," Finn says.

I stare daggers in his direction. They don't understand. None of them do.

"I'm going for a walk. I need a minute." I tear aside the curtain and storm off.

TWENTY-TWO

Hannah

Christmas #3, 2010

"Fries?" Finn asks as we pass a glowing orange open sign in the grease-stained front window of a diner.

"Fries," I confirm.

Everything in Boston closes early. It feels miraculous to stumble on a diner open at 11:00 p.m. on Christmas, especially when we still have an hour to kill before the midnight Chinatown bus. Brooke suggested we stay the night, but nothing about sharing the pullout couch in the middle of her living room, which now smelled like charred ham, felt appealing. And if we stayed, we'd only have another awkward meal with Brooke and Spencer to look forward to in the morning, although at least his family wouldn't join for that.

When she offered, I gave Finn the signal we devised for parties when one of us wanted to leave and dipped my right ear to my shoulder like I was stretching my neck. "You know what, I have to get back tonight. I forgot to feed my pet turtle before we left and he's probably hungry," he lied.

"You have a pet turtle?" Brooke asked.

"Big turtle guy," Finn deadpanned.

I made fun of him for the turtle when we made it outside. "The first rule of improv is *yes, and*," he rebutted, "If you'd *yes, anded* me, you could have had a fictional exotic pet of your very own."

"Are turtles exotic? I don't think that counts."

"I'm just saying that you lost your opportunity to *yes, and* a pet parrot into existence."

Inside the diner, I shove my backpack into the red vinyl booth before sliding in and stripping off my winter layers. A sixtysomething waitress in a pink bowling shirt embroidered with her name takes our order. Martha's bleach-blond hair is shellacked into a beehive and the smell of hairspray radiates off her in waves.

"That sucked, right?" I ask Finn after Martha retreats to the kitchen to put in our order and tempt fate by standing anywhere near an open flame with her choice of hairstyle.

"I hope Brooke's not holding her breath for a Michelin star."

It wasn't that Brooke burnt the ham, which she did, it was that she so thoroughly erased any glimmer of our family's Christmas traditions. She was all manic smiles as she tripped over herself to suck up to Spencer's family, who drove down from Maine for the day.

First of all, ham? We always had lasagna on Christmas. Then

there was the white elephant gift exchange she insisted on where three different people brought taffy, some dumb in-joke with Spencer's family. Grandma Betty was not thrilled to get stuck with my gift, a throw pillow screen printed with a bare-chested Nicolas Cage with his lower half encased in a banana peel for modesty. I bought it at a joke shop on Newbury Street hoping Finn would pick my gift.

The nail in the Christmas coffin was when Spencer suggested we turn off *The Grinch* and put on *It's a Wonderful Life* and Brooke actually agreed with him.

Martha drops off a plate piled with fries doused in cheese sauce and two chocolate milkshakes.

"We should have stayed on campus." I take a long pull of shake to drown my sorrows.

"Reginald Tiddlywinks could have joined us," Finn laments. Reginald Tiddlywinks III—heir to the inventor of the children's game—is the ritzy alter ego Finn invented for himself last Christmas. We scrimped and saved all of fall semester to book a room at the Copley Plaza hotel for the weekend. On Christmas, we went downstairs to the swanky wood-paneled bar and drank candy cane martinis in outfits borrowed from BC's drama department pretending to be Reginald Tiddlywinks and his mistress, Miss Scarlett Oglethorpe.

The bar's signature holiday cocktail was dangerous, it tasted like melted peppermint stick ice cream, and not at all like booze. The more we drank, the smoother Finn's British accent became— he was perfecting it for an upcoming audition to play Henry

Higgins in the drama department's spring production of *My Fair Lady*—while the addition of alcohol sent my attempt at an accent careening back and forth on a spectrum between *The Godfather* and *Cool Runnings*. No one believed our fake backstories, but it didn't matter, we spent the evening in a bubble of our private jokes laughing so hard Finn shed actual tears.

"Reginald has an open invitation next year, because I'm never going back there for Christmas again. Or maybe ever. I haven't decided."

"Fine with me." Finn tips his milkshake toward mine to seal the promise with a cheers.

I feel lucky that Finn was there with me today, both as moral support, but also as a witness to my sister's Olympic-level effort to replace our family with a shiny new one of her own. It's clear now that ours was a pity invite. Not having a "real" family won't be so bad. What Finn and I have is better than family anyway, because we chose it.

"Plus, I'm sure we'll have way cooler plans next year," Finn says. "Next year, we'll live here."

That's the plan. After we graduate in May we'll move to New York. Finn will become a big Broadway star. He has a plan to work his way up through the ensemble into feature roles within two years, and win a Tony by twenty-five. I, on the other hand, am less certain about the future. The career counselor at the campus career center gave me a worn copy of *What Color Is Your Parachute?* to read over the break.

This morning, before going to Brooke's, we walked around

Tompkins Square Park pointing out which buildings we'd live in when we moved to the city.

"These are definitely the best part of Christmas," I tell Finn as I drag a fry through the pool of cheese sauce on the plate.

"Here's a burnt one," Finn points to a dark brown fry. Our complementary fry preferences—the well-done fries for me, the undercooked ones for him—seems to validate the perfection of our pairing. I look at Martha, standing behind the counter marrying the ketchups, and I feel bad for her. Alone, on Christmas. She doesn't have a Finn.

"Okay, enough about Brooke," Finn says. "What I really want to talk about is Spencer's shirt. The white cuffs with the blue shirt, who does he think he is, Gordon Gekko?"

His comment catches me so off guard that I shoot milkshake out my nose laughing. No one can snap me out of a bad mood like Finn.

TWENTY-THREE

Hannah

This year, December 25

I've been sitting outside the rec room of the children's wing for twenty minutes and I already have a nemesis. A teenage boy, jaw speckled with acne, stole a Christmas cracker from one of the younger kids. He's a bully. Sure, he probably has cancer, but he's still a dick. Plus, hating him is better than hating myself. What if Priya is right and I am a bad friend?

After I left, it felt good to slam the crash bar of the stairwell door and climb until I was out of breath. When I was panting, I stepped out on the ninth floor, aimlessly roaming the halls. But even after I recovered from the climb, my heart banged in my chest, and I could feel tears prickling behind my eyes.

On the verge of a panic attack, I wandered onto the children's ward. The unit is oddly cheerful, the hallways painted with murals of Candy Land. I'm watching the theater troupe, which is really more of a folk band, sing Christmas songs to a circle of children through the rec room's plate glass window.

I startle when someone appears at my side. I look over, expecting a nurse telling me I'm not allowed to be here, but it's Finn.

"How'd you find me?" I ask.

"Are you kidding? You're wearing a bright red ball gown and a feathered headpiece. Everyone in this hospital has heard about us and thinks we're total freaks. I overheard two of the nurses speculating that we're in some kind of cult. One of them told me you were up here. I think she was worried you were recruiting the children."

I laugh in spite of myself, but I'm secretly disappointed that he wasn't frantically searching for me. Ideally, because he needed to tell me how wrong Priya was. How unfair her words were.

But instead he says, "Our costumes are better." He nods at the music group in the rec room. "I'm also a better singer than him." The lone man in the group is butchering "Christmas (Baby Please Come Home)," an ambitious song choice for his limited vocal range. His attempted falsetto comes out crackly and sharp, but no one else notices. The kids are too hyped up on sugar and their parents are nearly catatonic, grateful for any distraction.

"We could challenge them to a duel?" I offer.

"I'm gonna guess dueling is frowned upon here. Also, what are you even doing up here? Isn't it kind of messed up to gawk at all these sick kids like it's some kind of sadness zoo?" He scrunches his nose in distaste.

"Shit, is that what I'm doing? I just wanted somewhere to think."

"What are you thinking about?"

"Do you remember that Christmas we went to my sister's? Our senior year of college?"

"I remember," he says. "But why were you thinking about that?"

I shrug. The honest answer is that I've been trying to shove thoughts of what Priya said out of my brain. If I don't think about it, I don't have to deal with it. At least for a little while longer.

"Do you remember how awful that night was?" I ask.

"Oh god, yeah, your sister is a terrible cook. Not that you're much better. Glass houses and all that." He raises his eyebrows at me. "That ham she made was, like, black on the outside, but somehow still raw in the middle. And those rolls! We could have played hockey with them. You know, if one of us knew how to play hockey."

"Sure. But do you remember how insufferable she was?"

"What do you mean?" He gives me a blank look.

"How she completely erased every single trace of our parents and moved on like: *Poof! Brand new life!*"

He's silent for a minute while he mulls this over. "That's not what I remember. I mostly remember how bad the ham was and how the whole apartment smelled like burnt meat. Although, in hindsight, who were we to complain? I'm pretty sure we showed up empty-handed."

"No, you must remember. She was sucking up to Spencer's mother and we had that stupid white elephant with all that taffy because that's what Spencer's family does every year? We didn't even watch *The Grinch*. We used to watch it every year when I was a kid, it was our favorite part of Christmas."

"Hannah, she probably didn't want to watch *The Grinch* because you were twenty-one, not twelve."

I puff out a breath. How could he have forgotten how bad that Christmas was? Time must have dulled his memory. In mine, that Christmas was painful. I wouldn't have survived it without him.

"I remember one other thing," he says with a finger poised in the air. "I remember her telling the story about her trip and how she went to all the places in your mom's journal. I thought that was really nice."

"What?" I would have known if that's what Brooke was doing on her gap year. "No. Trust me, she was just gallivanting from one hostel to another following Spencer around like a little duckling."

"I swear I remember her telling a sweet story about how much that trip meant to her and how she used your mom's list as a guide. Maybe you were in the bathroom or something? Or you were talking to someone else?"

A seed of doubt plants itself in my gut. If she did say that, I definitely wasn't there to hear it.

"Well, even if that's true about her trip, it doesn't counterbalance her abandoning our family."

"I don't know if I'd put it that way. Maybe she . . ." He hesitates. ". . . Moved on?"

"Exactly! She moved on! From me, from her only family. Who does that?"

"She invites you to every Christmas and Thanksgiving. Weren't you complaining that she invited you to a Fourth of July barbecue last year?"

"Yeah, but they're pity invites. She's glad when I don't come. You don't abandon your family like that. You'd never do that to me."

"Wait." He turns to look at me. "Is that why you didn't go to David's parents' house for Christmas?"

"What are you talking about? Brooke has nothing to do with that." I can't believe how out of sync Finn and I are right now. I wonder if he's still a little buzzed from the champagne at lunch.

"Sure, I mean, not directly. But you know it's alright for you to spend Christmas with David, right? It's okay for us to move on from this tradition, to grow as people. Healthy, even."

"What if I don't want to move on? What if I like things the way they are?"

Why is everyone in such a rush for the next thing? What about appreciating what you have? Because I know from experience that it could be gone any second. I finally have Finn back, things are good with David—or they were until the past month. Why can't that be enough?

He puts a hand on my knee. "Hannah, you know that just

because we met on Christmas, you'll still be my family even if we don't spend Christmas together. Like, we can have Arbor Day or Halloween instead. Oh, and I definitely want National Margarita Day. Or we can do something special on Valentine's Day or Flag Day. What I'm saying is, you couldn't get rid of me even if you tried. And it doesn't matter what arbitrary holiday we celebrate that on. It'll be special because we're together, not because of the date on the calendar. Hell, we can make up our own holiday. July twenty-third! I've always felt like there are too few summer holidays."

I launch myself at him and wrap my arms around his neck, my tears soaking into his rainbow cape. "I wish I could think of something bigger than I love you," I say into his shoulder.

"I bigger than I love you, too," he says into my neck. I think he might be crying, too. "And it's okay if you love David, too. It's not one or the other."

Suddenly, it all clicks. What if after my parents died, I made my life small: existing like a magpie, clinging to my friends like hoarded treasure? Positive it was only a matter of time before anything good was taken from me. That disaster lurked around every corner. What if Brooke did the opposite, and made her life big? Leaping headfirst into every new experience—travel, dating, motherhood—since the time we get here isn't guaranteed.

Oh god, what have I done?

I think of the ring, the one missing from David's sock drawer this morning. His words from our fight ring in my head: *I'm not sure you need me or even want me now that you have Finn back.* What if I pushed him away one too many times? What if it's too late to have both?

"Finn, I think I really messed up."

"Priya will forgive you. But I think she was a little right. Maybe more than a little. We've all been so caught up in Christmas."

"I can't believe we didn't know about Ben or that she got fired. I feel awful she was going through that alone. How was I so blind? I've fucked everything up so badly. Definitely with Priya, but David, too." I tell him about the ring that was and then wasn't. About our fight this morning.

While I wait for him to tell me that yes, I have single-handedly ruined my own relationship—the only serious relationship I've ever had—a woman in dress pants and a crimson sweater walks by us. I recognize her from inside the rec room. "I'm sorry for whatever you're going through. I know how hard this is," she says in a hushed whisper and as she passes. At first, I think she's talking about Priya or David and wonder how she knows, but then I look at Finn's tear-streaked face, which must match my own. The two of us sitting on a bench in the hallway of the children's wing of a hospital.

"Oh no, we're not—" I rush to cover.

"Thank you," Finn says at the same time. When she reaches the end of the hall and ducks into a bathroom, we exchange a look. Finn's shoulders heave with silent laughter.

"It's not funny," I tell him.

"Hey, you were the one gawking at the sick kids in the first place. I was going along with your bit. I was *yes, and*ing you." He straightens his shoulders, and a serious look comes over him. "Look, I don't think it's too late to fix things with David. You need to talk to him, tell him that you messed up. Call him and tell him everything you just told me. There are still"—he looks down at his phone in his lap—"four and a half hours left of Christmas."

"Okay. Yeah, okay." I feel anything but okay. I feel panicky and out of breath. "I can do that," I say mostly to convince myself. I grab my phone from my dress pocket and tap David's name in my favorites list.

The phone rings.

And rings.

And rings.

Voicemail.

He's probably sitting around the Christmas tree with his family, fielding questions about why I'm not there. By now they've collectively decided that they hate me and are telling him how much better he can do. When I end the call, it feels like pressing the red disconnect button signals the end of our relationship, as well.

"He didn't answer," I say, even though it's obvious. I try again, but get the same result "We should probably get out of here before someone else thinks our kid died. And I need to talk to Priya, too. At least maybe I can put things right with her."

"I'll meet you down there," Finn says, "I should go find Theo.

I think he's still wandering the hospital looking for you." He gives a guilty grimace.

I'm standing outside what I think is Priya's ER cubicle. It's the third one on the right past the door, but is that the correct door? Was it actually the fourth cubicle? Since there's only a curtain and no real door, I take a deep breath and say, "Knock, knock!" I sound like a nosy neighbor in a sitcom, but it's better than walking in on a half-naked old man in the midst of a heart attack.

"Hello?" Priya's voice comes from inside the cubicle in front of me. She sounds groggy.

I pull the curtain wide enough to let myself in, and Priya looks up at me expectantly.

"If you think I'm about to tell a knock-knock joke, you're about to be very disappointed."

She doesn't laugh at my attempt to lighten the mood. She keeps staring at me. Her eyes are glassy. I can't tell if I woke her or if she's been crying. I'm really screwing up today on all fronts. "While I don't have a knock-knock joke, I do have an apology. I'm sorry I'm a self-obsessed bozo. You were right, I have been a bad friend to you."

"Yeah, you kind of have been," Priya says. "The self-obsessed bozo part, not the bad friend part. You're a great friend, Hannah. Honestly, sometimes you're way too intense about it. You're stupidly loyal."

"I think you're being too generous. Plain stupid is more like it.

Don't go easy on me. I've been a narcissistic asshole the past few months." I grimace and correct myself, "Maybe years?"

"No, I was pretty harsh before. They gave me some painkillers and I think they're starting to work." She shrugs. "So, you're going through a self-obsessed phase. So what? Do you remember when I dated Charlie the *New Yorker* cartoonist and I was convinced he was cheating on me, and it was all I could talk about for four solid months?"

"He *was* cheating on you. You were right." When I saw him on Hinge, I shrieked and threw my phone across the room. I recognized him from my role as Priya's accomplice on many evenings of light internet stalking. She insisted I try and match with him to catch him in the act of cheating on her. We flirted for a few days in messages Priya ghostwrote, and on the night of our first date, Priya showed up instead of me to confront him. He stormed out, but I was waiting at the bar. We closed down the restaurant toasting the success of our mission, the thrill of catching him dulling the sting of his betrayal. He didn't matter; we had each other.

"So, I'm saying everyone gets a main character phase once in a while."

Priya *was* pretty insufferable that spring.

"Speaking of dating . . . do you want to talk about what happened with you and Dr. Ben?"

Priya pats the sheets next to her good leg. I climb in bed with her, scrunching myself as small as possible against the guardrail so I don't jostle her injured leg, which is nestled atop a stack of pillows while she waits for a cast. Somewhere in the distance a heart-rate monitor emits a steady beep-beep-beep.

Priya shifts so her head rests on my shoulder and she can whisper the story directly in my ear, as if the people in the neighboring cubicles might be listening through the curtain-walls. Although, with the wait times tonight and no other entertainment, they might be.

"I'm an idiot, Han. The problem with us was always distance, so I thought once he moved here our problem would be solved and we'd be together. He said from the beginning he wasn't looking for anything serious. That the first year of internship is super intense and he didn't have time for a relationship, but I thought he was bluffing. So, I thought we were dating, while he thought we were having post-shift cocktails and casual sex." She covers her eyes with both hands. "He told me exactly what it was, and I didn't believe him. I'm not even sure if it counts as a breakup if both people aren't on the same page about being in a relationship in the first place.

"When I asked him what we were doing for Christmas, he got all freaked out and ended things. I think that's why I was so hard on you the past month. You were complaining about not wanting to spend Christmas with David, while I was bending over backward to get Ben to invite me to spend Christmas with him. And here you had this great guy who loves you so much and wants to build a future with you, and you were pumping the brakes."

"Well, joke's on Ben. You are spending Christmas together. You kind of won this one."

"Not funny," Priya says. "Or intentional."

"I'm sorry I was rubbing all my David stuff in your face. I didn't know. Also, Ben is an idiot if he doesn't want to be with you. You're the dream girl."

I press a kiss to Priya's forehead. Our roles in this conversation are familiar from any number of times we pretended a frog was a prince and were disappointed when he turned out to be a frog after all. "If it makes you feel any better, I think I'm about to be single again, too. I think David's going to break up with me. He's super pissed."

She finds my hand between us on the bed and squeezes. "He should be."

"Wow," I deadpan, "great to have friends who are unconditionally on my side. Finn basically said the same thing. Did everyone take truth serum when I was in the bathroom?"

"It's your friends' job to tell you when you're being stupid, and you are. So, are you going to stop being so dense and go do something about it?"

"I tried. I called David but he didn't answer. He's probably screening my calls."

"Oh my god!" Priya shrieks. If the people in the surrounding cubicles weren't listening before, they are now. "This isn't a conversation you have over the phone. You need to go there."

"Yeah, but didn't we just have a fight about me being a bad

friend? You're in the actual hospital, so . . . I think I should probably stay here."

"Ugh," she groans, "be a good friend to me tomorrow. Tonight you need to go to Connecticut and find David."

She's right. I do need to go find him. This isn't a phone conversation. This is a grovel on my hands and knees situation. Even then, I'm not sure we can come back from this.

"Are you sure you don't mind? Finn and Theo can stay. And you can call me if you need anything and I'll come right back."

"I'm not going to need anything. They're keeping me overnight. They can't reach the orthopedist on call. And take Finn and Theo, I think you need them more than I do. Ben offered to wait with me when his shift ends at eleven." Her expression is unreadable. I can't tell if she's hoping they're not as over as she thought.

"You're not going to get back together with him, are you?" I ask.

"No, but we still need to talk. I think I need some closure. I'm not over him yet, but I'll get there. This time was finally the last."

"And we're okay?"

"We're fine. That's what sisters do, we fight." She grins at me and I dip my head onto her shoulder for a second. "Ow! Seriously, Hannah, get out of my bed and go to Connecticut right now."

"Jeez, I'm going."

I text Finn and Theo to meet me in the lobby. While I wait, I pull up Uber and plug in David's parents' address. The fare will be astronomical, but I don't care. This is too important.

No cars available.

I open Lyft and enter the address. No cars available.

I check the Metro North schedule, but all trains are canceled for the rest of the night. The tracks must be frozen.

I step through the automatic doors out to First Avenue. Being inside a hospital for four hours is like being in a sensory deprivation tank—it was afternoon when we came in, but now it's full dark—I blink at the lights of the building across the street as I try to find my bearings. The city is oddly quiet, like the entire population of New York is at home on the couch in elastic-waist pants after a long day of food and family.

I scan the street for a cab. A handful pass, but none have their light on.

By the time Finn and Theo make it to the lobby, I'm in a full-blown panic, pacing back and forth in front of the main doors. I downloaded every transportation app I could find and struck out with all of them. And still not a single open taxi.

Theo's arms are loaded with a giant stuffed teddy bear and a bouquet of red-and-green-dyed carnations, while Finn has a balloon that says "It's a boy!"

"We stopped at the gift shop," Theo explains.

"Theo insisted you shouldn't show up empty-handed for a grand romantic gesture. He was dead set on doing posters, like in *Love Actually*, but they didn't have any poster board in the gift shop. This was the best we could do," Finn says.

"Well, I don't think we're going anywhere. There are no cars. I've tried every app."

"We could rent a car? Did you try Zipcar?" Finn suggests.

"They don't have anything until the day after tomorrow. Same with all the rental places."

"What about a car service?" he asks as if I haven't tried every possible option already.

"Tried it. Nothing." I stop pacing and lean against the building's facade before sliding down it into a crouch with my head in my hands. "I also tried calling David five more times and still no answer."

"Did you leave a voicemail?" Finn asks.

"I know you're trying to be helpful right now, but you're making me more stressed."

"Also, who wants an apology voicemail? That feels like a cop-out," Theo says without looking up from his phone. He sets the stuffed bear and the flowers down next to me, and wanders to the other side of the door with his phone to his ear.

From where I squat next to the automatic doors, I hear him say the words "desperate," "Phillip Benson," and "important client."

Finn and I exchange a look. I've never heard Theo use his

father's name for special treatment. I've actually heard him use a fake last name more than once to avoid the fuss altogether. He's shockingly low-key about the whole *my dad is a billionaire* thing.

Theo ends his call and returns to us with a huge grin on his face. "A car is on the way!"

I jump up from my crouch and gather him in a hug. "Seriously, if David and I decide to have kids, I'm naming our firstborn after you."

I should have asked more questions before promising naming rights, because the car that pulls up is a rusted white limousine from the eighties that bears a strong resemblance to the one in my mom's prom photos. A uniformed driver pops out and walks around the car to open the door for us. I duck my head into the back seat and take in the strobing laser lights.

The driver catches the expression on my face and apologizes. "It's all we had available tonight, unfortunately."

"All I care about is getting to Connecticut before midnight," I tell him.

"That we can do," he assures me.

I'm frustrated but completely unsurprised when the limo breaks down on I-95 in Mamaroneck, thirty minutes into our drive. There's a loud pop, then a sputtering noise, before the limo chugs to a stop in the right lane. I look over at Theo and Finn with an expression that I hope conveys *What the fuck?!*

"That's not good," George, our driver, says in the front seat. He looks at us through the partition like we might know what to do. He tries starting the engine again, but it makes a sad, sick noise like a cat getting ready to vomit.

Somehow, Finn, Theo, and I are elected to get out and push the car into the breakdown lane, while George, claiming a bad back, shifts the limo into neutral and steers. "I hope you're getting a refund," I say to Theo through gritted teeth as I heave my hip into the limo's bumper. "And you can forget about baby Theo or Theodora."

"Don't hold this against Theo Jr., he's innocent in this." Theo sticks out his bottom lip in a mock-pout.

Two hours later, we're shivering in the back seat waiting for AAA. George calls for updates every thirty minutes, but the best the dispatcher can tell him is "Soon." It's already eleven.

"This is stupid," I say to Finn and Theo. "We're not going to make it before midnight."

"It's not stupid, it's romantic," Theo reassures me.

A blinding set of headlights pulls up behind us. They're so bright that they light up the interior of the limo even through the two inches of snow that have accumulated on the rear window.

By now we have very little faith in George, so when he gets out to talk to the tow-truck driver, we follow to eavesdrop. I hear the door of the truck slam, but can't see anything because I'm blinded by the headlights. Oddly, I hear jingle bells moving closer to us. I shield my eyes with my hand to try to see better, but it doesn't help.

"Finn?" says the disembodied voice of an older man.

"Who could you possibly know out here?" I ask him under my breath. I wonder if the cold is making me hallucinate.

"And Liam? Hannah? Is that you?" the voice calls.

The man comes into view, backlit by headlights. He's wearing a Santa coat over a pair of coveralls with a belt of sleigh bells draped over one shoulder. He has a thick gray beard. I recognize him, but can't place him. I briefly wonder if I know him from TV and we're on a *Cash Cab*–type reality show, where we'll have to answer Christmas-themed trivia to earn a ride.

It's Kevin, I realize. Or Pete? Richard? The man from the parade all those years ago. "Keith!" Finn yells.

Yup, that's it.

"What are you doing out here in the burbs?" Keith bellows from where he stands a few yards away.

"What are *you* doing here?" Finn retorts. "I can't believe this! How do you even remember us?"

"Oh, you four made an impression. Wait, where's your other gal?"

"In the hospital," Finn says, and Keith looks shocked. "She's fine, it's a long story. You were saying?"

"Do you know, in all my years of going to the parade, no one has ever invited me to join their plans after. Except for you all. Usually I'm home by lunchtime, I have a PB and J, and then I take the evening shift so my guys can have Christmas dinner with their families."

I feel guilty that I barely remember him, and our interaction made such an impression on him. I wrap an arm around Finn's waist.

"Well, we're glad you're here," Finn says. "We're, uh, having some car trouble."

"What are you doing this far from the city? You're not running from the law, are you?" Keith laughs at his own joke.

"We're actually trying to get to Hannah's boyfriend's house in Fairfield. They had a fight, and she needs to talk to him."

"Let's see what we can see," Keith says, "I like our odds. We've got Christmas magic on our side. I see the magic worked for you two." He points two split fingers at Theo and Finn. "I'm glad to see you're still together."

"Us?" Finn chokes. "No, we . . . uh . . . you must be mistaken."

Keith gives him a funny look, but let's it slide. "So, let's see about this car."

Keith spends fifteen minutes banging around under the hood of the limousine while George stands beside him holding a flashlight and positing unhelpful theories about what might be broken. At one point, Keith asks Finn to try turning the car on and it sounds promising for a few seconds, but then nothing.

"I'm sorry," Keith says. "I think we're going to need to tow her."

"And then you can fix the limo at your garage?" I ask hopefully.

"Sure, eventually. But I'm going to need to order some parts."

"But we have to get to Fairfield," I say. "Tonight."

"I might be able to help with that," Keith says.

We pile into the back seat of Keith's tow truck, and are surprised to be greeted by a woman dressed as Mrs. Claus in the front seat. Keith introduces her as Elaine, his new wife. He tells us how he traded in his parade tradition for something new this year, but still kept the costumes as a nod to his late wife. At least one Christmas love story went right.

An hour later, we're in a beat-up old pickup truck Keith loaned us. Finn's driving, and I'm sandwiched between him and Theo on the truck's bench. The clock on the dashboard reads 12:34. "I guess I'm not going to be able to salvage this Christmas after all," I sigh.

"What do you mean?" Finn says. "We'll be there in an hour according to Keith's directions." All of our phones are dead so we're navigating nineties style, pre-GPS. Keith assured us Fairfield was a straight shot once we got back on I-95, and there are maps galore in the glove compartment if we need them. I'm pretty sure I remember the way to David's parents' house from the highway.

"Yeah, but it's not Christmas anymore."

"Oh, stop being so literal. It's Christmas until we go to bed."

He flips on the radio and "Last Christmas" wafts into the truck's cab. *Last Christmas, I gave you my heart. The very next day you gave it away.* How fitting, given that this is probably our last

Christmas together and David's about to break up with me on December 26. I feel a deep kinship with George Michael in this moment.

An hour and a few wrong turns later, we pull up to David's parents' house. "Is this a bad idea?" I ask as we stare at the darkened house, everyone inside has likely been asleep for hours.

"I think that depends how it turns out," Finn says, "and we don't know how it'll turn out until you ring the doorbell."

I nudge Theo so he can let me out of the car. "Here goes nothing. Wish me luck," I tell them.

"Luck!" Finn says at the same time Theo says, "You don't need it. Love is stronger than luck."

TWENTY-FOUR

Finn

This year, December 26

Hannah swishes up the snow-covered front walk, a flash of crimson against a backdrop of pristine white. I can't decide if the symbolism is grim (the first drop of blood marring a snow-covered battlefield in a World War II epic) or hopeful (a single flower pushing its way through the ground after a long, cold winter). In my head, a cinematic soundtrack accompanies the tableau, the music swelling with every step she takes toward the front door.

"I can't look," Theo says even though his eyes are glued to her through the passenger-side window. He reaches across the seat for my hand like the suspense is too much.

For a minute she stands in front of the door and does nothing. My mental soundtrack glitches like a scratched record.

Is she going to chicken out? If she does, I'm prepared to shift the car into drive, and leave her on his parents' lawn. I'd come back eventually, but I'm not above forcing her hand. I will not let her ruin this moment. It'd be for her own good. She has something real with David, she's just scared. And, selfishly, I like knowing that she'll have someone there for her after I move.

Finally, she lifts a finger to the doorbell. "YESSS!" I pump my fist like she's my favorite sports team and she just scored the winning goal. Theo jumps in his seat, surprised by the volume of my reaction.

A light flicks on in the upstairs window, and a minute later an older woman in a fluffy white bathrobe answers the door. Her chin length hair stands up straight on one side and is matted down on the other in an unintentional Flock of Seagulls look.

"Crack the window," I tell Theo. "I want to see if we can hear them."

He pushes the button to lower the window, but nothing happens. "I think it's frozen shut."

We watch Hannah and David's mother have a quick exchange, but less than two minutes later they hug, and Hannah turns on her heel and walks back towards the car.

"Do you think he didn't want to see her?" Theo asks. "That's cold."

"Shhh, pretend we weren't watching." I whip my head forward and look straight ahead through the windshield. "Fake laugh at something I said so it looks like we were having a conversation this whole time." Theo is a less-than-generous scene partner and stares at me blankly.

When Hannah opens the passenger door, she announces over Theo's lap, "He's not there. He went back to the city."

Theo and I groan. Keith was kind enough to loan us his truck, but he didn't have a charging adapter for the cigarette lighter and the truck is too old for a USB port. At the time, our mission seemed too critical to pause and plug in our phones, but it might have saved us a lot of time and headache.

"So, we go back to the city?" I ask. Hannah nods, her face set in a look of grim determination.

The ride back is quiet. The combination of the holiday, the late hour, and the snow means we have the highway to ourselves. I leave the radio on low, playing oldies Christmas songs. Around New Rochelle, Hannah says, "His parents probably think our relationship is on its last legs. First, I don't show up for Christmas, and now I don't even know where David is."

"Who cares what they think," I say.

"Come to find out, I think I do," she says. It feels kinder not to point out that Hannah's always cared more than she lets on. There's a stretch of silence where we mull on that while "I'll Be Home for Christmas" changes over to "Let it Snow."

"What do I do if it's too late?" she asks.

"We could do the *Golden Girls* thing and the four of us could move to a house in Miami and eat a lot of cheesecake and talk shit about our exes," I suggest.

"Doesn't sound like the worst plan," Theo says. He'd been dozing against the passenger window. I didn't realize he was listening.

It's almost two thirty in the morning when we pull up to Hannah and David's building. All but two windows in the mid-rise building are dark. "We'll stay close," I say. "And I'll find a phone charger. Call or text to let us know everything is alright. We can come back and get you if you need us." I press a kiss to her temple. "I'm proud of you," I whisper into her hair.

We park in an overpriced garage—$60 for up to two hours plus a $15 oversized vehicle fee—and leave the most ostentatious parts of our costumes in the truck. I scrubbed the last of my eye makeup off in the hospital bathroom with hand soap and paper towels. We look wrinkled and rumpled, but almost normal if you don't happen to notice Theo is wearing gold lamé breeches instead of pants. I feel like I've lived a whole week in the eighteen hours since I woke up yesterday morning.

The only thing open this time of night is a twenty-four-hour deli on Greenwich Street.

"What are you getting?" I ask Theo as we survey the giant menu board behind the counter.

"Just coffee."

"Can I get a patty melt?" I ask the young man behind the counter. He's probably in college, and I wonder if he's here because he's another Christmas orphan or maybe because the holiday overtime is too good to pass up. I hope it's the latter.

I catch Theo giving me the side-eye for my order. "What?" I ask. "We didn't eat dinner, aren't you starving?"

"Too nervous to eat."

We tuck ourselves into a scratched wooden table in the window.

"You don't think he'll forgive her?" I assumed Hannah and David were having make up sex in the front hallway by now. He'll be glad she finally came to her senses.

"I don't know." Theo takes a contemplative sip from his paper coffee cup. "But I think she's brave."

"For telling her boyfriend she's been a stubborn idiot the last month? I think stubborn is Hannah's resting state. I don't know if I'd call that bravery."

"No, I mean for putting herself out there for love. Being willing to go outside her comfort zone. That's vulnerable and I think it's brave."

I wonder, not for the first time, if we're still talking about Hannah, or if maybe we've veered into talking about us. I've always wondered if Theo knew how I felt; knew that my fight with Hannah wasn't just about Jeremy. His words feel like a challenge: if I were brave, I would tell him. We stare at each other, the sound of the burger patty sizzling on the grill fills our silence.

Fuck it. I'm done being a coward. I'm done feeling less than. I'm exhausted and light-headed with hunger, and in my half-delirious state, it doesn't seem like such a bad idea to tell him. A Hail Mary pass before I leave New York.

"In that case," I begin, "I have something to tell you."

His green eyes lock onto mine and my stomach drops like we're hovering at the top of a rollercoaster.

"I have feelings for you. Romantic feelings, not friendly feelings. I've always had those feelings for you, and I wanted you to know that." I keep it short, not giving myself time to back out. Better to rip the Band-Aid.

He blinks at me. His face is blank. My skin feels translucent under the harsh fluorescent lights, and I wonder if he can see through my shirt and straight through my chest, all the way down to my frantically beating heart.

"Is this a good idea?" he asks.

The lone spark of hope I've been tending all these years gloms onto the fact that I have not been summarily rejected and flickers a little brighter. "Of course it's not a good idea. For a whole host of different reasons." I tick them off on my fingers. "I'm leaving, and we're friends, and we might make a mess of it. It's a terrible idea." He looks like a bobblehead figurine, avidly agreeing with my reasoning. "But I love you and sometimes love is messy and inconvenient."

"I love you, too . . . ," he says. His tone makes it clear his declaration of love ends with a comma, not a period, and I brace myself for the but. It will crush me if the rest of that sentence is *but only as a friend,* and I might slap him if it's *but I'm not in love with you.*

But apparently no further sentence is forthcoming. He stalls out there. I want to grab the collar of his shirt and shake the rest of the sentence out of him. Not knowing how it ends is too much to bear.

I'm not willing to back away from the brink this time. I've come this far. "I haven't heard you say you don't have feelings for me. So do you?"

The moment has an electric charge to it. "I think this is a bad idea," Theo reiterates.

"You already said that. So, do you? Do you have feelings for me as more than a friend? Because if you do, I think we should explore this."

Out of the corner of my eye, I spy the kid behind the counter gawking at us. When he sees me look his way, he jerks his head down and busies himself assembling my sandwich, which I have no appetite for anymore.

"You're leaving, so what does it even matter?"

"I'm not leaving you, I'm just going to LA. You could come with me. Or you could visit."

He makes a dismissive sound.

"You don't have a job. Your father owns a goddamn airline. This is a minor inconvenience, at most. This is not a dealbreaker and I won't pretend otherwise. Tell me, do you or do you not have feelings for me?" I'm playing a dangerous game. I will get my answer tonight.

"I . . ." The word hangs in the air between us for an unbearably long time before Theo takes a breath and finishes, "I don't."

He reaches for my hand on the table between us, and I whip it away like I've been burned.

"Oh," I say.

He wasn't scared to admit he had feelings for me. He was trying not to hurt mine by telling me he didn't. Bile rises in the back of my throat while tears prickle behind my eyes. I feel like a leaky water balloon threatening to burst.

The kid behind the counter hovers by the register with my sandwich on a paper plate waiting for the right time to bring it over. I can't pretend he didn't hear every word, it's pin-drop-silent in here and we weren't keeping our voices down. I'm as confused as he is about what to do next.

"Now I know," I say, treading water in our conversation.

My tears threaten to spill over at any second, and I don't want Theo to see me cry. "You know what?" I forge ahead before he can guess, "I should probably go check on Hannah. I didn't charge my phone like I said I would, and I don't want her to worry." I pop out of my chair, pull my wallet from my front pocket, and throw down all the cash I have—three singles. It's not enough, but now isn't the time to worry about *fair* with Theo. Life isn't fair. If it was, he'd love me back.

"Finn," he says, "this doesn't have to change anything."

Is he really dumb enough to think that? This changes everything.

As I leg it for the door, the kid holds up the plate with my sandwich and shouts, "Do you want this to go?"

I can't answer because of course I don't want it, but if I tell him my voice will wobble and I will not let myself cry until I'm out of Theo's sight line.

I push through the door and power walk past the front window of the cafe. Theo gets up from his chair and for a second I wonder if he's about to come after me. Instead, he stands stock-still and stares at me through the window with an anguished look on his face. Like he knows he ruined us.

And he has.

I hustle past, snow flurries sticking to my eyelashes, and the minute I'm out of sight, the tears come.

TWENTY-FIVE

Hannah

This year, December 26

I've always thought the hallway of our apartment building looks like a hotel, not a home. When I get to our door, I pat my pockets for my keys. Nothing.

I wedge my phone between my chin and chest and turn the pockets inside out looking for the keys, and when I don't find them, a hole in the pocket's seam. Oh god, what if they're lodged somewhere in the gown's many layers of lining? But my search turns up neither keys nor holes. They must have fallen out in the truck or maybe I left them at the hospital with my regular clothes.

The most pessimistic corner of my brain wonders if I'll need them after tonight. David would keep the apartment if we broke up. I can't afford my share of rent as it is.

I knock lightly on the apartment door.

What if David isn't here? What if he got a hotel room or is sleeping off his anger on his brother's couch? I'm about to head back to the lobby to get the spare from the front desk when David opens the door. He's wearing his chinos from this morning and an untucked white undershirt. He looks wide awake despite the hour. His hair stands on end like he's been raking his hands through it over and over.

Instinct takes over and I launch myself at him, wrapping him in a suffocating hug. I cling to him like if I can physically hold on to him, he can't leave me. Even if he broke up with me, he'd have to carry me around like a barnacle, stuck to him for the rest of his days. I sag with relief when he hugs me back and presses a series of quick kisses into my hairline.

"Where have you been?" he asks. "I was so worried. You called me fifteen times, didn't leave a message, and then wouldn't pick up your phone. I thought there had been some kind of emergency."

"My phone is dead." I let go of him and hold up my phone to prove the veracity of my statement.

"Are you okay?" His voice is thick with concern.

"I'm fine. Everyone's fine," I answer, before remembering that's not strictly true. "Actually, Priya's in the hospital—"

"Oh my god! What happened?"

"She fell ice-skating. Broken leg, but she'll be alright."

"Is that where you were?"

"I was in Connecticut."

"Connecticut? Why were you there? I've been back since seven thirty. I didn't see your calls because I fell asleep on the couch." I suppress the urge to laugh. David was here all this time.

He got home before we even left the hospital. Tonight was all a wild goose chase.

"I went to your parents' house. I needed to see you, in person, to apologize. David, I'm so sorry, I've been such an idiot. Not just this morning, for months. And you deserve so much better than me, but I love you and I want to love you better, if you'll let me. I should have been there today. If spending Christmas with your family is important to you, then it's important to me, too. I should have realized it sooner, but I promise I'll be there next year."

"Hannah," he starts. Then heaves a big sigh. "I don't want to be second-best. I don't want spending Christmas with me to be some consolation prize after Finn leaves and you don't have a better offer." He doesn't sound mad, he sounds sad.

"That's not . . . ," I begin, before realizing that's exactly how it sounds.

All at once the fear that our fight has already gone too far hits me square in the chest. I wonder where the uncrossable line in our relationship is, the one that marks a step too far for his forgiveness. Worse, I wonder if I accidentally wandered past it these last few months without even knowing, blind in the haze of my own stubbornness.

With that realization I forget how to breathe. My breath comes out in quick, jagged pants. David gathers me into his chest. He smooths my hair and makes quiet shushing noises. "Breathe," he tells me. "It's okay. You're okay."

"I'm not okay, I'm an idiot," I whine miserably.

He laughs next to my ear.

A laugh is good. People don't usually laugh during breakups.

I pull away from him and we stand staring at each other in the front hallway. It feels crucial for me to make him understand how serious I am. About him, about us.

"You're not a consolation prize. Not at all. I realized today that I think I was holding on to Christmas because of Brooke—"

"Brooke? You haven't spent Christmas with her in years."

"Exactly. I always thought Brooke abandoned our family. That she bailed as soon as something better came along and put me and our parents in the past. At least, I thought she did. Some new information has come to light there, but I can only handle one apology at a time. The point is, I guess it made me want to not abandon Finn and Theo and Priya and our traditions. I know you don't get it, but they're family to me, too."

He reaches for my hand and weaves our fingers together. He looks down at them as he speaks. "I know they are, and I'm not asking you to give them up. I know how important they are to you. And I love how passionate and loyal you are when it comes to your friends." He looks at me, his expression open and vulnerable. "I'm just asking you to put me first. Not all the time, but sometimes. It's not really about Christmas. I don't care where we spend Christmas. We can spend it in a dive bar or in the desert or on the moon. As long as we're together." He squeezes my hand for emphasis, then adds, "Unless we have kids. Then we kind of have to spend Christmas with my family or my mom would flip."

"We can do that," I tell him. "I want to spend Christmas with you. I'm not just saying that." Now I understand why grand gestures exist. I want to make him understand that this is not lip service. This isn't an empty promise I plan to forget about in the next 364 days. This is real. I wish I had a skywriter or a fireworks display in the shape of a heart or a picnic of all of his favorite foods to prove to him the depth of my love.

My eyes lock onto a bag of sourdough bread in a ceramic bowl on the kitchen island.

I walk toward it pulling David with me and remove the twist tie that seals the bag.

"What are you doing?" David asks, confused by the break in our conversation and my seemingly sudden, overpowering need for toast.

I turn back to him and drop to one knee. I haven't thought this through at all, but it feels right. My bright red gown pools on the floor around me. I look up at him and try to telegraph all the love I feel for him right now. "David?" I ask.

"Yes . . ." His lips curve into a surprised smile.

"I want you to know that I'm in this. I want Saturdays at the greenmarket and Sunday mornings doing the crossword together. I want to get you your favorite ramen before a big work presentation, and I want to know what's next after you finally master your at-home pizza recipe. And I want to finally go on that trip to Italy. But most of all, I want you. I want you to be my family, too. Will you marry me?"

"Yes, I already told you yes." There are tears in his eyes as I wrap the twist tie around his ring finger. He pulls me up to standing and gathers me in his arms. Then he lowers his lips to mine.

It's a kiss that holds promise for a lifetime of future kisses—a kiss that's leading somewhere.

He pulls back for a second to say, "I love you so fucking much, Hannah," before he backs me against the kitchen island. I pull his lower lip into my mouth and give it a playful bite. His hands fall to my ass and lift me onto the counter. I wrap my legs around his waist as his tongue brushes past my lips.

"I have no idea how to get you out of this dress," he says against my mouth.

"It's going to be a nightmare, there are so many tiny buttons."

He runs his hand up my back and starts to fiddle with the top one. "Can I rip it?" he asks.

"It's not mine. I need to return it. Whole, ideally."

He's gotten through about half the buttons—his progress is slow, doing it blind while we continue our feverish make-out—when there's a knock at the door.

We break our kiss and exchange a look. I almost suggest we ignore it, but then I remember I told Finn I'd let him know everything was okay and I didn't. "I think it's Finn," I tell David. "This will only take a second."

When I open the door, I find Finn with a hangdog expression on his face. His cheeks are wet—from snow or tears, I'm not sure.

"What's wrong?"

"Can I come in?" he asks.

I look over my shoulder at David, who is still standing at the island, and remember the promise I made that I would try to put him first. This feels like a cosmic test. I look back and forth between them, unsure what to do in this impossible position. It almost kills me to say it, but I tell Finn, "This actually isn't the best time. Can we talk tomorrow?"

David comes up behind me, taking in Finn's stricken expression. He leans over my shoulder and says into my ear, "This isn't a time I have to be first. Sometimes it's fine for me to be second."

"Thank you," I tell him, and pull Finn into the apartment.

"Do you want me to make you both some tea?" David offers. "It's three thirty, I guess I could make sandwiches or some French toast before this goes stale," he says, eyeing the open bag of bread on the counter.

"Do you have any tequila?" Finn asks.

"That kind of night, huh?" David says and gives a decisive nod.

I lead Finn to the couch, while David goes to the kitchen cabinet where we keep the hard liquor.

The minute we sit, Finn collapses into a fresh wave of sobs. "I told him," he says.

He doesn't need to say who he told or what he told them. "No?" I ask.

He shakes his head no.

I pull him into me and rub his back while he cries.

TWENTY-SIX

Finn

This year, December 26

I wake up in Hannah and David's guest room alone. I fell asleep with Hannah big spooning me, but she must have slipped out at some point during the night. I make my way to the hall bathroom where I know they keep the Advil. I feel hungover, even though I'm not. David couldn't find any tequila, and after I wrapped my crying jag I just wanted to go to bed and turn the page on another disastrous Christmas. I feel like a dried-out husk. My head pounds and my throat is raw from crying.

After I pee and take three Advil, I make my way back to the bedroom where my phone lays on the nightstand. I check to see what time it is: 9:05. Five hours of sleep. Also five texts from Theo, one every hour like he was pacing himself, so he didn't seem too desperate.

4:45 AM: I'm heading back uptown. I'll be there when you get home if you want to talk.

5:34 AM: You're still not home. Call me and let me know you're OK. I'm worried about you.

6:19 AM: Can we talk? I feel like I messed everything up.

7:54 AM: I'm sorry.

8:42 AM: Please don't shut me out.

Rage floods through me. I start to delete these messages, so I won't have to look at them again, but instead I decide to delete my entire text history with Theo so I'm not tempted to comb through our old texts to figure out where I got it all wrong. Where I misinterpreted things so badly and thought he might like me as more than a friend.

The minute I do, I feel hollow. I stare at our empty text thread, five years of memories gone in the click of a button. I think about googling how to get them back, but shove the phone under a pillow instead. I need a clean break.

Over the next days, Hannah and I fall into an easy rhythm marathoning Nancy Meyers movies on her overstuffed couch. The middle-aged protagonists give her an excuse to tell me that it's not too late to find love at least once per movie, or in the case of *It's Complicated*, that maybe things aren't actually over with Theo, prompting me to throw a decorative pillow at her face, because it's definitely over.

"Can we not talk about him?" I ask her.

It feels like we're in college again. We exist in a space outside of time—me, unemployed; Hannah, off work until the New

Year—so we sleep until eleven, drink wine with breakfast, and wander down to the bodega on the corner for breakfast sandwiches at six in the evening. Sometimes David watches movies with us. One day he makes a giant glass casserole dish of stuffed shells and serves it to us in shallow bowls topped with parmesan cheese. "Comfort food," he says.

It takes Hannah three days to admit that she and David got engaged on Christmas. She doesn't actually admit it, but I force her to tell me when a vintage-looking diamond ring mysteriously appears on her left hand. It turns out the ring was only missing from David's sock drawer because he realized the first one he bought, with his sister-in-law Jen's help, was completely wrong. In its place, he asked Brooke if he could use their mom's ring— Brooke wasn't using it; she had some five-carat monstrosity from her tacky husband. Hannah strokes her mother's ring lovingly as she relays the story to me.

I offer to get a hotel, but she refuses. At least I negotiate that her and David go to dinner without me to celebrate, which she begrudgingly accepts.

While they're gone, I find the journal I kept for Hannah the year we weren't speaking tucked into their bookshelf. There's a coffee stain on the cover and its pages are warped like it's been reread frequently. The discovery makes me feel even sadder to leave her.

Theo leaves voicemails I don't listen to, I only read the transcription before deleting them. I can't bear to hear his voice.

After the voicemails come the deliveries. First, he sends a spread from Zabar's; the next day, my favorite cookies from

Levain. On the third he sends a messenger with the suitcases I left at his apartment. Each comes with a note that says: PLEASE CALL ME XX.

Then, on the fourth day, he sends Clementine.

David is beet red after he answers the door and leads her to the sofa where we're halfway through *The Holiday*. "Erm, someone's here to see you," David stammers.

My first thought is, *Wow, the hits keep on coming*. First Theo rejected me, now he sent his ex-lover to do his dirty work. My second thought is that she looks fantastic. She's wearing a fuchsia sweater with giant balloon sleeves and a pair of acid-wash mom jeans. It's an outfit no one can pull off outside of a fashion magazine, but, of course, it works on her.

"Oooh! I love this film," she says by way of greeting.

Before I can come up with a withering response to call her out for showing up here uninvited, she's settling into the spot on the couch between me and Hannah and pulling her legs up underneath her to sit crisscross applesauce like this is totally normal and she's here for movie night.

"Clementine . . . uh, what are you doing here?" Hannah asks before she can commandeer one of our blankets.

"Theo said you had some kind of podcast emergency and I'm here to help."

"You want to be on my podcast?" Hannah repeats, her voice dripping with shock.

"Sure. If you want me, I mean," Clementine replies.

Hannah looks between me and Clementine like she can't decide what to do. "And that's the only reason you're here?" I jump in, sure Theo must have an ulterior motive.

Clementine looks slightly guilty. "If you're asking if I heard about *your* thing, I wasn't going to say anything, but I heard the broad strokes. Honestly, try not to be too torn up over it. You know Theo, he can't handle anything real. That boy is the ultimate Peter Pan. I told him I'm on your side."

"Uh, thanks . . . ," I say, my head still spinning from this turn of events.

"Welcome to the club, by the way. Of people Theo binned, I mean. Trust me, I've been there. I think we probably have enough for a football club by this point. There might even be a professional footballer or two in our ranks if the rumors are true."

A nervous laugh escapes Hannah.

"Do you mind if we finish the movie, then, before we do the podcast thingy?" Clementine asks.

"Fine by me," I say.

New Year's is a somber affair. David makes more pasta—this time with lobster in a white wine and butter sauce with lots of garlic and burst cherry tomatoes—and opens a bottle of Krug, but the champagne makes me think of Theo and that makes the pasta feel like glue in my throat. At midnight, Hannah and David kiss while I stare straight ahead at the TV and watch Ryan Seacrest announce the dawn of 2019.

"It's a clean slate." Hannah squeezes my thigh and I nod back at her, not wanting to correct her that my current slate feels more barren than clean.

On January 2, we say our goodbyes in the front hallway. Saying goodbye to Hannah feels inconceivable. How do you say goodbye to part of you? It's absurd to imagine saying goodbye to your elbow and leaving it at home while you head off into the wider world to go grocery shopping or have a first date or visit the Taj Mahal. Hannah is my elbow, this weird knobby part of me that feels impossible to leave behind. Not in a cerebral way, but in a very physical way.

I still haven't accepted the fact that she won't pop out from behind a magazine kiosk while I'm deplaning at LAX and yell, "Just kidding!"

But at the same time, I'm relieved to go. I've been a storm cloud darkening her and David's apartment in what should be a celebratory time. "You'll text me when you land?" Hannah asks.

"I promise."

"And you know you can call anytime. And I'll see you in February." The other night she impulse bought a flight to LA the first weekend in February while David will be out of town on an annual ski trip with his brothers.

"I know." I pull her in for a hug. "And thank you for letting me crash here the last week."

"You don't have to thank me," she says. "That's what family is for."

We stand toe to toe, and I'm unsure how to leave her. "I love you," I tell her.

"I love you, too. Forever." She offers me her pinky to swear on it. We lock pinkies and take turns kissing our fists to seal the promise.

My desire to be done with New York has turned me into one of those awful people who hover near the gate before boarding, like it will get them to their destination faster. The only thing I have to look forward to is the chocolate chip muffin in my backpack that I'm saving for the plane.

A man comes running up the concourse and everyone turns to stare because someone running in an airport is fairly alarming. Sure, he could be running to make a tight connection, but he could also be running away from something awful or on his way to do something awful. Airports always put me on edge.

I don't have a good view of what's happening because I'm buried in the scrum of people crowding the gate. I crane my neck to assess the potential threat and catch snippets of a man doubled over at the Jamba Juice kiosk beside our gate. All I can see is a mop of dark, curly hair. He has his hands on his knees as he heaves deep inhales trying to catch his breath.

When he rights himself and begins scanning the gate area, I catch green eyes.

Theo?

He's in a heather-gray T-shirt and a pair of jeans, looking more disheveled than I've ever seen him.

When he spots me, relief cascades over his features. "Finn!" he shouts.

I feel the urge to pull up the collar of my coat and hide. Pretend it's not me. He jostles his way to where I'm standing in a not-quite-line waiting for them to finish boarding comfort plus and move on to main cabin. A man behind me grumbles to his wife that Theo is cutting, and she shushes him.

"Hi," Theo says. "Can we talk?"

I don't want to talk. I'm five minutes away from being on this plane and closing the chapter on my life in New York. A failure on pretty much all fronts. The last thing I want to do is rehash my rejection in a crowded public space.

The gate agent calls, "Main cabin one," and the not-quite-line surges forward.

"What are you doing here?" I only have to stall the time it takes for the fifteen people in front of me to scan their boarding passes and then I'll be gone. I decide I'll get a Bloody Mary once we take off to purge whatever conversation he's trying to have from my brain. I think I'll ask for an extra mini bottle of vodka.

"I've been texting and calling you all week. I need to talk to you before you leave," he says. He keeps pace alongside me as the line advances.

"No, I mean, how are you even here? I thought they don't allow people past security without a ticket since 9/11."

"I got a comped ticket. That's not what I'm here to talk about." He presses his fingers to his temples.

"To where?" I only have to run the clock ten more passengers before I'm on the plane.

"I don't know, it doesn't matter. I'm not using it." I wait him out until he looks down at the paper ticket clutched in his hands. "Bogotá, I guess."

"Can we please talk for a minute?" He tugs at my arm, trying to pull me out of line, but I stand firm.

"My group is boarding. So if you have something to say, you can do it here." It's harsh, but I'm pissed it didn't occur to him I wasn't answering his texts or calls because I didn't want to talk to him.

He takes a deep breath and eyes the distance between us and the front of the line. "Finn, I got scared. I panicked the other night when you told me how you felt. I guess I don't have a lot of friends—"

"That's absurd, you have more friends than anyone I know." I'm not going to stand here and let him twist the truth like his. How dare he try to get me to feel sorry for him after he shattered *my* heart on Christmas?

"I have Saturday-night friends, but not Tuesday-afternoon friends. I don't have anyone else to watch movies with on a weeknight or run errands with me. I don't have other friends who want to talk at two a.m. when I can't sleep. My other friends aren't there when there aren't tickets or parties or connections to be had. And I don't want to go back to not having Tuesday friends."

"So, you aren't attracted to me, but you want to run errands together?" This is a thousand times worse than I imagined. I'm not even a friend, I'm the help. Or at best, maybe a human replacement for the Calm app.

"No . . . I'm explaining this wrong. I'm . . . can you get out of line so we can talk? Finn, of course I'm attracted to you. Have you ever seen yourself sing? How could anyone see that and not fall a little in love with you. But it's not just that, it's your strong hands, and the way you walk—it's so graceful, like the whole world's your stage—and your gorgeous brown eyes, and the way they crinkle when you laugh. And your heart, let's not forget your huge, beautiful heart. I've been attracted to you since the very first night. I didn't think I could have both." I'm at the front of the line now and I have my phone out, poised to scan the QR code, but this makes me hesitate.

"Either scan it or get out of line," the line dictator behind me says.

"One minute," Theo says through gritted teeth, an octave below yelling.

"Can we?" He points to the wall of windows on the other side of the gate agent's podium in front of a row of abandoned chairs. All my fellow passengers are in line.

"Fine," I relent.

"Did you hear what I said back there?" he tries again once we're off to the side. "I was so out of line on Christmas. Of course, I love you, but I was scared and I choked. And I know I hurt you and I can't even begin to tell you how sorry I am, but I'd like to try—"

"You love me? You're attracted to me?" I interrupt, needing to hear the words a second time. I switch my iced coffee to the other hand and draw my cold, damp palm across the back of my neck to jolt myself out of it if this is some kind of dream or delusion. I never expected to be having one of the most important conversations of my life with a Dunkin iced coffee in my hand. This must be what it feels like to be Ben Affleck.

"Finn, for chrissakes, I went home with you the very first night we met. You could have had me then. I didn't think you wanted me. And you—all of you, Hannah and Priya, too—became so important to me so quickly. It felt like too big a gamble to risk losing you. You know my dating track record is shit. So I thought I would be your friend instead. I thought it would be better . . . for both of us."

A slightly hysterical laugh bubbles up the back of my throat. It starts as a giggle and builds to a full guffaw. "Let me get this straight—" I say between gasping laughs.

"Well, not straight, certainly. At least, bi," Theo corrects. His expression melts into a sly smile that makes my internal temperature tick up a few degrees.

"We both wanted to be together this whole time?"

He nods. "The whole time," he confirms.

"And you waited until now, a literal minute before I'm leaving, to tell me this?"

"That's about the size of it." He looks around the gate area and the rapidly shrinking line of passengers like he's not sure what to do now. "Finn, will you please stay?"

Stay?

It's like he took a safety pin to my soap bubble of happiness.

How could he ask me to do this? Anger wells inside me, and I'm so blindsided by his request that all I can manage to spit out is, "I will not be your Andie Anderson!"

"Who?" His voice is panicked, his eyebrows knitted together in confusion. "I'm not asking you to be him. I don't even know who he is!"

"Not him! Her. From *How to Lose a Guy in Ten Days*." His blank looks remains. "You know, when Matthew McConaughey recklessly drives his motorcycle across the Manhattan Bridge to track down Kate Hudson who's on her way to an interview in Washington, DC, because it's the only place where she can pursue her dream of serious journalism. Which, of course it's not the only place she can pursue her dream of journalism, but also how could he quash her self-determination and ask her to stay in New York for him?"

Theo looks more confused than before I launched my word vomit at him. The two gate agents, done checking in passengers, have turned to gawk at the scene I'm making.

"Finn, I'm not asking you to give anything up," he says, putting an arm on my bicep to calm me down. "I'm just asking if you can take a later flight."

In all the times I've imagined this, us getting together, the fantasy always flickers out with the declaration of love. I've never considered what will come after, and now I'm panicking.

"How will this work?" I demand.

"I thought we already covered that my father owns an airline, I'm sure we can figure something out."

"Not the flight. Us."

"Well, you said it. I don't have a job. I'm sure I could come up with all sorts of reasons to be in LA, if I needed an excuse. I was thinking that maybe we could try the *Golden Girls* thing where we live together and are best friends and eat a lot of late-night cheesecake, but also, we're in love. But I think that's the least of our concerns."

"Okay, what's at the top of your list?" I ask.

He gives me a shy smile. "That we haven't had our second kiss yet."

My insides melt into a molten puddle as he leans closer and brings a hand to cup my jaw. I watch his eyes flutter closed before I lean in. And then our lips meet. At first, it's tentative, but then he wraps his arm around my back and pulls me closer. At the last minute I swing my iced coffee to the side so it doesn't get crushed between us.

I'm stunned that I can't remember our first kiss. How could I forget a kiss this incredible? I feel electrified, like fizzy particles of energy are surging through his hands and his lips and his tongue and everywhere we're touching and pinballing around my body. I bring up my free hand and wrap it around his neck, burying my fingers in his curls.

We kiss for what could be five minutes or five hours. When we break apart, one of the gate agents wolf whistles and I remember where we are. We lean together, our foreheads still touching, while we recover.

"Yeah, I'll take a later flight," I tell him.

SEVEN MONTHS LATER

Hannah

I'm slathering my body in SPF 70—the mineral kind that's a workout to rub in, but still leaves behind a white pallor—when there's a knock at the door.

When I open it, Finn is standing there shirtless in a pair of red-and-green-striped swim trunks with gold-rimmed aviators resting on his head. His skinny chest is bronzed after three days in the sun. "What are you doing here?" he asks.

"We switched rooms; the walls are not as thick as you and Theo think they are." Theo rented out all twelve rooms of the boutique hotel, so we have the run of the place, and with only three rooms occupied there was no reason to stay in the room next door to Finn and Theo, listening to their marathon reunion sex.

"Whoops," he says, not sounding at all chastened. "We haven't seen each other in a month." Theo and Finn have been doing long distance since Finn left New York. Theo let it slip after dinner our first night on Holbox, after a couple of mezcal margaritas, that he's looking at houses in LA, but he made me swear not to tell

Finn. He wants to ask Finn to move in with him on Finn's birthday next month.

"Did you want something?" I ask.

"I wanted to see if you were up for an adventure. Apparently you can walk the sandbar out to the tip of the island and sometimes there are flamingos. We wanted to go before lunch."

"Yeah, let's do it." I pull on a pair of cutoffs over my bathing suit and slide my ponytail through the back of a Yankees hat for shade. There's no need to bother with shoes on the island; there aren't any real roads, just sandy pathways that golf carts take at an alarming clip.

We step out the front door and onto the teak pool deck. The hotel is built around a triangular swimming pool and each room has a back door that opens directly onto the small turquoise pool. Theo got the staff to set up a twelve-foot artificial Christmas tree in the middle of the deck. It's wrapped in gold garland and decorated with a hodgepodge of ornaments, some of which I recognize from years past at Theo's. The hot dog was always a favorite. I'm glad it made it here.

Hidden speakers play "Dog Days Are Over" by Florence and the Machine. At first, Theo asked them to play "Feliz Navidad" on a loop, but we got sick of it within an hour. So I whipped up a playlist for the trip—this one not depressing at all, but rather a compilation of songs that remind me of our happiest memories as a group.

Finn and I pass through the outdoor reception area and take the short path down to the beach. "Oh, I listened to your podcast on my run this morning!" he tells me. I had kicked him and David out of the apartment while Clementine and I recorded. It was too much pressure having an audience. "It was incredible. I had no idea that Clementine's record label sold her masters and she had to find a way to buy them back in secret. No wonder her last album was so angry."

The launch of *Aural History*, the first episode of which aired last week and immediately hit number one on both Apple Podcasts and Spotify, is just one of the things we're celebrating this week in Mexico. Finn's first show at Netflix has been greenlit to start production, and Priya's starting her new job at Estée Lauder next week, helping to build a brand-new content vertical for them. And, of course, it's our first Christmas in July.

For actual Christmas this year, David and I have plans to spend Christmas Eve with Brooke and her family in New Jersey and Christmas Day with his family in Connecticut.

When we get down to the beach, David is asleep in the shade on a lounge chair with an issue of *Bon Appétit* open on his chest, while Priya and Marcus, the orthopedist who put her cast on last Christmas, have waded into the crystal-blue water and appear to be deep in conversation. They're new. He asked her on a date after he took off her cast in March, and they've been inseparable ever since. We're supposed to be vetting him, but we unanimously decided we adored him before the plane even left the tarmac at JFK. I've never seen Priya happier. For all its disasters, last Christmas managed to work some magic for us all.

When Theo spots us walking down the beach, his face splits

into a grin. He's wearing a Santa hat with his candy-cane-striped swim trunks. "Having a good Christmas?" he asks when we reach him.

"Maybe our best ever," I say.

"I think we've got a new tradition on our hands," Finn says.

The only thing better than Christmas is two Christmases.

Acknowledgments

I always read the acknowledgments first, so it's quite a thrill to write my own and recognize the many people who made the book you're reading a reality.

Thank you to my incredible agent Allison Hunter for being my fiercest champion, always texting back in two minutes flat, and giving the best pep talks and advice. I am so grateful that we found each other and cannot imagine a better partner for this wild ride. Thanks to Allison Malecha, my amazing foreign rights agent, who continually floored me by selling the shit out of this book abroad and giving life to dreams I truly didn't even know to dream, and to Maddalena Cavaciuti, my brilliant UK agent. Many thanks also to Natalie Edwards, Khalid McCalla, and the extended Trellis fam.

To Marie Michels, my US editor, you have made this book un-equivocally better. First and foremost, thank you for "getting it" and for loving Hannah and Finn as much as I do. Thank you for your astute notes and line edits, for pushing me to make this book better, and then fielding my panicked phone calls when I was sure I couldn't do it. I have treasured building our relationship, and hope this is only the beginning. To Pam Dorman, thank you for being this book's fairy godmother in every way and championing me and my writing. To Hannah Smith, my UK editor, I am so grateful for all your insight, enthusiasm, and careful line edits to Theo's speech (and also for teaching me the phrase "rat-arsed").

Thank you also to the entire team at Pamela Dorman Books and Penguin who have worked so hard on this book, and especially to Paul Buckley and Liz Casal Goodhue, Christine Choi, Bel Banta, Nicole Celli, Janine Barlow, Matt Giarratano, Claire Vaccaro, Alexis Farabaugh, and Clarence Haynes. And to Patrick Nolan, Andrea Schulz, Brian Tart, Lindsey Prevette, Kate Stark, and the Penguin sales team, your belief in this book truly means the world to me.

Thanks to my team at UTA. First and always to Shelby Schenkman for being the first to see something in my work and remaining my biggest cheerleader. I'm forever grateful. Thanks also to Addison Duffy and Olivia Fanaro. If this book ever becomes a movie (imagine!), it's because of them.

Thank you to Grace Atwood for asking all those years ago if I wanted to start a podcast. If not for that question, I'm not sure I would have ginned up the courage to write a book in the first place. Thank you for so many years of friendship, and for always being my loudest supporter. And to Olivia Muenter: Writing this book would have been a lot lonelier without you. I am so glad to have you in the trenches with me, both as a cohost and as a fellow first-time author!

A huge, giant, outer-space-sized thanks to the entire *Bad on Paper* community. Thank you for being the best (and oftentimes weirdest) corner of the internet. I'm bowled over by your support and enthusiasm for this book. Thanks also to Terrence, just because. I hope you are still an inside joke when this book comes out; if not, I just made things awkward.

Thank you to my earliest readers—Ashley Mahoney, Ali Miller, Grace Atwood, and Lydia Hirt—for your enthusiastic support and offering the perfect mix of criticism and praise that allowed me to keep going. And thanks especially to Rachael King for giving such detailed and thoughtful notes and edits that undoubtedly elevated this story. Thanks also to Jessica Camerata for sharing your Peachtree City tips.

Thank you to the Mangy Ravens—Elizabeth Manley, Molly Hale, Ali Kelly, Ashley Mahoney, Peter Heyer, Kyle McCulloch, Betsy Spang, Julie Crowley, and Kate Page—for letting me mine an entire friendship's worth of inside jokes, being the funniest people I know, and loving me and absolutely dragging me in equal measure. Thanks to Boston College for giving me these people. I hope Elizabeth's bike is still chained to the sign outside 24 Strathmore Road to prove we were there.

Thank you to Hannah Orenstein, Kate Spencer, Kate Kennedy, Laura Hankin, Lindsey Kelk, and John Glynn for offering me advice, insight, and commiseration throughout this process.

Thank you to Aya for giving me my love of Christmas, and for making so many of my past Christmases so special. To Uncle Dee, I'm so sad you're not here to see this, but I know you would be so incredibly proud of this accomplishment.

Thank you to Bon Bon: without your candy, I truly am not sure if this book would have ever gotten finished.

And last, but certainly not least, thank you to the readers: I know that reading a book is an incredible investment of your time and money, and I am so appreciative you chose to take a chance on me and mine. I hope you're glad you did.

He just wanted a decent book to read ...

Not too much to ask, is it? It was in 1935 when Allen Lane, Managing Director of Bodley Head Publishers, stood on a platform at Exeter railway station looking for something good to read on his journey back to London. His choice was limited to popular magazines and poor-quality paperbacks – the same choice faced every day by the vast majority of readers, few of whom could afford hardbacks. Lane's disappointment and subsequent anger at the range of books generally available led him to found a company – and change the world.

'We believed in the existence in this country of a vast reading public for intelligent books at a low price, and staked everything on it'
Sir Allen Lane, 1902–1970, founder of Penguin Books

The quality paperback had arrived – and not just in bookshops. Lane was adamant that his Penguins should appear in chain stores and tobacconists, and should cost no more than a packet of cigarettes.

Reading habits (and cigarette prices) have changed since 1935, but Penguin still believes in publishing the best books for everybody to enjoy. We still believe that good design costs no more than bad design, and we still believe that quality books published passionately and responsibly make the world a better place.

So wherever you see the little bird – whether it's on a piece of prize-winning literary fiction or a celebrity autobiography, political tour de force or historical masterpiece, a serial-killer thriller, reference book, world classic or a piece of pure escapism – you can bet that it represents the very best that the genre has to offer.

Whatever you like to read – trust Penguin.